SWEETEST HEARTBREAK

Sweetest Heartbreak is a work of fiction. Any references to historical events, real people, or real places are used fictitiously. Other names, characters, places, and events are products of the author's imagination, and any resemblance to actual events or places or persons, living or dead, is entirely coincidental.

ISBN-10: 0-9975354-2-3
ISBN-13: 978-0-9975354-2-6

SWEETEST HEARTBREAK

heather bentley

To Mom

You come to love not by finding the perfect person, but by learning to see an imperfect person perfectly.

—SAM KEEN

ONE

Leah

I firmly believe that every person on this planet deserves a fair chance at a good first impression. No preconceived notions. No letting others' opinions sway my own. Give them every opportunity to prove themselves, one way or another.

But, by the way my knees bounce in a poor attempt to settle my frayed nerves, I'm failing myself miserably. Worse yet, my best friend, Eli, doesn't miss the clues my body gives away. Like right now. I can feel him watching me as I run my clammy palms down my thighs.

"What are you so nervous about?"

I turn to find him smiling at me as he tenderly grips my shoulder before returning his hand to the steering wheel. Considering Eli lives only a mile or so away from where we're headed, this has been a painfully long car ride.

I trap my fidgeting hands under my thighs and turn to stare out the passenger window. "I've never met a drug addict before. How do I act? What if I say the wrong thing?" My racing heart beats stronger with each word.

A small laugh escapes him. "You're overthinking this. Besides, Heath is hardly an addict. The only thing he's addicted to is pissing off his dad. Although I do think for being almost twenty-five years old, he needs to grow out of that shit."

"You're not very convincing." I sit back with a huff and cross my arms over my chest, shooting him a doubtful side-eye.

"I've known him all my life, Leah. He has his moments, but deep down, he's a good guy. You've got nothing to worry about."

I circle back to the first part. "If he's not an addict, why did he just spend six months in one of the most expensive treatment centers in the country?"

"Because his dad didn't know what to do for him anymore. Heath's never gotten over his mom, and his dad thought this place might be able to help him finally work through it." Eli turns the wheel, directing the car down a long and winding paved driveway bordered by trees, effectively hiding what is ahead.

"Work through it? I thought you said she left them when he was a toddler. What is there to work through anymore?"

Eli stops the car and turns to me. I mirror his pose.

"If there's anything you need to know about Heath, it's this. He feels things deeper than most people. If something makes him happy, then he's *really* happy. But, if someone hurts him, he can't move past it the same way you or I would. He has a bad habit of holding grudges and ruining anything good that comes his way. And between you and me, I think he's still holding out hope that, one day, she'll walk back through those doors." He lifts his chin, motioning behind me to the double doors that swallow the space just beyond Eli's car.

My head tilts back to better take in the sight before me. A deep two-story portico with a large lantern-style chandelier illuminates the beautifully aged, dark wood that encases tall leaded glass doors. More glass surrounds them, inviting you into the foyer of the home and beyond. From there, weathered sandstone highlights full-length windows that stretch out for what seems like a city block in either direction.

The home looks like it's been plucked up by a tornado in Vail, Colorado and dropped into an unsuspecting suburb of Dallas, Texas.

"It's something, huh?"

Frozen at the sight before me, I whisper a weak, "Yeah." It's so much more than *something*.

I've driven by many elaborate homes, even been in a few, but other than their size, they were nothing special. This house though, it speaks to me in a way that is equally awe-inspiring and comforting.

I push open the car door, and my chest warms when my eyes catch a sparkle near my feet. A shiny copper penny. Heads up. I recite the familiar wish in my head before safely tucking it into my pocket.

Eli appears at my side. "His dad built it for his mom back when he thought they'd be filling it with kids and building a life together. Spent every dime he had on it. Unfortunately, the big family never came to be."

"So, you're telling me only two people live in this house?"

"Actually, three. Louise runs the house and has basically been like a mother to Heath over the years."

At that, one of the massive doors slowly opens. Standing in the center is a petite brunette woman who appears to be in her sixties, wearing a navy sheath dress and flats. Under the mouth of the portico, she looks like a pixie coming out from a tree trunk.

"Eli! Come here and give me a hug. Then you can introduce me to your friend."

Eli leads me forward with a hand on my upper back. The second we reach the woman, she wraps him in a tight, familiar embrace, only coming up to Eli's chest. She lets him go and turns to me. I extend my hand, ready to introduce myself, but she catches me by surprise when she sandwiches my hand in both of hers and gives it a light squeeze.

"You are just lovely. Oh! Where are my manners? I'm Louise."

Between the kindness in her eyes and the genuine smile that brightens her face, my nerves during the car ride are a distant memory. "Hi, Louise. I'm Eli's friend, Leah."

With an arched brow, she glances between Eli and me. "Friends?"

We turn to each other and laugh lightly. She's not the first person to question our unusual friendship.

Eli answers for both of us, "Yes, just friends."

Louise peeks back as she leads us into the house. I'm immediately impressed with the sheer size. Although the ceiling is soaring and the space seems to travel on forever, it's open and comfortable. Made for a family, just like Eli said.

The ski-lodge look from the outside carries into the interior as well. To the far left is an oversized fireplace encased in rounded river stone that reaches up to a high ceiling covered in wide timber beams. Open to the family room on the opposite end is the kitchen. An impressive island takes center stage among creamy white cabinets and stainless steel appliances while floor-to-ceiling windows line the entire back wall of the home, guiding your attention to the expansive wooded property and flooding the interior with natural light. The subtle peace and warmth to this home draws me in and calms my mind.

"Leah?" Eli asks.

I'm so engrossed in my thoughts, I didn't hear him and Louise talking.

"Let's go. Heath is in the field house."

"Louise, it was so nice meeting you."

"Hope to see you again soon, sweetheart."

"I'd like that." I give a small wave and catch up to Eli.

We travel down a long hallway and out a side door, following a stone path until we come upon an enormous rectangular building done in the same style as the house. It's not quite dark yet, but I can see an amber glow that rises from the building's skylights.

I stop him and pull back on his arm. "Wait a minute, what is this?"

"It's the field house," he states, as if it were as common as a living room.

"A field house?"

"Yes, Lee, a field house. Come on, let's go."

I'm silent the rest of the short walk. When we reach a pair of double doors that mimic those on the house, Eli pulls one open, allowing me to step inside first. I find myself in the center of a large room, surprised when I turn to my right and see a full-sized bar, like you'd find in a thousand restaurants across America.

It's constructed of thick, dark wood that runs the length of the substantial space with tall swiveling barstools lining the front. Blue glass pendants hang strategically overhead, highlighting the glass shelving along the back wall. It's what these shelves hold that catches my attention though. Row after row of every type of alcohol, glowing from the lights from above, and all ready for consumption.

Isn't that a little much for someone just out of rehab?

On the opposite side is a lounge area, complete with not one, not two, but three TVs lined up end-to-end, horizontally. Across from the screens sits an enormous U-shaped sectional and a massive square coffee table.

"Ready?" Eli strides forward to a set of thick glass doors finished with long brushed nickel handles and flanked by even more glass.

Beyond them is a full-sized basketball court. He slides a door open, and I'm instantly bombarded with the sounds of what I know well enough from Eli to be "Enter Sandman" by Metallica.

And there he is, in black basketball shorts and a sweat-drenched gray T-shirt. My best friend's best friend. Heath Braeburn.

He moves on the court like a man without a care in the world, his dark hair swinging as he bobs his head to the music between shots. He's tall and lean but definitely muscular enough that it shows through his fitted shirt. He looks more like a guy trained to run a marathon than someone fresh out of rehab.

An unfamiliar tingle travels up my spine and my insides flip. My feet are cemented to the floor as I watch him move like he invented the sport.

He finally notices us and pulls a remote from his pocket, pausing the music and walking our way. He smiles at the sight of Eli. But when he sees me, his mouth flattens as his expressionless eyes hold mine.

The two meet for a brief hug. With them standing side by side, I can't help but take in their differences.

Where Eli has short sandy hair and chestnut-brown eyes, Heath's dark waves fall over his forehead, framing cool ocean blues. He carries himself with a confidence that gives his easily six-foot-two frame the illusion of towering over Eli's five foot eleven. As the two face me, Heath's mouth lifts in a sneer while Eli's smile couldn't be brighter. They are opposites in every way.

The ball held at his hip, Heath openly inspects me from top to bottom. "So, you're Leah," he says, unimpressed.

My body jolts forward as I begin to ramble nervously, "Heath, it's so nice to finally meet you. I can't believe it's taken this long. Eli talks about you so much, I feel like I know you."

He uses the bottom of his shirt to wipe the sweat from his face. "Can't say the same." With that, he turns away from us and runs in for a layup.

My shoulders deflate the slightest bit at the rejection. When I look to Eli, his only response is a casual shake of his head. *Don't listen to him.* Now, I regret not pressing Eli more to meet Heath over the years. But, with Heath bouncing around from college to college before rehab and me completing my internship that rolled right into a full-time job at the advertising agency, we couldn't seem to make it work anyway. Until now.

He easily makes one layup and then turns to run in for another as the two of them continue to catch up like I'm not even there. Finally, he rolls the ball off to the side and leads us back out the glass doors. I follow quietly as they carry on.

When Heath throws his head back, laughing at something Eli said, he catches me watching him, causing his eyes to narrow and my steps to falter. The corner of his mouth rises in triumph before he turns back to Eli. I quicken my pace to keep up with them as they enter the house. When I make it to Eli's side, I give him a quick poke in the back.

He turns, his forehead scrunched in confusion.

I narrow my eyes as we continue to walk. *Did you forget I'm here?*

We head up to Heath's room, which ends up being more of an oversized suite than a bedroom, as it takes up the entire space over the house's four-car garage.

Even though it's one enormous room, the furniture serves as a divider, with a deep sectional breaking it into two. At the opposite end of the expansive space is a simple bed and dresser.

Heath takes a seat at one end while Eli takes one in the center, patting the spot next to him while smiling up at me. Heath grabs a remote, bringing a giant TV to life, before fishing under the sofa and pulling out a slender wooden box. As he and Eli continue to talk, he casually takes a bag from the box without missing a beat in their conversation. A matte black pipe with a shiny silver bowl is next, and I watch, slack-jawed, as he fills it with contents from the bag. He twists the top back in place and then reaches for the box once more to retrieve a lighter.

I fail to control the shock on my face as he takes a long hit from the pipe before holding it out to Eli. Eli shakes his head and continues their conversation. Heath has yet to release his breath when he turns to me and holds out the pipe, his brows raised in challenge.

"No, thank you," I answer politely, as if he were offering something as mundane as a piece of gum.

I went through four years of college. I've seen people smoke pot; that's not my problem. My problem is, the guy just got out of rehab, which his dad probably paid tens of thousands of dollars for.

I focus on Eli, waiting for him to catch my stare and hopefully get an idea of where this falls on the Richter scale of WTF. I'm thinking we're at a nine out of ten, but that's just me. Eli finally looks my way, but his expression is the same as it was before the box came out. He's smiling, at ease.

Heath turns his head from me just enough so that, when he exhales, I still manage to get hit with a cloud of smoke. Nonchalantly as I can, I lean away and hold my breath.

"Sorry about that," Heath mutters with a grin, effectively turning his apology into anything but.

I don't respond, just continue to hold my breath until I can't take it anymore.

"Where's your dad?" Eli asks.

I know he's happy to see his friend after all this time, but his obliviousness to my internal freak-out is starting to piss me off. He's definitely getting an earful from me on the ride home. I focus on keeping my hands in my lap, so I don't *accidentally* pinch him in the side.

"Work, I guess. Where else does he ever go?" Heath replies before taking another hit.

Just then, Eli gets a call. "Shit. Speaking of work, I'll be right back. You good?" He looks down to me as he stands. I nod the same time he answers the call and walks out of the room, leaving Heath and me alone.

Eli has been a statistician for the Dallas Cowboys since we graduated. He loves numbers almost as much as he loves sports, so he found a way to put the two together. The only downside is that the coaches and management work all year long, and if they ask for data, then, as the new guy, it's Eli's job to get them the information they want when they want it. Weekends be damned.

Hopefully, he won't have to go into the office. And, if he does, he's taking me with him. No way am I staying here with Heath.

I'm struggling to think of something to break the silence when he beats me to it.

"What's your story, Princess?"

"Princess?" My eyes roll at the unoriginal name.

"Jesus. Don't tell me you don't know Star Wars." His tone is more disgusted than accusatory.

"Of course I do," I answer defensively.

The first time I saw *A New Hope* was a few years after my dad died. Seeing this tough woman who fought alongside men, carried a gun instead of a purse, never shed a tear, and also happened to be royalty, I couldn't get enough. In the privacy of my bedroom, I'd pretend that I was Leia, fighting Darth Vader like he was the cancer that had taken my dad. Except for the fact that we shared a similar name, she was everything I wasn't. That I was sure I could never be.

Heath shakes his head, his obvious irritation with me growing as he tucks the box back under the sofa. I watch the door, willing Eli to walk back through it, thinking this can't get worse.

"So . . . you and Eli, are you two fuck buddies?"

"No! Nothing like that." The words fly from my mouth.

He grins at my shock and discomfort, exposing a perfect dimple on his cheek. I shake away the thought.

"I'm his friend. His best friend." I wince as soon as the last word drops from my mouth and rush to repair the damage. "I mean, his *other* best friend."

His jaw grinds, and his shoulders stiffen the tiniest bit. My chest fills with guilt as I witness the effect my words have on him.

I look down and notice my thumb rubbing over the face of the penny. I didn't even realize I'd pulled it from my pocket, but it must have been minutes ago because it's warm to the touch.

Heath's eyes move from my face to my hands and back again as his silence heightens my anxiety.

"Sorry, nervous habit, I guess." I shove the penny back in my pocket as he watches me.

There's neither a sneer nor a smirk on his face. Just his eyes locked on mine, holding me in place.

When Eli told me I'd finally be meeting his oldest and dearest friend, I pictured the three of us becoming some kind of corny trio. Cooking dinners together. Bickering over which movies to watch. Exactly what Eli and I already do in real life.

But, so far, it's the exact opposite. Heath makes my neck hot, my stomach queasy, and my pulse race.

This is not going well. This is not going well at all.

TWO

Heath

J *esus, what a bitch.* Rubbing it in my face that she's spent more time with my best friend in the last few years than I have. *Well, I was here first, Princess. And I'll be damned if I let you forget it.*

When Eli told me freshman year that he'd started hanging out with a chick, I figured she was homely, or he was using her to pass his classes. I mean, why else do you hook up with a girl once and decide you're better off as friends? Then, actually *stay* friends? Seriously, who thinks like that? Eli—that's who. The only guy I know who collects friends the way I collect phone numbers.

But, after hearing about her for so long, he waits until the last minute to tell me that he's stopping by—and, oh yeah, bringing her with. Then she ends up being the total opposite of everything I was expecting. My nostrils flare and my jaw clenches at the sight before me. All that long, wavy dark blond hair framing stormy-gray eyes and a small nose perched over full lips. It doesn't help that she's wearing short shorts on her goddamn tan, lean legs and a ridiculous pink T-shirt with a giant silver heart.

"I'm sorry. I shouldn't have said that." She shakes her head before looking down at her lap.

My eyes lock on her hands as she runs her palms up and down her smooth thighs.

"I know you two have been friends forever. It's just, Eli talks about you all the time. You should know, he was really worried about you when you were . . . away."

What has Eli told her?

When my narrowed eyes rise to meet hers, she turns silent. If I didn't know better, I'd swear they were pleading for forgiveness. But I won't let her have it. I can't remember when I've had this much fun.

I reach over to the small fridge at the end of the sofa and grab a beer. The look on her face when I pulled out my stash was priceless. Too bad the pot was old as shit and tasted like it. Not what I had planned after going through rehab the last six months, but I don't care. It was worth the stunned look it put on her face. In fact, I liked it so much, I think I need more.

Like the pot, the beer is so old, I don't even remember buying it. I push thoughts of my dad's disappointment out of my head and force down half of the can before slamming it on the coffee table.

And there it is—exactly what I was hoping for. Her eyes grow wide, her mouth drops open in a soft *O* shape, and her cheeks flush a warm red. The best kind of trifecta. For a minute, I'm lost, imagining her beneath me with her lips barely parted, watching and waiting for my kiss, until my head drops, and my cool lips meet hers.

I shake it off and remember that I need to be a dick. Otherwise, I might have to admit what Eli failed to tell me. That my best friend's best friend is everything I don't need. The worst kind of trifecta—sweet, innocent, and beautiful.

"So, what's your plan?" Eli asks as he tries to spin the basketball on his finger. It's been a few days since he brought Leah to the house. Thankfully, he didn't bring her back again today.

I smack the ball away and run in for a layup. When I land, he's standing there with his hands on his hips, annoyed.

"My plan? First, I'm going to kick your ass on the court. Then, I'm going to get laid." I'm messing with him—at least, partly. I had this same conversation with my dad last night. And I get it. Now that I've been home for a week, I need to get my shit together.

"Don't be an ass. You know what I mean."

I turn with the ball just as he rushes me and steals it away. He runs back to the three-point line and makes his shot.

"Are you thinking of going back to school? Third time's the charm, you know. Oh, wait. For you, it'd be the fourth." He laughs.

"Very funny, asshole. For your information, I got the last of my credits while I was away at Lakeland. Just waiting for my diploma to show up in the mail." That was the only productive thing to come out of rehab.

He passes me the ball and I move to where he just made his shot. I aim and . . . miss.

"Ha! That's Y. You're officially a pussy!"

I let my middle finger do the talking as we move toward the glass doors.

Behind the bar, I toss him a bottle of water as he takes a seat in front of me.

"So, seriously, Heath, what are you going to do next? Are you going to take your dad up on his offer? You'd be stupid not to."

I sigh, annoyed with the subject that my dad's been pushing for months. "Just because my degree is in computer science doesn't mean I want to spend my days updating software and busting people for watching porn."

"What did you think you'd really do? Work for the CIA and intercept communications from ISIS? Seriously, dude, your dad is the best litigator in Dallas. Hell, probably all of Texas. Just think of some of the batshit crazy clients he's taken on over the years. You'd be like a cyber sleuth, digging up dirt that could help your dad win his cases. That is, when you're not busting employees for watching porn, of course."

I refuse to admit he's right even though I know it would make my dad happy. Something he deserves after I've been such a pain in the ass all these years. Not to mention, the trouble it would save me from actually going out and finding a job. To anyone else, this is a no-brainer. I don't know what my problem is. Oh, yeah, I do. Getting up every day and being responsible.

Eli gives up and changes direction. "What did you think of Leah?"

I was wondering how long it would take him to ask. I shrug a shoulder and down a bottle of water, giving me time to come up with an answer that won't hurt his feelings too badly. Because, let's be honest, she doesn't fit. Eli knows every fucked-up thing I've done in my life, mostly because he was either a part of it or was there to bail me out. He will always accept me and all the arrogant shit I say and do. Leah, on the other hand, doesn't know me well enough to give me that same courtesy. And she never will.

"Whatever. She's fine, I guess." I crush the plastic in my fist, but Eli sits, restrained. "What?"

"Don't sleep with her, Heath." His eyes are hard and his mouth is pinched in a flat line. "She's not like that."

"Not like what? And what makes you think I'm even interested? I don't do sloppy seconds."

I know I've gone too far when his fingers tighten around the rail of the bar.

"I've put up with a lot of your shit over the years. So, I'm asking for this one thing. Be nice to her. Get along. But hands off. Okay?"

He has no idea how happy I am to oblige that request. I'm not interested in girls who have sticks up their asses, no matter how much they smell like fresh laundry and vanilla.

"Relax, man. Your princess isn't my type." My phone on the bar buzzes with a text. "Ah, speaking of my type." I hold it his way. "It's Laurie. She must have heard I was back in town. That girl doesn't waste any time—a trait I can appreciate."

"Laurie Cantano? Heath, she's a fucking stalker. Are you forgetting how psycho she was in high school? Don't go back there, dude. It won't end well."

"Relax, that was, what? Five years ago? She's got to be past all that crap by now. Besides, I heard she has her own place and a decent job at a hotel downtown. She can't be that crazy if she pulled that off."

"Your funeral. Just do yourself a favor and wrap it."

"Look who's talking. When was the last time you got laid?"

Water jostles out of his bottle as he slams it down on the bar. "None of your business."

It's clear I've gone too far, but I just can't stop myself. "Wait, was it Leah? Is that seriously the last time you got any? Because, if it is, that's just sad."

"Fuck off. At least one of us has standards."

He's right. He does have standards. While I have criteria, namely, likes to party and get naked.

"So, explain this to me. How could you like this chick, sleep with her once, and then decide to just be friends? Tell me how *that* works."

"It's not as easy as that." He focuses intently on his water bottle as he pulls at the label. "First semester of our freshman year, we got seated next to each other in Econ. We met up to study and started hanging out after class, and pretty soon, we were seeing each other every day. We did that for a while till I asked her out. We dated for a couple of months until we finally slept together. It got weird right away, so, we ended things."

I interrupt, "You mean *she* ended things?"

He gives me a dirty look, confirming my suspicions, before continuing. "At that point I'd gotten so used to seeing her every day that being away from her was harder than I realized. Turned out, she felt the same way, so we talked and decided to go back to being friends. And only friends." He shrugs a shoulder while keeping his focus on the bottle. "Four years later, and here we are."

"I don't know how you do it, man. Being friends with a hot girl like that." I stop as a thought hits me. "Are you gay? Because I won't judge. I have no problem with that. Unless you think I'm hot. Which, let's face it, I am. But, seriously, I've known you since we were practically born. You can—"

I don't see the water bottle hurl toward my face in time to block it. It's still half-full when it hits me, leaving a nice crescent-shaped dent in the center of my forehead.

"Fuck, dude! That hurt!" I rub at the tender spot as he sits back and crosses his arms.

"You can have Laurie Cantano kiss it better for you. And, if you call Leah hot again, I'll kick your fucking ass."

"Wow. For a guy who says he's just friends with a chick, you sure are defensive."

His glare tells me what I already know. He's not fooling me. He's got a thing for his best friend.

THREE

Leah

"Mom! I'm ready to make a run up to Goodwill. Is there anything else I'm missing?"

While I'm standing at the bottom of the stairs, waiting for her answer, my brother, Connor, comes around the hall.

He moves in close, his voice low. "Do you think she's okay?" He motions his head toward the stairs.

Our mom's familiar humming floats through the house.

"I think so. I mean, she's been smiling and singing all morning."

"It's just odd; that's all," he says quietly. "After twenty years, she finally decides that today is the day to get rid of Dad's stuff? Just like that?"

We stand side by side, eyes locked on the rise of the stairs.

"Well, I, for one, am happy for her," I whisper. "You can't keep a closetful of your dead husband's clothes for that long. It's not healthy." I watch my brother close his eyes and take a hefty breath. "Are *you* okay? Do you want to look through the boxes again and make sure there's nothing you want to keep?"

"No," he sighs.

I wrap him in a supportive hug that he quickly returns.

"She needs this, Con," I say into his shoulder.

Other than our hair color, you'd never guess we're twins, seeing as he's a broad six feet tall to my narrow five foot seven. He's grown into a younger version of our dad while I'm the same as our mom.

"I know. I guess I just liked knowing that his stuff was always there. It gave me something to hold on to. It made up for not having a single memory of him other than the stories Mom tells."

I squeeze him just a bit tighter. "Don't be so hard on yourself. We were only three when he died. But at least we've got pictures and a few of his things that are the most important to us. Now, we need to focus on Mom. She deserves to be happy after all she's done for us."

His chin bumps my shoulder as he nods in agreement.

"Uh-oh. What's going on here?"

We both turn at the sound of our mom's voice. She's standing on the bottom stair, hands on her hips. Before either of us can come up with an answer, she steps in between us and wraps an arm around each of our waists. We instinctively do the same in return.

"This is good, guys. It's something I should've done a long time ago." She looks from my brother to me, a sympathetic smile warming her face.

"We just want you to be happy, Mom," I reply.

"What makes you think I'm not happy? You two bring me more happiness than anything. But I'm not getting any younger, and now that you've both graduated college and you're starting to live lives of your own, it's time I put a little of the focus back on myself."

"I think that's great, Mom. Really," Connor agrees. "Just tell us this doesn't mean you're going to start skydiving or bungee jumping."

I tense, worried she might actually say yes.

Instead, she throws her head back and laughs. "Good Lord, child. The day I say I'm jumping out of a plane is the day you can check me into a psych ward."

My shoulders sag in relief.

"But now is as good a time as any to tell you that I've decided to start dating."

Connor and I look around her, catching one another's wide eyes and gaping mouths. My mom kisses each of our heads and then turns and walks to the front door, laughing all the way.

"C'mon, Lee. I'll ride with you to Goodwill."

Connor turns to me. "I think I would've been happier if she'd said she was going to go skydiving."

"Me, too, Con. Me, too."

"Let's stop at the grocery store on the way back, hon. I thought I'd throw some chicken on the grill tonight."

"Sounds good. Eli was planning on coming over, if that's all right."

"Of course. Eli is always welcome. I was beginning to worry. We haven't seen him around as much the last couple of weeks."

"Well, his friend Heath is home now. I'm trying to give them some space." *More like, I need space from Heath.*

I've seen him a few more times at Eli's house, and each time was a variation of the same. He treats me like I am invisible, answers my questions with one word, and—my favorite—looks at me like I have a large boil growing out of my forehead. It's that look that usually sends me to seek out any one of Eli's three younger sisters. But it's all really starting to mess with my head.

"Ah, the boy from rehab. Do I need to say it out loud that I'm not thrilled you're hanging out with him?"

"I'm not hanging out with him, Mom. But he's Eli's best friend. If I want to be friends with Eli, I have to learn how to coexist with Heath."

"Mmhmm." She's not convinced.

"Don't you trust me, Mother?" I sigh, eyes glued to the road.

"Lee, I always trust you. It's the outside influences I don't trust."

"Well, for now, I'm making the best of it. Besides, Eli would kill anyone who tried to hurt me. Even Heath."

She shakes her head. "I just don't get why you two don't date. He's such a good guy, Lee. And let's face it, he still has feelings for you."

"That's not true. Besides, he knows how I feel about him. He's more like a brother. At least a brother who doesn't tattle on me or tell his friends my bra size. Besides, you've got your own love life to focus on now." I move my foot to the brake as it hits me. "Oh my God!"

"What?" She turns to me, frantic.

"My mother is going to have a love life. I don't know if I can handle this." I groan as I turn into the parking lot.

"Well, handle it, sweetheart. Because I happen to have a date this weekend with Bob Crandall."

"My old tennis coach?" My eyes fly to meet hers. "What? How did that happen so fast?"

"It's actually not fast at all. I saw him at the grocery store a few weeks ago. We met for coffee once, and then, the other day, he asked me out. Easy as that."

Easy. Right.

Meanwhile, I'm dealing with Heath, who's anything but easy. But I just can't let it go. What did I do to make him hate me so much? And, more importantly, why do I care?

Because you need everyone to like you.

Oh, yeah, that.

"Dinner's ready, Lee. When will Eli be here?"

"I'm sure any minute, Mom. At this time of day it'll take him over an hour to get here."

Just then, I hear the front door open.

"Hey! Sorry we're late. Traffic was crap."

We?

I step out from the kitchen to see Eli heading my way while Heath stays put at the door, hands in his pockets and head turned away.

"No worries."

Eli pulls me in for a hug as Heath remains frozen in place.

Here we go. Commence Operation Kill Him with Kindness.

I give Heath my brightest smile before wrapping him in a short, loose hug. "Hey, Heath, glad you could come."

He mumbles back nervous and shy, "Thank you."

It's a side of him I would have doubted even existed, but who cares? Because, here, in my foyer, with his chin

25

down and his bangs hanging to his eyes in a poor attempt to hide, he's actually kind of adorable.

My hand is loose around his bicep as I pull him toward the kitchen. "C'mon. I'll introduce you to my mom and brother."

A flash of something crosses his eyes, and for a second, I think he might actually be afraid.

"Mom, Con, I'd like you to meet Heath Braeburn. Heath, this is my mom, Madeline Dawson, and my brother, Connor." I motion to my mom and then Connor.

I hide a deep exhale as I watch my mom offer her usual warm smile while Connor gives a silent head nod.

"Nice to meet you both. Thanks for having me."

I direct him to the table and am surprised when he pulls out the chair next to mine. But, at the last second, he switches with Eli, and a small twinge of disappointment swirls in my belly.

Heath is quiet through most of dinner. Polite but quiet.

When I catch a glimpse of Connor giving him the death stare from across the table, I kick him in the shin. Lucky for him, I'm barefoot. He flinches anyway and turns his eyes to me, silently asking what that was for. As if he doesn't know.

I mouth the words, *Be nice*, before taking a drink of my sweet tea.

His eyes narrow in defiance, and there's no doubt I'm in trouble.

"So, Heath, I hear you just spent six months in rehab. What was that like?"

My fork clangs against my plate as my head whips to my mom, seated next to my brother, and my jaw drops in shock and disappointment because she's the only one I've shared this information with.

"Connor!" my mom scolds.

"It's all right, Mrs. Dawson. It's no secret." Heath pauses to push some food around on his plate.

I wish so badly he were sitting next to me, so I could give him some kind of reassurance. Instead, I lean forward, sending muted thoughts of apology and support.

He puts his fork down and clears his throat. "The last few years, I acted like an immature idiot. Pretty much all of college. And high school. So, I guess that's more than a few." He chuckles lightly. "And it's just me and my dad. My mom left us when I was two, and Dad works a lot. Really, I think I was just acting out because I knew I could get away with it. And, because I'm an ass, I did it to see if I could get him to pay attention to me. And he did. My dad is awesome. It wasn't the first time he dropped everything for me. But it took thirty grand in a treatment center for me to realize that."

My eyes are glued to him, my heart breaking a little with each of his words.

He turns his attention solely on my mom. "I was there because my dad didn't know how to help me get my shit together."

Between his time in rehab and his use of a four-letter word in her home, I brace, waiting for my mom's terse response.

She leans in and crosses her arms on the table, giving him her full attention in return.

Here it comes.

"So, do you have your shit together?" She stares him down, waiting for his answer.

Both Connor and I are still. We've never heard her swear. Never.

27

"Yes, ma'am. I have my shit together." His words are firm, his tone unwavering

"Good." She sits back in her chair. "Now, wait till you try my pecan pie. It's the *shit*." She gives Heath a wink as she stands from the table.

Connor is staring at me with his mouth hanging wide open as we simultaneously try to process the midlife crisis that has taken over our mom. Add to the fact that I just witnessed Heath's soft side, and my head is spinning.

FOUR

Heath

What the hell did I agree to?

Of all the idiotic things I've done—and there have been plenty of them—agreeing to dinner at Leah's house *with her family* is currently ranking number one on my all-time top ten list.

Eli's ramblings on everything related to the fabulous Dawson family only made the hour-long drive worse. Then, just when I thought I'd have a minute to get my nerves in check, Eli walked right in the house, like he's one of the family. I, on the other hand, took as few steps in as possible. Just enough to close the door behind me.

I'm not like Eli. I don't easily adjust to new surroundings. And, aside from Eli's sisters, I don't have female friends. This is all new and uncomfortable territory for me.

I didn't move away the door until Leah came from around the corner, wearing a navy-blue tank top and white shorts. *Short* shorts.

Jesus, doesn't she own anything else?

I willed my eyes away from her legs only to have her shoot me an incredible smile I felt low in my gut. Just when I thought the situation couldn't get any worse, she wrapped her arms around me in a quick a hug. I barely got my arms around her in return, but it was enough to catch a soft floral scent from her long, wavy hair.

If it wasn't for her delicate fingers around my bicep when she led me to the kitchen, I have no doubt I would have bolted for the door.

Although introductions and dinner were painless, it didn't take a genius to see her brother did not like me.

To make matters worse, when I went to take the seat next to Leah, Eli nudged me to the next chair down, a silent reminder that I was the outsider here.

I stayed quiet during dinner, just answering the occasional question or adding something small to one of Eli's stories. They all smiled and laughed their way through the meal, slowly drawing me in and making me feel like I might actually be a part of something. Until Connor opened his mouth.

Whether his purpose was to humiliate me or to protect his sister, I don't know. But this is something my dad and I have talked about many times during rehab and since I've been home—owning your mistakes.

When Connor put me on the spot, my dad's words recited clear in my head. *"When you know better, you do better."*

It was time to put this strategy to good use.

I took a full breath and then answered honestly because I'm ready to be more than the guy who always slacks off. So, when I told Leah's mom that, yes, I do have my shit together, I actually meant it. Although that doesn't change the way I feel about Leah. If Eli wants to be friends with her, that's his choice. I, on the other hand, find it more productive to spend my free time with girls who serve a purpose beside friendship. Girls like Laurie.

"Dinner was great," I say as I hand my dishes to Leah at the sink.

She takes them with a smile before giving them a quick wash and placing them in the dishwasher. I lose myself for a minute, watching the swing of her hips as she bends, that I almost don't hear Mrs. Dawson call my name from the next room.

I turn toward her voice and find her a few steps away in the living room.

"Heath, come here. Let me show you something." Her back is to me as she motions toward a frame.

The picture inside, older and slightly yellowed, is of a young Leah and Connor curled on each side of a small golden retriever, all three asleep in a large dog crate.

"After the kids' dad passed, I bought them a puppy." She leans in a little closer. "Word of advice: Bringing a puppy into your home when you're dealing with a traumatic loss is *not* the best idea."

I can't even begin to imagine, so I just nod.

"But I don't regret it for a minute. I would have cut off my own arm if that could've taken away an ounce of the pain my kids were feeling." She turns from the picture to face me. "What I'm trying to say is, knowing what it's been like for my kids to go through life without a dad, I have a pretty good idea of how hard it's been for you to go through yours without a mom. Your dad sounds like he's doing an amazing job, but if you ever need to talk,

I'm willing to lend out my services. Despite what my own kids think, I actually know what I'm talking about."

I don't fight the laughter that escapes my chest. It feels too good.

Madeline Dawson is genuine and kind and now I know where Leah gets it from. When Leah held my eyes at dinner, the last of my nerves evaporated, replaced with the courage I needed to talk to these strangers about my mistakes. But here, after a home cooked meal and warm conversation, I realize, that's no longer what they are.

"Thanks, Mrs. Dawson," I say quietly.

And, for a minute, I let myself think about what it'd be like to have a mom who cared enough to stick around.

"Hey, have you decided if you're going to look at condos tomorrow?" Eli asks.

We're sitting in Leah's family room, watching some boring movie that Leah and Eli bickered about for fifteen minutes before he gave in. I have a feeling that happens a lot between them.

"Who's looking at condos?" Leah asks.

She's curled up with a blanket at one end of the sofa while Eli sits at the opposite end, and I'm sitting in a chair off to the side.

Connor got frustrated and left during the movie selection, muttering something that sounded like, "Not again."

"Heath is," Eli answers.

"I love looking at real estate. Mind if I come along?"

I'm not prepared for this. At all.

If I were at home, in my own space—or even at Eli's for that matter—I'd have no problem telling her that I neither need nor want her help. Then, I'd watch, waiting for the satisfying moment the hurt fills her eyes.

I keep my focus on the TV because I can't do that here, in her house. Especially not after her mom was so nice.

"It's true, dude. She's always looking at magazines and websites about house stuff," Eli confirms while staring at the screen. Some red-headed high schooler is making herself an awful pink prom dress after she got dumped by her boyfriend. I should've gotten out when I had the chance.

"Uh, yeah. Sure, I guess. It'll be pretty boring though." I shrug a shoulder, never once looking her way and stall a few extra seconds, hoping she'll rescind her offer. But she doesn't. "Be at my house by nine tomorrow morning."

"Can't wait," she says with an enthusiasm that causes my pulse to unexpectedly race.

Tomorrow, it'll be just me and Leah. Spending the day together. Alone.

I can totally handle this.

Who am I kidding?

"Do you have the address of the first place?" my dad asks before taking a sip of his coffee. He's seated across from me at the kitchen table.

"Yeah, and Joan texted. She'll meet us there."

"Us?"

"Yeah, Leah is coming with me. Her idea," I say indignantly.

"Isn't she Eli's girlfriend?"

"No, they're just friends." I almost say, *just his other best friend*, but stop myself before I sound like a total chick. That's the last time I watch a movie with Leah. "She offered to come. I guess she likes this kind of shit."

He hides a smirk behind his mug, his bullshit meter fully functioning.

The doorbell rings, and from somewhere in the depths of the house, Louise announces that she's got it. I hear mumbled talking before they both break out in laughter and enter the kitchen, smiling.

When I look over to Leah, I don't pay attention to the two coffees she's holding or the giant purse on her shoulder. All I see is how the sun glows golden behind her, highlighting the lightest blond strands of her hair that frame her makeup free face. Her gray eyes hold a hint of blue today as she walks up and offers me a coffee. I force my eyes back to the table.

"I got you a latte. I figured we could use the energy."

A latte. I don't drink *lattes*.

If my dad and Louise weren't here, I'd say those words out loud.

"You must be Leah. I'm Heath's dad. John Braeburn." My dad is up and striding her way while wearing a fascinated smirk. Since I have yet to acknowledge the coffee, he takes one and holds it in front of my face, forcing me to grab it, before shaking Leah's hand. "Nice to meet you."

"Nice to meet you, too, Mr. Braeburn. You have an amazing home."

"Well, not nice enough to convince Heath to stay a little longer." He gives her a jaunty wink even though we both know it's time for me to be on my own.

While they exchange niceties, I grab my keys and wallet and start walking to the door, shouting my good-byes to my dad and Louise and giving Leah a not-so-subtle hint in the meanwhile. I need to get out of here before my dad thinks this is something it isn't. But, when they all ignore me and I'm forced to turn back, I catch the ridiculous grin on my dad's face and I know I'm too late.

While I'm driving to the first address, Leah talks the entire way. Something about a color wheel, floor plans, and comparing comps. I keep my eyes on the road and focus on my driving instead of her legs that stretch out from underneath her khaki skirt. She pauses only to take a sip of her coffee. Mine sits in the cup holder, untouched.

When we pull up to a large high-rise at least twenty stories tall, I open my door and step out.

"Don't forget your coffee."

Damn.

"I'm not really a latte kind of guy, but . . . thanks," I grumble.

"Oh, let me guess. Guys don't drink lattes. Did you even bother to take a sip before you judged?"

Of course not.

She appears in front of me, holding the cup up to my face. "Just taste it," she challenges.

"Maybe later, Princess." She blows out an agitated breath at the nickname. *Victory.* When she raises it a speck higher, I give in and take it, thankful that at least it's still warm.

Just steps away from the main entrance, she stops short, bending to pick something up.

"Heads up, good luck." She turns to show me a dull penny.

"Sorry?"

"Pennies. They're good luck. Well, not all pennies. They have to be heads up."

My brows squeeze in doubt. "Since when are there rules to good luck pennies?"

"No rules. It's just something small I do to honor my dad. And they've never failed me." She admires the coin pinched between her fingers.

"Ooookay." I exaggerate the word, so she doesn't miss the fact that I think she's crazy.

She gives my shoulder a playful nudge. "Don't make fun of me, Heath Braeburn. This lucky penny could mean good things for you today."

"Well, considering you're the one who found it, I think the luck goes to you."

"Good thing for you, I'm willing to share." She takes my free hand and twists it palm up before planting the coin firmly in the center. When she turns to the door, her hair whips by my face, filling my nose with the scent of vanilla.

I'm left alone, mesmerized by the sway of her hips, as I watch every step. Tucking the penny in my pocket, I take a sip of the latte and follow her inside.

Joan is waiting for us in the lobby, eager to lead us to a two-bedroom unit on the nineteenth floor, before leaving us to tour the space on our own.

Even though she's out of earshot, Leah leans into me, her shoulder brushing mine, and whispers, "I was thinking there'd be some work to do. I didn't realize we were looking at places so . . . incredible."

Who cares what the space looks like? I'm sold on the awe stretched across her face. She's too fucking cute as she runs her hands along the quartz countertops, opening cabinets and babbling something about a wine fridge.

Her smile explodes when she turns and places her hand on my wrist, tugging me forward. Her fingers slide down until our hands meet, the softness of her palm colliding with the coolness of my own. She doesn't bat an eye, just continues to lead me forward, as she rambles on about bathrooms and closets. Between the feel of her small hand in mine and her blinding smile, I follow willingly.

"Oh my God!" She splits from me and bounds into the shower of the master bath, arms out and body spinning as her laughter bounces off the glass and across my chest.

"I've never seen anyone so happy about a bathroom." I cross my arms and lean back against the wall, enjoying the show.

"This isn't just a bathroom, Heath. I mean, look at it. It has a *sitting area*. Like an actual place to sit other than the toilet. I've never seen anything like this before!"

She's right. It's been staged with an upholstered chair and a small side table in the corner.

I take a sip of my coffee and then smirk, anticipating what my next words will do to her. "Well then, Princess, better not let you anywhere near the *master closet*."

She freezes, and her eyes widen at those two magical words. She springs from the shower and charges back into the master bedroom. I hold my position at the wall, ankles crossed, anxiously awaiting her return. Any second now.

"Where is it?" She's at my side, cheeks pink and voice flustered.

In all of her spinning, she didn't notice that the mirror along the wall is actually a wide pocket door. I tilt my head back, and with the speed of a freakish gazelle, she runs past me and slides it open, gasping at the sight in front of her.

"Ho . . . ly . . . shit." She takes two steps in, her head whipping left then right before turning to me. "This . . .

this isn't a closet. It's a room. No, it's not a room. It's a *department store*."

I follow her inside, impressed myself because she's not far off.

Dark-chocolate cabinets with glass doors line the walls and rise to the top of the twelve-foot ceiling. Resting a hip against the large island in the middle of the room, I watch her at the far end, standing near a three-paneled mirror that allows me the opportunity to study her without being caught.

I get a full view of her toned legs that lead up to a white top that scoops just low enough to frame a small pendant that rests on her chest. She turns and tucks her hair behind her ear with the same fingers that held mine just minutes before, and out of nowhere, all I can think about is touching her again. But I will my body to stay in its spot.

"Is this place in your budget?"

"Sorry?" I force my guilty eyes to hers.

"Is it in the budget? Because, if it is, you have to get it."

She's serious and anxious, as if someone else might just walk in the door and buy it out from under me. It's kind of cute.

"We haven't even checked out the entire space yet. What if the view from the balcony sucks?"

When her eyes light up yet again, I feel like I've just won a prize. Finding new ways to excite her is becoming increasingly addictive.

I push off from the island and follow her to the family room, not even bothering to hide my smile. As I turn into the kitchen, she's already stepping out onto the outdoor space. As much as I want to stand next to her, I can't get over the sight in front of me. Her hands grip the railing and her body leans back to absorb the sun as a strong breeze travels in, lifting her hair up and back. I commit the image to memory. If I wasn't sold on this place before, I am now.

I step out beside her as she motions to the spot on the railing next to her. As if I'd go anywhere else. We turn our sights forward, above the crowded streets of downtown, and it's surprisingly quiet.

"This view definitely does not suck."

I close my eyes and replay the image of her from just seconds ago. "No, it definitely does not."

Something about seeing her here only makes me want more. I shake off the thought because Leah is a relationship girl, and I am the furthest thing from that. Whether it's Laurie, the girls I hooked up with in rehab, or the countless others, it's what I do. It's what I'm good at.

I know I need to do something and quick to cut myself off from whatever this is I'm feeling. I bring my phone to the side and text Laurie, asking her to meet me tonight. It takes all of ten seconds to receive her emoji response—thumbs-up, heart, lips, eggplant.

"What's up with the eggplant?" I mumble to myself.

"What did you say?" Leah asks with a smile as she glances at my phone.

"Uh . . . nothing. Nothing." I slide my phone into my pocket with one hand while I hold the balcony door open for her.

Downstairs, we meet Joan to discuss the property. We still have a few more to look at, so I make it a point to keep Leah at arm's length for the rest of the morning, no matter how good her skin felt against mine.

Just before I get in the car, I take a sip of coffee. Only a few cold, sweet drops hit my tongue because I drank the whole damn thing.

FIVE

Leah

"I thought you said Heath was coming over," I say to Eli as I come around with the chips and salsa and join him on the sofa.

We're spending the night in with his family at his house.

"He said he might stop by later. I guess he made plans tonight."

"That's odd. He did get a few texts this morning but never mentioned anything." *Just when I thought I was making progress with the guy.*

Eli shrugs off my comment. "So, how did it go? Anything worth putting an offer on?"

I stop the chip before it reaches my mouth. "Eli, we looked at four condos, and each was more incredible than the last. They were all brand-new and absolutely stunning. Steam showers and wraparound balconies. One even had a hidden door to an office. Crazy!" I say the last word before taking a bite.

"Well, they should be nice for a million dollars."

I start to choke on my chip. "I'm sorry, what?" I slap at my chest and take a sip of water.

"That's his budget. One million dollars."

"You're serious."

"You were with him all day. I assumed you knew."

"No, he never mentioned a number. And, trust me, *that* number, I'd remember." My head shakes at the thought.

I've never known anyone at our age who has access to that kind of extravagance. Even Eli, whose family is better off than most.

"Pizza should be here soon. Want to pick the movie?"

We're seated near each other on the sofa as he brings up Netflix before passing me the remote control.

Just as I'm about to take it from him, he pulls back. "But I call that the word *love* can't be in the title." He looks at me matter-of-factly.

"What? That's not fair," I whine.

"Lee, what were the last few movies you picked?"

"Well, there was—"

"I'll tell you," he cuts in, counting on his fingers for dramatic effect. "*Love Actually*, *Can't Buy Me Love*, and *Shakespeare in Love*." He looks triumphant and smug. Because he's right.

"Fine," I say in defeat. "Then, what are we going to watch? But nothing with fighting, superheroes, or aliens."

He rolls his eyes. That pretty much eliminates everything he likes.

"Looks like you're fucked, dude." The voice comes from behind the sofa.

We both turn to see Heath, dressed in ragged khaki cargo shorts and a black T-shirt frayed along the bottom.

When he takes up the open space between us, the smell of pot hits my nose.

With a lazy smile on his face, he puts an arm around each of us and looks from side to side. "How are my two best friends?"

I try to pull away, but he holds me in place, his fingers digging into the bare skin of my shoulders.

"What? If you're his best friend and I'm his best friend, doesn't that make us *all* best friends?" He thinks the annoyed look on my face is from his words, not the wretched odor wafting off every inch of him.

I catch what looks like smeared lipstick on his neck and jerk out of his hold, standing at the same time Eli elbows him in the chest.

"Jesus, Heath. You're wasted. You'd better not have driven here."

"No, Laurie dropped me off." The cocky smile on his face turns my stomach sour.

"I'll go see if the pizza is here," I mutter even though I've suddenly lost my appetite. I need an excuse to get out of this room.

After spending the day together, I thought we were actually becoming friends.

I am such an idiot.

In the kitchen, Lucy, the oldest of Eli's sisters, is clearing the long island to make room for the pizzas that are stacked at one end. "Hey, Leah. I was just about to get you guys. Did Heath make it there in one piece?" Lucy gives me a raised eyebrow.

I shake my head in frustration. "Luce, that guy . . . what a . . . I mean . . ." I'm walking around the island, helping her lay out the boxes and put out the plates and napkins.

"Who are we talking about?" Sienna, the middle sister, asks as she enters the room.

"Heath just got here," Lucy answers, her tone flat.

"Ah," is all Sienna says as she grabs a plate.

I'm a little shocked at their lack of surprise.

Sienna turns to me. "We love Heath, Leah. He's like family, but, man, does that boy have some growing up to do."

"Let me guess. We're talking about Heath," Megan, the youngest of Eli's three sisters, announces as she joins us. "He's a perfect example of what happens when you give your kids everything."

"Listen to you three," their mom, Elaine, chastises as she closes the refrigerator door and sets out the salad. "We all know that, without his dad, Heath would be dead in a ditch somewhere. So, better he be spoiled and immature than six feet under."

All three girls roll their eyes, and I can't hold in my laughter.

"You're so dramatic, Mom. Seriously." Lucy waves a hand in the air before filling her plate with food.

Eli and Heath enter the room, and Heath goes straight for the pizza, cutting in front of Sienna and piling his plate high.

"Hey!" she shouts as she shoves her body against him. "You're such an ass, Heath."

He ignores her, instead choosing to take a large bite of a slice right in her face. All three girls spear him with sharp eyes, ready to pounce. But he grabs a bottle of water and leaves the room, completely oblivious.

I watch his back until he's out of sight, disappointed that the guy I spent the day with is gone, replaced by a total jerk that has taken up residence in his body. Just when I think I'm getting to know Heath, I see this other side of him again that I don't understand. And, quite frankly, that I don't like.

I don't go back to the room where Eli and Heath are. Instead, I sit at the kitchen table with Eli's sisters and pick at my food before helping Sienna wrap up the leftovers.

"Don't go there, Leah." Sienna gives me a knowing look as she turns to the fridge.

"What are you—"

"I saw the way you looked at him. And I get it—to a point. I mean, he's good-looking, rich. He's the ultimate player in a game that every girl thinks she can win. But I've been around long enough to tell you that they lose. Every time. And I don't want to watch that happen to you. Not just because I care about you, but also because of what that would do to my brother."

"Sienna, it's not like that. We're barely friends."

"Heath doesn't make friends with girls."

I eye her with doubt.

"My sisters and I are different. Heath is family. Just don't go there, okay? What you think you see there, lingering under a facade of equal parts confidence and arrogance, isn't as it seems. Trust me."

"Cynical much?" I try for cool but can't help but replay her words.

Visions of the lipstick on his neck and the roughness of his hand on my arm have me cringing at the thought of where else his hands have been tonight. She's right. That guy has heartbreak written all over him.

I don't bother to say good-bye to the guys. Instead, I text Eli from the driveway that I'm leaving.

SIX

Heath

Shit. Leah smelled good when I sat next to her on the sofa. Way better than Laurie had. Laurie smelled more like a dirty ashtray. Whatever. She got the job done. But she hadn't felt like Leah; that's for damn sure.

When I wrapped my hand along Leah's shoulder, it took me back to the condo and when she'd slid her hand into mine. I wanted to tell her I put an offer on it—partly because it had everything I wanted, but also because it was the one that had made her eyes light up the most. But I didn't get the chance.

"Good job, asshole."

"What? I'm just sitting here. What did I do now?"

"Leah just texted. She left."

Shit. My already fading high begins to bottom out. I took this too far. All I was trying to do was distract myself from her, but all I managed to do was piss them both off.

My phone vibrates on the coffee table with a text. It's my dad wanting to know where I am. We were supposed to have dinner.

"Jesus, Heath. You've barely been home from rehab and you're getting high, screwing around, and blowing off your dad. Do you have your shit together, or not? Figure it out."

I grab my bottle of water and chug it down because all I want to do right now is tell Eli to fuck off—or worse, admit that he's right.

When he gives me a ride home later that night, I let my arm hang out the window and casually toss my newly purchased bag of pot out into the trees.

SEVEN

Leah

Eli is dead. He just doesn't know it yet.

"I thought we were supposed to be packing." Standing with my hands on my hips, I huff as Heath takes a shot from the three-point line.

Eli promised he'd be here, and if he doesn't show up soon, I'm going to hunt him down and kill him myself. I did not give up my Saturday to watch Heath work up a sweat. No matter how good he looks doing it.

"I figure, since Eli's not here yet, we can get a game of Horse in."

I stomp to the door and shout over my shoulder, "I'd rather start packing."

"Afraid I'll beat you, Princess?"

With my hand on the cool metal handle, memories of years of competition with Connor come rushing back. I turn to see Heath spinning the ball in his hands, looking smug as hell. There's no way I can walk away.

"Pig!" I shout back.

"Elephant."
What?
"Ox."
"Gorilla."
Jerk.
"Jerk," I fire back. "And I shoot first." I storm back to the court.

"Of course." He passes me the ball, not even bothering to hide his cocky smile.

As I take a few warm up shots, he asks, "Care to make it interesting?"

My shot bounces off the rim. "What do you have in mind?"

He crosses the court, so we're practically toe-to-toe and looks down at me with a mischievous grin. "How about, if I win, you have to unpack the entire kitchen in my new place?" He doesn't miss the obvious confusion on my face. "What? Louise has been buying me every kind of spoon and plate and pan they make. I don't know what to do with all that shit. And, honestly, I have no desire to figure it out."

"Fair enough." With my hands to my hips, I rock back on my heels in thought. When it hits me, I rise onto my toes and point into his chest, holding my eyes to his. "And, if I win, you have to stop drinking and getting high."

His jaw shifts as he considers my bet. "For how long?"

"One month." I want to say, *forever*, but I know he'd call the whole thing off.

He's staring me down as he considers my offer. I don't budge.

"Deal."

"Seriously?" I was expecting anything but that.

He puts a hand out, ignoring my surprise. "Care to shake on it?"

I don't hesitate to take his hand in mine and grip firmly. He squeezes even harder in return as the corner of his mouth rises, and his eyes narrow. I have got to win this bet, if anything, to knock that ridiculous, pompous, self-righteous attitude down a few notches.

I take my first shot from the far right on the free-throw line and sink it. I stand in place, waiting for him so that he can stand exactly where I am.

"Easy, Princess. I think I get how the game works."

I move out of his way and watch him easily sink the shot.

I manage to make my next shot and step aside as he gets into position. He bounces the ball a few times and then spins it between his hands. I'm growing impatient when he spins it once more.

Then, he says the one thing that throws me off my game. "I'm sorry about being an ass at Eli's house."

I stand there, silent.

"It was a shitty thing to do to both of you, and I just want you to know . . . I'm sorry." Although he's speaking the words to me, he never pulls his focus from the basket.

"Thanks." Stunned, it's the only response I can manage.

He takes his shot—and misses.

We go round for round, finally tied at three letters each—*J-E-R*—when I decide to go in for the kill shot.

As I get myself aligned at the center of the free-throw line, Heath laughs. "C'mon, don't make it so easy for me."

I fail to mention that Connor and I have played this game out on our driveway more times than I can count. I raise my chin in challenge, take one more look at the basket, and then turn around to face the opposite wall. I can hear him stifling a laugh from beside me, but I shut him out and focus only on the ball in my hands. I lift it once, twice, and on the third time, release it backward over my head.

I turn just in time to see it bounce from the backboard to the rim and then . . . in the net.

"Yes!" I jump with both hands in the air. "Make that shot, Braeburn!"

He shakes his head, smiling in disbelief as he walks to the line. He turns his back to the net and peeks over his shoulder before closing his eyes and swinging the ball just once before launching it back over his head. I hold my breath as I watch it bounce off the top of the backboard and then onto the court below.

"I win! I win! I win!" I shout as I run across the court and launch into a celebratory cartwheel, followed by a flip-flop. When I turn back and run his way to gloat over my victory a little bit more, I'm met with the last thing I expected from Heath. A huge, radiating smile. "You know what this means, right?" I ask, out of breath from my impromptu gymnastics routine.

"Yes, Princess. I know exactly what it means." He rests an arm over my shoulders and says with a wink, "It means no fun Heath for a month."

We head for the doors, in need of a drink. My body is vibrating, not so much from the victory, but because of what it means.

"Well, for what it's worth, if this is boring Heath, I like him much better."

He slides a door open for me as we exit the gym, and goes behind the bar to grab us a couple of bottles of water.

He holds one out to me, all the while shaking his head and fighting a smile.

I don't bother to hide my own. Not just because I won, but because I would've been just as happy to lose. I'm dying to organize his new kitchen.

EIGHT

Heath

I've never seen anyone so happy to win. When she started flipping across the gym floor, with her hair flying all around and her face flushed, the smile she rewarded me with was absolutely worth me throwing the game for. I doubt I'd have made that backward shot anyway, but I didn't want to risk it. I definitely could have made the two before it though. Not that it matters. I'm done with the drinking and drugs. I need to show my dad that not only can I handle the responsibility of living on my own, but I also deserve the kick-ass condo he's paying for. So, I'm officially retiring from partying.

As we left the gym, I didn't even realize that I'd put my arm around her shoulders until after I did it. Better than that though, she didn't flinch. She just kept talking, like we casually touched like this all the time. Like I could pull her close and kiss her, and she'd kiss me back. Because, with the sun streaming in and casting a warm glow to her skin, I was itching to feel her lips on mine.

I'm standing on one side of the bar with her sitting on the other when the door opens, and in walks Eli.

"Sorry I'm late. Did you get my text?"

She ignores his question. "Eli! Heath and I played Jerk, and I won with a backward shot. It was awesome!"

Eli takes a second to process her words before he looks at me, eyes narrowed and walks to her, taking one step too many into her space. He might as well pee on her leg. "Nice. What did you get for winning?" He knows I always bet on my games.

I begin to stutter out an answer but stop, knowing no matter what I say, I'm screwed. Quitting for her, especially after I promised to keep my hands off her, won't be good for our friendship. But when have I ever done the right thing?

"Nothing actually," she says. The words are effortless. Convincing.

I'm impressed. Not only does she tell a bald-faced lie, but the loyalty she's just shown me with those two words pinches at something deep in my chest.

"Nothing?" He looks from Leah to me and then back again, doubtful.

"Nope. Guess I should've bet big though, huh?" She turns to me. "Can placing a bet be retroactive?"

I lock eyes with her in solidarity and copy her word. "Nope."

"Well, let's get to it," Eli interrupts our silent conversation.

I'm not able to pull my eyes from her just yet, and fortunately, neither is she. Because, with her loose hair falling out around her face and the red from her cheeks fading to a soft pink, I'm using every ounce of energy I have to communicate to her just how beautiful she is right now.

NINE

Leah

"Mrs. Dawson, your chicken and dumplings are the best I've ever had. Hands down," Eli says as he scrapes his plate clean.

Heath echoes, "Definitely. Louise is a great cook, but she doesn't make anything like this."

"Well, thank you, boys. That's sweet of you. Even if you are kissing my ass."

"Mom! What has gotten into you?" I whisper harshly. A thought hits me, and I drop my voice lower. "Are you . . . are you going through . . . the change?"

"Good Lord, Leah. No, it's not menopause." She rolls her eyes. "You kids are old enough. It's time to turn off the filter. No more, *Oh my goodness!* Or, *Jiminy Cricket,*" she says as she swats her hand in the air.

As I scrub a pot, Connor places a dirty plate on the counter and leans in with a feigned whisper, "The other day, I swear, I heard her drop an F-bomb in the laundry room."

I turn to her, my jaw falling open in horror.

"What? I spilled detergent all over the floor. It made a horrible mess."

"Who is the person who taught me that's not how a lady acts?" I scold, as if I were the actual parent here.

"Oh, Lee. My sweet, sweet Lee." She comes up behind me, resting her warm hands on my shoulders. "You'll be where I am one day. Then, you'll understand." She kisses my cheek and leaves the room.

"What the heck is that supposed to mean?" I look at the three guys left with me in the kitchen, hoping one of them has an answer.

"It means, you can't live life with a stick up your ass," Connor says as he brings me more dishes from the table.

"Jerk." I flick soap bubbles at him, hitting him in the nose, which emits a laugh from the room.

Eli, always the peacemaker, attempts to cover for my brother from his chair at the table. "I think what your brother is trying to say is, don't take life so seriously. Have some fun."

I turn to him, irritated, when I catch him about to lick a small spot of gravy off his plate. I cross my arms at my chest and silently dare him to do it.

His shoulders drop in defeat as he hands it to me. "It's just, as long as I've known you, Lee, you've followed every rule, planned out every moment."

"What? I've broken rules before. Don't you remember when I signed you in for our European Studies class even though I knew you weren't coming? That's breaking a rule."

"You only did that because I was sick in bed with a fever, and if I had one more absence, I'd drop a letter grade. You did it because you're a good friend. Not because you're a rebel."

I dry my hands on the kitchen towel with a little too much force, unwilling to admit he's right. "Well then, I'm definitely not a planner."

A rough scoff escapes Connor's throat.

"What?" I ask haughtily. "For your information, I have no idea what I'm doing tomorrow. A true planner would at least know what they were doing the next day."

"Just because you have one day with no plans doesn't make it true. Besides, you're more of a big-picture planner." Connor looks to Eli. "Has she ever told you about her dream proposal?"

Eli looks from me to Connor. "Like, a wedding proposal?"

"Yep. She's got it all planned out."

I swat him with the kitchen towel. "I do not, Connor. Just stop!"

He laughs and pulls the towel away before I can hit him again. "She has this whole cliché dream about candles in the sand or some shit."

I smack him once in the arm, hard, because he's embarrassing the hell out of me. But he just laughs as he moves to the other side of the table.

"Give me a break, Connor. That's not true anymore. Besides, I was, like, ten when I said that."

"No way. Try more, like, eighteen."

Now, all three guys are laughing at me, and my face is burning red in embarrassment.

"But the best part is the costumes!" Now, he's laughing full force, having to catch his breath before attempting to continue.

I know where he's going with this, and it needs to stop. Now.

"Connor Michael Dawson, this is not funny. Shut up *right now!*"

"Oh no, man. Tell us. This, I've got to hear," Heath encourages, enjoying my panic.

Really? After I covered for him and our bet?

I lunge at Connor, but he's faster than me, making it to the other side of the table and out of reach.

"She made a list of all of her favorite couples costumes. Like, whoever the poor sucker is that she marries will be forced to wear coordinating costumes every Halloween for the rest of his life."

"Seriously?" Eli and Heath ask in unison.

I grip my hips and raise my chin. "What's so wrong with couples costumes? It's my favorite holiday. Is it really such a big deal that the man I marry will need to like Halloween as much as I do?"

Heath is the first to speak. "So, like, he's Superman and you're Wonder Woman?"

Connor jumps in. "Or he's Fred and she's Wilma!"

Now, it's Eli's turn. "Or he's bacon and she's eggs!"

Connor injects, "Cinderella and Prince Charming!"

They all think this is hilarious, throwing out costume ideas, as I turn my back on them. I scrub at a dish before shoving it in the dishwasher, all the while fighting to tamp down my rising humiliation. With every plate and fork I jam into the machine, I vow to never share anything personal with Connor ever again for as long as I live.

"Hey, Leah," Heath speaks from behind me, my shoulders hunched over the sink as I grab another dish and begin to scrub. "You know the chances of that happening are slim to none, right? No normal guy likes to dress up."

The three of them don't bother to hide their laughter as my eyes burn.

I drop the dish in the sink and lift my eyes to Heath's, not bothering to hide the hurt that shows in every line of my face. "The right guy will."

Their laughter fades as I leave the room.

TEN

Heath

"Shit. I think we hurt her feelings. I'll go talk to her," Connor says as he moves toward the doorway Leah just exited.

He stops when his mom enters the room. She's not happy.

"Anyone care to tell me why my daughter is out back while you three are here, in the kitchen?" She stands tall in the doorframe, arms crossed over her chest.

None of us are brave enough to answer.

"I'll tell you why. Because her brother, the person she adores more than anyone else in this world, teased her about things she'd shared with him *in private*." She looks pointedly at Connor.

He opens his mouth, about to speak in his defense, when Mrs. Dawson raises a hand and effectively silences him.

"You boys don't think I could hear every word from down the hall? Shame on all of you. Especially you." She points to Connor. "I taught you better. And, for the record, she was twelve when she shared that with you, so give her some slack."

"Sorry, Mom."

"Sorry, Mrs. Dawson," I reply sheepishly. God, I feel like an ass. I know I'm not the only one at fault, but knowing I'm even partly to blame weighs heavy on my mind.

Eli steps forward. "Yeah, sorry, Mrs. Dawson. Should I go talk to her?"

A hot wave of jealousy hits me at his words. The thought of him being the one to console her pisses me off.

"No. You, Eli, can finish the dishes. Heath, you take out the garbage, and, Connor, you wipe down the table and sweep the floor."

A collective, "Yes, ma'am," comes from the three of us.

As we get to work on our newly assigned chores, she turns to leave the room but not before sharing a few parting words. "A man who makes a woman feel anything less than valuable is no man at all. Remember that."

We nod in silent understanding.

As the other two continue working, I step out the side door with the garbage in hand. The deck is dimly lit, but I don't miss Leah sitting in one of the teak chairs. It's a typical warm night, but a light breeze whistles through the trees. I set down the bag and walk over.

"Hey," she says with a weak smile as she stands.

The wind pushes a lock of hair in her face, and I tuck the piece behind her ear. "I'm sorry. I was an ass."

"Don't worry about it. I'm more irritated with my brother. Besides, I get it. Couples costumes and all. Stupid." She shrugs her shoulders. "We tease each other all the time. I think I'm just on edge because Connor will be moving out soon."

"He's moving? He didn't say anything at dinner."

"Well, he doesn't want to jinx it, but it's basically a done deal. He's just waiting to hear back from Burger."

"Burger?" I laugh.

"Yeah, Kyle Heisenburger, but we've called him Burger ever since we were kids. He's a recruiter and is helping Connor with his job search. Connor had his third interview with an engineering firm in Houston and now he's just waiting for their offer." She looks off to the side. "It'll just be weird. Him living somewhere else. His room empty."

"Or maybe it'll be like when you were both away at college?"

She shrugs again, keeping her head turned away. "We went to the same college." Her shoulders rise and fall with a heavy breath.

She still won't look at me, and I can't stand it. How my words affect other people is something I've never considered before. But this, seeing her hurt because of me, stirs up feelings I'm not used to.

With a finger to her chin, I gently turn her eyes to mine.

"I really am sorry, Leah."

I lower my face to hers until we're just a breath apart. Her mouth opens slightly as her eyes soften and the crinkle of her nose disappears. That urge to feel her lips against mine returns with an urgency I want to give in to. I've never given much thought to kissing. It's never been anything more than a means to an end. But, with Leah, I want to know what it's like to kiss her. More than that, I *need* to know.

As she stares up at me, I swear, she can read my thoughts. I close the narrow gap between us and brush my lips against hers before hesitantly pulling back. I need to be sure she wants this as much as I do. When her palm rests flat on my chest, I have my answer.

My fingers leave her chin and travel to the warm skin of her neck, gliding around to the back. Her skin prickles with goose bumps under my hand as I draw her forward until her lips are firmly, and *finally*, pressed against my own. We stay just like that, absorbing the feel of our connection. When she pulls my shirt into her fist with one hand and brings the other to my hip, I cup her face in my hands and swipe my tongue along the seam of her lips, thankful when her mouth drops open and she gives me what I've been thinking about since the first day she walked onto my court.

When a small moan escapes her throat and her hands glide around to my back, I know she feels the same way. I don't hesitate to kiss her the way she deserves to be kissed. Steady but strong. Soft but deep. Her tongue swirls with mine as our lips heat, and her fingers burrow into my skin.

She moves with me, like we've done this a hundred times before. I marvel at the thought that, if our first kiss is this amazing, I can't wait to discover all the ways it can get better. I know one thing for sure though. This is the kiss that all others will forever be compared to.

We break apart, and I run my nose alongside hers and kiss the apple of her cheek, her lashes brushing against my own as her eyes flutter open and I pull away. Her lips are red from the friction as our rapid breaths begin to calm, and her mouth spreads into a shy smile.

"If that's how you apologize, you definitely need to screw up more often."

I steal a kiss before answering. "I'll do my best, Princess."

If I only knew how true those words would someday be.

ELEVEN

Leah

"Can you come here a minute, so I can show you where I'm putting everything?" I call to Heath as he walks past with a box.

It's been six days since he kissed me on the back porch. Six days of talking on the phone and waking up to his texts.

I discovered he hates emojis, so I always make sure to throw a few random ones in just to drive him crazy. Last night, before I fell asleep, I texted him a puppy, a paper clip, and the French flag among others. This morning, I woke to his text.

> **If that's code for "I want to see you naked," then my answer is YES.**

I smiled stupidly to myself and so badly wanted to play along and tell him yes back, but I wasn't brave enough. So, I just sent him a string of surprised faces.

It's been a long time since anyone has seen me naked, ever since I made that mistake with Eli. I hate to call sex with a great guy like him a mistake, but as it was happening, I knew it wasn't right. I confused feeling safe and open with him for having true feelings for him. So, we did it, and I almost immediately regretted it. It wasn't what we were meant to be. It felt like being with my best friend and nothing more. It was good. It was fine. I wouldn't wish it away because I do love Eli. I just don't *love* Eli. There's no spark like that between us. No heat or intensity. Thankfully, Eli said he agreed and we eventually worked past the awkwardness.

Now, if I could just get past the kiss I shared with Heath. The kiss that curled my toes and stole my breath.

Heath comes from around the corner as I snap out of my thoughts and stumble to open the first cabinet. He finally closed on the condo and he, Eli, and I have been working all day to get him unpacked.

With one hand, I direct his attention to what's inside and, more importantly, away from my flushed face. "So, here are your dinner plates, salad plates, and cereal bowls. Above are a few serving bowls and over here"—I go to the next cabinet—"are your glasses and coffee mugs." I'm pointing to the inside of the cabinet, but he's yet to look anywhere but at me. "Heath, are you paying attention?"

He moves close, his bare feet on either side of my own, as his mouth drops dangerously low. "I'm paying very close attention."

"Oh." That one syllable is all I can manage. I'm too focused on the curve of his lips to say more. The same lips that are currently smiling down at me. I will him to move in and kiss me. I need him to kiss me.

Kiss me.

70

His warm chest leans into mine, and just as his hands wrap around my hips and my eyes fall closed, Eli shouts as he enters the room. "Where do you want this box marked *Crap* to go?"

Heath drops his hands the same time I jump back, bumping into the countertop behind me. But it's no use, and we both know it when we turn to see Eli standing ramrod straight, his eyes as wide as his mouth. Although we're not touching, two people couldn't be physically closer than we are right now. There's no denying that something other than unpacking was about to take place.

His body locks, and his face falls. "Never mind. I'll figure it out," Eli growls as he turns and storms from the room.

"Shit." I drop my head to Heath's shoulder and take a deep breath. *God, he smells good.* "I'd better go talk to him," I mumble as I force myself away.

Eli's easy enough to find in the first door on the right—the spare bedroom and Heath's new office. I stand in the doorway, watching him move boxes from one side of the room to the other, not really accomplishing anything.

"Hey."

"Hey," he answers, his body bent over a box.

I shift my weight from one foot to the other. "So . . . about what you saw in the kitchen . . . "

"I don't want to talk about it," he mumbles.

"Eli . . . "

"Damn it, Leah." He throws a book down into the box at his feet, the sharp noise causing my body to instinctively jump a step back. When he turns to me, his eyes are wild and bloodshot. "Haven't you figured out by now that Heath gets everything he wants? Money, cars, this condo . . . you." His arm juts out in my direction before he turns away again. "I knew this would happen. I knew he would see how much you meant to me and go after you. Just to prove that he could do it." His body swings back to mine. "Because that's what he's doing; you understand that, right?"

"Eli, that's not what's happening here. I promise . . . "

"Don't. Just don't, Lee. I've known him his whole life. I've seen firsthand, more times than I can count, how he takes something good, only to go and sabotage it. And, this time, that something will be *you*. I thought I was doing the right thing by keeping you apart, giving you time to consider giving us another chance . . ."

I stare at him as his words penetrate. "But . . . but that's not us. I thought we worked through that."

I take one step toward him, and he raises a hand, holding me to my spot.

"You're my best friend, Eli. My very best friend. I thought you were good with that. I thought *we* were good."

"I was good with it because I *had* to be good with it. I had no other choice. I just thought you needed more time, so I gave it to you."

"Eli ..." I dare to take a step toward him. But just one, as I see his fists ball at his sides.

"God, I'm so stupid! All the time I've wasted on waiting for you to see me, to see what I could give you. Just forget it. Forget all of it." He stomps the few steps dividing us and gets in my face. "He will hurt you, Leah. Heath only cares about one person. Himself. He will suck you in, take all the good from you that you have to offer, and then toss you aside, broken and used. It's what he does. And he's good at it. And, in the process, I'll lose both of you."

I shake my head, pleading. "That's not true. No one is losing anyone."

He lets out a strained laugh, but I don't give up.

"Eli, no one is losing anyone," I repeat my words with unconvincing conviction.

"I can't watch you with him. And I won't be the pussy who waits around, hoping to pick up the pieces when he breaks your heart. And I promise you, Leah, he *will* break your heart."

He bolts from the room, and a moment later, I hear the condo door slam.

What the hell just happened?

TWELVE

Heath

I come around the corner just in time to see Eli storm out of my office, grab his keys, and then tear out the door, looking like he lost his best friend. When I get to the office, Leah is standing motionless, wearing a similar expression. I give her shoulders a slight jar until she raises her eyes to mine.

"What happened? Did Eli do something?"

She shakes her head as the tears start to fall. "No. He didn't do anything. It's my fault."

I pull her into my chest and wrap my arms around her. She hesitates before doing the same and takes a few deep breaths before backing out of my hold.

"I should get going, but we got a lot done today, so you're pretty well set." She moves around me and out of the room, her focus anywhere but on me.

"You're going? Leah, what happened? What did he say to you?" My neck heats with panic as I follow on her heels, down the hall and into the kitchen.

"Nothing, Heath. I just have some of my own things to take care of today; that's all." She's looking for her purse, wiping at her eyes as she goes. She finds it on the kitchen table, hidden under some bubble wrap and quickly throws it over her head and across her chest as she heads for the door.

I step in front of her, blocking her with my full body. "You're not leaving."

"Heath, please. I need to go." Her head remains down as she digs for her keys, but I don't miss when she wipes fresh tears from her cheeks. "Just let me go."

"Not until you tell me what happened, Leah."

Her eyes are bloodshot and pained as red splotches now cover her chest and throat. "I'm sorry if I led you on, Heath. I honestly never meant to do that."

"What? You're not making sense right now." Fear rolls through me. It's foreign and unsettling, before quickly brewing into something more akin to anxiety.

She wraps herself in a hug and moves away from me, still afraid to raise her face to mine. "What I'm saying is, if I gave you the wrong impression, that there was something here, then I'm sorry. I'm really sorry."

Without thinking, I move close and grip her arms a little too tightly. "Leah, what the fuck? Talk to me." Anger is the winning emotion right now. I'm trying my best to rein it in, but I'm failing miserably.

She finally looks at me with exasperated, shiny eyes. "I just need to go, Heath. If I want to leave, then I should be able to leave."

She wants to leave? No problem. I'll give her a reason to leave.

I drop my hands and step back. "Fine. I see. You're one of *those*." I know this is stupid, and I should stop, but covering up my fear with resentment has always been one of my specialties. "A tease. You like to lead guys on, play games, like you've been doing with Eli. Almost had me fooled."

Her face falls in shock. "What? No . . . it's not like that."

"Bullshit. You've been leading him on for years, and now, you think you can do the same with me. And I almost fell for it, too. Well played, Princess. Well played." I pull the door open and wait for her to get the message. She's about to talk when I cut her off. "I speak for both Eli and myself when I say, get the fuck out and don't come back."

Her body jerks before she scurries out the door. I slam it and fall against it, catching an echo of a sob from down the hall.

What the hell just happened?

THIRTEEN

Heath

Clink.

I pick up another bottle cap from the small pile I've amassed on the coffee table and flick it from between my thumb and middle finger. I watch it sail into the TV screen.

Clink.

"You keep doing that, and you'll put a chip in the screen," Eli says from the kitchen.

He's been coming over more and more, and it's starting to annoy the shit out of me.

"I don't really give a fuck." I lay my head back on the sofa and try to stop the spinning. I've lost track of how many beers I've had. Or shots of Fireball. There's a reason a fire-breathing demon is on the label.

Tomorrow is going to suck. *Looks like I'll be going in late.* Just one of the many perks of nepotism.

A bottle of water hovers in front of my face.

"Drink this." Eli waits for me to take it.

I smack it away, only for it to reappear.

"Sit up, and drink the damn water, Heath."

I grab the bottle with a grunt and force my body upright.

As I begin to drink, Eli slides a plate onto the coffee table in front of me.

"Where did we get pizza?" I lean forward with a drunken smile.

"I ordered it. Shut up, and eat."

I inhale a few pieces before reaching for my beer on the table. "Where the hell's my beer?"

"We're out of beer. You drank the last one." He slides the bottle of water closer and continues to eat, never once taking his eyes off the screen.

"Since when do you care so much about my welfare? And how the hell did we run out of beer? I just bought a couple of cases."

"That's what happens when all you do is work and drink."

"Aw, are you worried about me, Eli? You're like the mom I never had. And just as big of a bitch."

He glares at me before looking back to the TV, never speaking a word in rebuttal.

"Somebody needs to make sure you don't choke on your own vomit."

"I don't need your help, dude. Fuck off."

He ignores me and takes another bite of pizza. I lay my head back and close my eyes, and before I know it, I fall asleep.

I startle awake to the sounds of bombs going off and lights flashing.

"What the . . ." I run my hands down my face and realize it's coming from the movie Eli's watching.

Only he's not watching it. He's sitting with his elbows on his knees and his head in his hands. One guess as to what he's thinking about. Watching him, I remind myself for the hundredth time that Leah's a tease who played us both. Eli should be thanking me instead of sulking like a girl.

"I'm going to bed. You can crash on the sofa if you want," I mumble as I force my body forward.

"No. I was just about to go. I've got an early meeting. You going to work tomorrow?" he asks.

What he really means is, *You blowing off work tomorrow?*

"Yeah, I'm going in. At some point." I take in the mess on the coffee table. Beer bottles and a half-eaten pizza cover the table, but as usual, I ignore it and head for my room. "Lock up when you go, yeah?"

"Yeah."

I make it to my bathroom and lean back on the long countertop as I pop two aspirin and wash them down with a full glass of water. I take in the large space, and clear as day, as if Leah were here again, all I see is her, excited and smiling, twirling around in the shower as her laughter bounces across the room. I shake off the thought and go to bed, hopeful that tonight will be the night the dreams of her here with me will finally stop.

FOURTEEN

Leah

I swipe at the penny with the toe of my shoe before finally deciding to pick it up. "Heads up, good luck," I mumble the familiar line to myself. I clear the gravel away from Lincoln's face and slip it into my pocket. *Guess I should take whatever luck I can get.*

Stepping through the door to the deli, I scan the space of red booths, looking for Connor, just as my phone vibrates with a text. It's him.

Five minutes.

I head to the counter to place our usual orders and grab a seat.

I'm scrolling through my phone, torturing myself by looking at Eli's Facebook page to get an idea of what he's been up to these last few weeks. And, more importantly, if he's unfriended me. It wouldn't surprise me since he hasn't responded to a single text or voice mail. And, last I checked, Heath doesn't have a Facebook account. Unless he's blocked me. My shoulders hunch at the thought. I've run through so many emotions these last few weeks, mostly anger at them both, but the last few days have been stuck on plain old sadness.

"Hey, Leah!"

I raise my head to see a familiar face smiling down at me. I force one in return as he takes the seat across from me.

"Hey, Burger."

He doesn't miss the lack of enthusiasm in my voice.

"Bad day?" he asks as he brings his hands under his chin.

Burger is small, as far as guys go. Maybe five foot five with reddish-brown hair and brown eyes. Connor jokes that he looks like a leprechaun, and unfortunately, today, wearing a kelly-green polo shirt, he does.

"It's fine." I shrug. I don't mention that all I want to do is go home and crawl into bed. "I found a lucky penny in the parking lot, so that's something, right?"

"Actually, it is your lucky day." He jolts upright as his palms smack the table. "A major ad agency is hiring in Chicago. You'd be perfect for it!"

I give him a blank stare, which he ignores.

"They just won a national retail account and need to build their team fast."

"Burger, I'm barely out of college. No agency out of Chicago is going to want me."

"I disagree. They need a team of junior-level reps to handle day-to-day maintenance and I think you'd be perfect." I eye him, suspiciously. "What do you say? Can I send them your résumé?"

"Sorry, you lost me at Chicago. Thanks for thinking of me though. Besides, when do you recruit for anything other than engineering?"

"Since they've run out of strong candidates. And, if I'm being honest, they're offering a bonus to anyone who can fill the roles." He leans over with puppy-dog eyes and a sad pout. "Will you just talk to them? It would really help to at least show my bosses that I'm trying."

His fingers clench in prayer, and I cave to his begging.

"Fine. But don't be upset when I graciously turn them down. Not that they'd even want me."

"You're the best. Thanks, Leah. I'll schedule something for later this week."

I roll my eyes at him, annoyed with myself for giving in. I really need to learn that it's okay to say no sometimes. Although it couldn't hurt to hone my interview skills a bit. You never know when you're going to need a change.

"What are we talking about?" Connor asks as he takes the chair next to Burger.

"Burger's trying to pimp me out."

"What? One Dawson isn't enough?" Connor jokes.

"Always looking to help out my friends, man."

"Yeah, more like you're looking to make twenty percent commission on our first-year salary."

"Hey now! That's not why I do it. And, besides, it's only ten percent." Burger stands as our food is delivered. "Thanks again, Leah. I really appreciate it. I'll be in touch."

"I'm sure you will. Now, shoo, so I can talk to my brother before he leaves me and breaks my heart." I manage a weak laugh, but it doesn't fool Connor as we watch Burger walk away.

His warm hand wraps around my wrist. I hesitate before meeting his eyes.

"You know I'll be less than four hours away, right?"

"Three hours and forty minutes actually," I say with a weak smile.

"Lee, this is a huge opportunity for me. Don't make it harder than it already is."

"It's not just that. It's . . ."

He sits back, arms crossed in concern. "It's Eli, isn't it?"

I push around a few fries. "How'd you know?"

"Because he hasn't been around, and you've been acting like a total crabass."

My only response is a pointed stare since I can't really argue with him there.

"So, what happened? He saw he had a little competition and finally mustered up the courage to tell you how he feels?"

I freeze, the fry dangling in front of my mouth. "How did you know?"

"Lee, come on. The guy has had it bad for you since you met. It was obvious the first time you brought him by the house. The way he followed you around and smiled at you like he was drugged."

I throw my fry at him, hitting him in the shoulder. He ignores it but I smile for the first time in a week.

"You're seriously telling me you never knew?"

"No. I mean . . . yes. Ugh." I throw my head back. "I guess I just wanted to believe we were good. And I thought we were when we *both* decided we'd be better as friends. Everything was fine after that. Or so I thought."

"Let me guess. Until you started hanging around his fresh-out-of-rehab stoner friend?"

Between his rip on Heath and my own obliviousness to Eli's feelings, my anger flares. And, when I'm angry, I cry. It's one of the things I hate about myself. I hang my head as my hair falls around me, helping to hide the building tears in my eyes.

Connor moves into the seat next to me and wraps an arm around my shoulders. "Lee, don't cry. It can't be that bad. Tell me what happened." He's leaning in to my ear, hiding our conversation from the bustling lunch crowd.

I take a few deep breaths and go over every detail from the moment I first met Heath playing basketball to our kiss and, finally, the day at his condo.

Connor and I might tease each other from time to time, but we have a bond built on not just being twins, but twins that have gone through the loss of a parent together.

Connor leans back and looks off to the side, grinding his jaw.

"Con?"

"Jesus, I never thought Eli would end up being the bigger tool of the two."

"Connor!" I hiss, eyeing the restaurant for curious stares. Fortunately, there seem to be none.

He leans back in and whispers sharply, "That's total bullshit, Lee, being your friend until he finds his opening to get in your pants. I swear to God, if you ever bring him by again, I will kick his ass out the fucking door."

Connor is madder than I can remember seeing him in a long time. Madder than . . . A thought hits me, and I start giggling. It feels good, and the increasingly irritated look on his face just makes my laughter grow.

"What?"

"I haven't seen you this mad since I shaved off one of your eyebrows!" I'm full-on belly-laughing now, and other customers begin to look our way.

He's shaking his head, trying to fight off a smile. "Lee, it was the night before homecoming and I was going with Kelly Evan, the hottest girl in school."

"Well, you deserved it. Remember when Aiden Bishop came over to study, and you walked into the family room wearing my bra around your neck and chewing on a three-pound hunk of salami?"

"What was wrong with that?"

"I had a huge crush on him and he never talked to me again after that."

"Hey, I was just helping by pointing out a major character flaw . . . fear of ladies' undergarments. Or he's intimidated by large pieces of meat."

I smirk and shake my head as I dip a fry in ketchup and take a bite. "What would I do without you?" I bump my shoulder against his.

He wraps an arm around my shoulder before planting a kiss on my head then stealing a fry as he moves back to his seat. "So, what are you going to do about Heath?"

"Heath? Don't you think my bigger problem is Eli?"

"Not at all. Eli is his own problem. He needs to get his head straight and see things for what they are. *You* need to talk to Heath."

"They're best friends, Con. I told you what Eli said. Being with Heath will only hurt him. They'd never be friends again, and I won't do that to them. Besides, things barely got started with Heath. I'm sure he's moved on by now."

FIFTEEN

Heath

"All right, ladies, make room for our special guest." I push the empty beer bottles aside before dumping the contents of the brown bag in the center of the table, the bet I made not long ago a forgotten memory.

Laurie moves in close to me on the sofa while her friend scoots in on my other side.

I take a second to appreciate their short skirts that rise even higher as they lean in toward me before fumbling with the plastic wrap knotted at the top. I'm tempted to give up and just tear it open to get to the white gold inside when it's suddenly ripped out of my hands from behind.

"What the fuck?" When I whip around, Eli is standing behind me with my newly purchased eight ball of coke.

I rise and swing an arm out to retrieve it, but he's faster than I am. I might have taken one hit too many off the bong.

"That's it. You're done, Heath. Ladies, it's time to go. I'll get you an Uber." He pulls his phone from his pocket and swiftly moves his thumb around, but I'm more interested in what he's protecting against his chest. "There. Five minutes. Laurie, I gave them your address, so why don't you both head downstairs?"

The girls hesitate, looking to me for direction.

When they don't move, Eli's tone darkens. *"Now."*

On that, they scurry out the door.

I lunge at Eli over the back of the sofa, my leg bumping the coffee table. A few bottles rattle and fall over, rolling to the floor and leaving a trail of beer as they go. I ignore it and reach for Eli a second time. All I'm concerned with right now is pummeling my supposed friend. I rush around the sectional and grab him by the shirt collar, jabbing a finger in his face, at the same time he hides the package behind his back.

"Give me my fucking blow, Eli," I spit, giving his shirt a rough shake. But he stands his ground. "Give it to me before I kick your fucking ass."

"No. This isn't high school, Heath. You don't get to fry your brain every time life doesn't go your way."

"What the hell does that mean?"

He doesn't answer, just stares me down. "Sit," he orders.

I tighten my grip, but he shows no signs of fear or fighting back.

"I said, *sit down*. It's time we had a talk."

"Give. Me. My—"

"Sit down!" His face burns deep red as he finally pushes me back from him.

We've been friends for more years than I can count, and we've never fought. And that's mostly thanks to him

90

for being one of the most laid-back guys I know. Until now.

"Sit." He takes a deep breath. "Down." Then, another.

When I grudgingly take a seat, he comes around to stand in front of me, wisely on the other side of the coffee table. With my coke stashed in his back pocket, he puts his hands on his hips and expels an audible sigh.

"I'm the reason Leah left." The words rush out, but I still manage to catch every one. "It's my fault, okay? It's all my fault."

He hasn't mentioned Leah since the day she left here, but he's been micromanaging me in the meanwhile. Like, nagging me to go to work, coming over with food, and now, taking my coke. That all leads to one thought. *Guilty.*

I stand slowly, shoulders back and feet firmly planted. My buzz evaporates, and my impatience brews. As much as I want to punch him in the face, I want an explanation more. Then, I'll punch him in the face.

"What did you do?"

Eli looks out toward the balcony while my fists clench at my sides. I'm losing patience while he musters up the courage to explain.

"So, you know how Leah and I dated in college and you know how we've been close friends and you know how, since the two of you met—"

"Eli, you're talking like a chick and not making any fucking sense. Just say it."

He rakes his hands over his face, up through his hair, and back again before looking me in the eye and forcing the words out. "I told Leah that I still had feelings for her and that she needed to stay away from you if she didn't want to cost us our friendship."

My body jerks. "What? Why?" I whisper in shock. When he doesn't speak, I stand taller. *"Answer me."*

"I just . . . it was . . . I've had feelings for her since college. And then she meets you, and just like that, she's yours. What I was always afraid of."

"That's why we never met?"

He looks away, embarrassed.

"Eli?"

"She'd ask about meeting you but I always found an excuse."

"You tell me this now? After all these weeks?"

"I had to. You've been self-destructing. Drinking. Laurie. Now, the coke. I can't watch it anymore."

I wring my fingers together behind my neck, squeeze my eyes shut, and inhale a deep breath. "You can't *watch it* anymore?"

"I just meant . . . I can't . . ."

My temper begins to wear thin, forcing me to walk to the far end of the room. The good thing is, my mind is clear of the pot and I'm in full control of my faculties. Resentment and anger are the only things flowing through my veins right now.

"Have you talked to her?" I ask as I begin to pace.

"Um, no. She texted a few times, left messages, but I didn't answer. I was more worried about you." He glances at the bong on the table.

I don't bother to contain my bark of laughter at his pathetic line of thinking. "And you say you care about her."

His body tightens at the venom in my voice.

When he doesn't answer, I stop and unleash on him. "How could you treat her that way?" I point at my chest. "Treat *me* that way?" I can't take it anymore. My rage wins out. Before he realizes it, I've got him up against the wall by his shirt, the pictures rattling around us as his head hits the drywall. "If you can't have her, neither of us will? Is that it, Eli? Do you know what I said to her? What an asshole I was, all because of you?"

He flinches when my spit hits him in the face.

"I'm sorry."

"Get out. Just . . . *get . . . out . . . now.*" I let up my grip and allow him enough room to get by, using every muscle in my body to keep me from turning him into my personal punching bag.

He stands at the island, out of reach. "Heath, let me try to fix this. If I—"

"*Out!*" I push that one word out with enough force that I'm surprised when the walls don't shake.

He finally has the sense to listen to me, and just as the door shuts, I grab a bottle and catapult it across the room, too outraged to take pleasure in the mess it makes against the wall.

"Fuck!" I shout to the empty room.

Every day since she walked out my door, I've grown angrier and angrier with her, and only with her. I went back to drinking, screwing around, and almost fried my brain on an eight ball of coke. All the while, that fucker hid the truth.

With an arsenal of supplies at my side, I start cleaning up any signs of the last few weeks. Next is a long, hot shower to remove every trace of Laurie. Just the thought of her ever touching me again makes my skin crawl.

With a clean house, showered body, and sober mind, I'm once again pacing my living room, debating the bigger problem. *What are you going to do now?* What if Eli and I fucked this up so badly, Leah is done with the both of us?

There's only one way to find out.

SIXTEEN

Leah

There's a double knock on my door a second before my mom walks in. "You still up, hon?"

"Yeah, just working on a proposal for a new client. We're presenting it on Friday, and I need to polish it up a bit."

"You never bring work home. And you've been working later than usual, too. Everything okay?"

"Yeah, Mom. Just really busy. Clients' new budgets kicked in, so they've got money to spend. It's all good."

"Okay, if you say so." She gives me a sympathetic smile. "Nothing from Eli?"

"Mom," I say, exasperated.

"All right, all right. I'll stop asking." She puts a hand up in defeat. "I talked to Connor tonight. He said you're going to visit him this weekend . . . again?"

"What's your point, Mom?" I ask, unable to hide my growing exhaustion.

"It's just, you've been out there almost every weekend since we moved him into his new apartment. I thought maybe you and I could do something instead?"

"Are you sure you don't have a date?" I ask her, mostly joking. "Part of the reason I've been visiting Connor so much is because you've had quite the social calendar, and I don't want to sit around an empty house. Or worse, walk in on something." I shiver dramatically at the thought.

"You're hilarious," she deadpans. "For your information, I've yet to have a first date lead to a second one. These men are all out for one thing."

"Okay, that's enough of that. No details, please." I dramatically wave the thought away.

She walks over and kisses me on the head before taking a step back to look me in the eyes.

"Tomorrow's a new day, Lee."

She closes the door behind her as she leaves but I know she's far from giving up. She's been fishing for weeks now for any information about Eli and Heath, but I just need to let it go. I need to let them go. I don't ever want to be the reason two lifelong best friends lose each other.

I give up for the night, closing my laptop and turning out the light. The upside to all of this is that I've never been more productive at work. The lead account executive on one of the largest clients I support has asked me to present at our next client meeting. Usually, I'm stuck in the back, taking notes and making sure the coffee is fresh. So, there's one silver lining to all of this.

I slide under the covers and stare at the ceiling of the pitch-black room, physically spent from the hours I've been putting in but unable to shut my brain off. I roll over when my phone pings with a text. It's from Heath.

Come outside.

I jump out of bed, suddenly no longer tired, and peek through my blinds. Fortunately, he can't see me in the darkness, but I can definitely see him.

Heath is in my driveway, leaning against his car.

His face glows from the light of his phone as he types another text.

I see you.

Can he? I duck down below the window when my phone buzzes again.

I'm waiting, Princess.

In just a tank top and sleep shorts, I quickly but quietly make my way down the stairs and out the front door. Even though the night air is humid and warm, goose bumps travel across my body. I stop a few feet short of him, running my hands back and forth over the bumps on my arms, but it's no use.

He pushes off from against his car but doesn't approach. Even in the dim light, I don't miss the dark circles under his eyes.

"Why are you here?" I ask, more curious than irritated, more surprised than elated.

He moves swiftly, erasing the last of the space between us, until he's hovering over me. "Ask me again," he says with an eyebrow raised in challenge.

I swallow and then speak each word, halting and shy, barely loud enough for him to hear over the buzz of grasshoppers and the whispering breeze that swirls around our bodies, "Why are you here, Heath?"

"This."

And, before I know it, his hands cup my face, and his lips crush against mine. Heath is kissing me. He's here and he's kissing me and it's just as good as the first time. I grip him in return, eliminating any space left between us, turning a simple kiss rough and desperate. He's making up for every kiss that would've been. I dig my fingers into his muscled back as everything that's been missing these last few weeks comes rushing back. My pulse races, and my breathing is heavy. With wonder. With excitement. With anger.

I push at his chest, but his hands move to my hips, gripping me in place.

"You shouldn't be here. You need to go," I order.

His grip loosens but he doesn't release me.

I stop fighting as we both stand silent in the darkness, the only light coming from a few random streetlights. His hands rise and his fingers push into my hair while his thumbs sweep over my cheeks. My eyes close as the tip of his nose brushes against my own.

"I'm sorry, Leah." The words float against my lips, faint and pained, like they've never been spoken before. "I was an asshole."

"Heath—"

"Jesus, I missed you." He pulls back, eyes fierce, taking me in like he'd forgotten every detail.

I fall into his chest as his chin comes to rest atop my head.

"I talked to Eli. He told me everything."

My body stills and his hands envelop my body in response.

"What he said to you, lying to you all this time, it wasn't right."

"He's entitled to the way he feels."

"And so are you."

I heave a deep breath, not sold on his words.

"Fine. He's entitled to have feelings for you, but you don't have to feel the same way back. And you sure as hell don't have to feel guilty about it."

I push against his chest in defense. "But he's my best friend and a big part of my life . . . and—"

"And he's my best friend, too. But he fucked-up. And, right now, all I care about is you."

"Really?" The guilt I've carried the last few weeks has me fighting back tears.

"Yeah, really." He pulls me back in close. "So, what do you think? Can we try this again?" By his confident smirk, he already knows my answer.

"I'd like that."

He takes my face in his hands once more before he takes my kiss, my heart not far behind. Then, we make up for every kiss we missed.

SEVENTEEN

Heath

I'm standing outside Leah's work, a latte in each hand, when she comes out, frazzled and stressed but still managing to look like a hot little executive in her slacks and blazer, complete with a messy bun atop her head and a pen sticking through it she most likely forgot about. The second she sees me, her eyes light up, and her full lips break out into a wide smile.

"Please tell me that's a latte." She moans as she reaches out a hand.

I pull my arm back. "It depends. What do *I* get?" I give her her favorite smirk, the one that always gets me what I want.

Her cheeks flush as her eyes flutter, and, Christ, just like that, she goes from hot to too fucking cute. I've never known anyone so easy to please. I'll give her a latte every day if that's all it takes to see that look on her face.

She rises up onto her toes as her small hand flattens against my stomach and her body leans in before she plants a solid, cool kiss on my lips. Here, in the middle of a bustling rush-hour sidewalk, surrounded by strangers, this intelligent, beautiful girl is kissing *me*.

"Heath?"

I shake out of the thought. "Yeah?"

"Everything okay?"

"Hell, yeah." I smile before handing her the cup and lean in for a second kiss.

I'm not really sure how to define what we've started. Partly because we haven't had a straight conversation about it and partly because I have nothing else to compare this to. Of all the girls I've been with, there's never been one I wanted something more with. Not a single one I thought about after the fact or considered putting before myself. Not until Leah. Now, it's like my head is swimming when I'm with her, and I'm crawling out of my skin when I'm not. It's foreign and awkward and really fucking addictive.

I tangle my fingers with hers and wait in anticipation as a second blush fills her face, pink and glowing, and all I can think about is being alone with her. We haven't gotten that far yet, but I need to know if other parts of her turn pink as well.

I hold open the door for her, and she steps inside the foyer of my condo. She's grasping the straps of her purse and waiting for me to lead the way, hesitant, both of us remembering the last time she was here.

"All good?"

She only answers with a silent head bob.

"C'mon." I take her hand, entwining our fingers, and guide her forward. I give a slight squeeze, and in this moment, realize that I haven't held a girl's hand like this since the eighth grade. Even then, it was nothing more than a tactic, giving the girl the impression I had only the purest of intentions—until I got what I wanted. But, with Leah, I'm content to hold any part of her she's willing to give.

When we reach the kitchen, I pull her purse from her shoulder and lay it on the island before leading her to the sofa where she takes the seat next to me and grips her hands together in her lap.

She's looking around, not like she's seeing the space for the first time, but like she's expecting everything to have changed. But nothing's changed. Not with us at least. There's only one thing different, one thing missing.

She shifts her focus to her hands. "Have you talked to Eli?"

I pull her over until her bottom is resting in my lap. She swings her legs to my side as I brush her hair over her shoulder, watching my fingers weave their way through. "No. And, honestly, I couldn't give a shit if I ever talked to him again."

Her face drops in disappointment.

"Leah, what did he think? That you'd wake up one day and realize you were as crazy for him as he was with you? If that's the case, he should've manned up a long time ago."

"Heath, he's my best friend. *Our* best friend. Just because we hit one bump doesn't mean we walk away forever. How much longer can this go on? He needs us."

"How can you say that? He's basically been lying to you for years. And I bet I'm not the first guy he's cockblocked you from."

Her jaw drops for a brief second before her eyes squint in aggravation. Shy Leah is cute, but I'm learning pissed off Leah is pretty damn hot.

She tries to twist in my lap as she huffs, "You can't just drop someone from your life without at least trying to fix it, Heath."

"Why not? My bitch of a mom did. She walked out and never looked back. There's your proof right there."

Her eyes soften along with her voice. "Heath, you might never know why she did what she did, but that doesn't make it right for you to do the same to someone else. If everyone acted that way, we'd all be depressed and alone. Sometimes, you just need to let things go."

She doesn't get it, and I'm not about to argue with her now that I've got her back. No one understands what it's like when the person who is supposed to love you unconditionally turns her back and walks out of your life, never to be heard from again.

She brings her hands to my face, steering me back to her. "I'd like to call him, make sure he's okay."

When she kisses me at the corner of my mouth and pulls back, I stand my ground. When she does the same to the other corner, my resolve wavers. It's not until she kisses me full-on, tangling her tongue with mine before pulling back and locking eyes, that I cave.

"Fine."

Between the glide of her tongue against my own and her soft hands on my skin, I'd say yes to anything. I'd give her anything.

I'm done talking about this. All I want is to drag her down the hall, undressing her as we go. I'm just not convinced she's ready for that. We've barely done more than kiss and I want to do this right, at her pace. The opposite of everything I've done before because she's unlike anyone I've ever known before.

But where to start? A first date? *What the hell do guys do on a first date anyway?* Dinner. They start with dinner at a nice restaurant. Shit, it's too late. Besides, she's settled on top of me, her body resting over mine and warming me from the inside out. *Why would I give this up for sitting across from her at a loud, crowded restaurant?*

I run my hand up her arm and watch with greedy pleasure as goose bumps rise over her skin. "Want to order dinner? There's a great Italian place down the street that delivers."

She quirks her lips as her gray eyes darken and her fingers run along the collar of my shirt. "Maybe in a little bit. I'm not all that hungry yet."

She's silently willing me to kiss her, so I do. And, the second before our lips touch, I swear, she smiles.

The kiss starts slow. I have to force my body to follow suit because, as much as I want to see her under me, I want her there because she wants it, not because I'm taking it.

I slide my hands up her legs and over her body, registering the feel of her skin and every slight curve along the way—something I've never done before now. All the others I've been with were all just a means to an end. Not with Leah. With her, I want to memorize everything—from the smoothness of her arms to the firmness of her thighs to the beat of her heart.

I slide my hand around to the back of her head, burying my fingers in her hair, unwilling to break the kiss as I twist my body over hers, coaxing her to her back before I brace my arm alongside her. Her hand skims my chest and rests on my neck where she wraps her fingers and tightens our connection. I grip the fabric of the sofa with my free hand and lose focus, my mind wandering to all the things I'd like to be doing to her but can't because I'm worried it's too soon. I fight with myself to hold back.

"What's the matter?" she asks between breaths.

"Nothing."

"Then, why aren't you touching me?"

"Because I'm trying to take it slow."

"Why?"

"Because I want to do this the right way. I don't want to scare you off when I've barely had you back."

"Heath, just because I don't have as much experience as you doesn't mean you can't touch me. All it means is that there hasn't been anyone worth touching me in a long time." Her mouth travels to my ear. "I want you to touch me, Heath. In fact, try to scare me off. I dare you."

The little vixen underneath the bun and blazer weakens my willpower and shreds my composure, but I manage to hang on.

"But this is supposed to be our first date," I reply teasingly.

She runs the pad of her finger over my bottom lip. "The way I see it, our first date was right here in this condo, the first time we came to look at it. Our second date was on your basketball court when I beat you playing Jerk—"

"Which makes this the third date," I announce with a wicked grin before stealing a kiss. "I like the way you think, Princess."

I'm off her and standing before my next breath. I scoop her up, *finally*, and head for my room.

Her laughter fills the hall until we make it to the bed, and I playfully drop her with a bounce on to the mattress below. Her legs hang off the end as she watches me pull at the neck of my shirt and yank it over my head. She rises up onto her elbows and her eyes fall to my pants and then back up again.

"Tell me what you want."

She decides to show me, starting by sitting up and reaching for my hips. I move in willingly, aching for what's coming next. She places a slow, warm kiss above the waist of my pants before undoing my belt and button and tugging them over my hips until they fall to the floor, leaving me in nothing but black boxer briefs. I'd much rather peel every inch of clothing off her body, but we're playing her game right now. And I'm loving every fucking minute of it.

I cross my arms at my chest, peering down at her before dragging my eyes from hers to her blouse and then back again. She smiles shyly and reaches for the top button. Then, the next and the next, painfully slow, until she pushes her shoulders back, allowing her navy blouse to cascade down her tan arms.

I'm rewarded with a black bra trimmed in silver lace, the kind that pushes everything together, creating a deep dip down the middle. Perfect for a shot of tequila.

Satisfied, I nod to her pants, disappointed that she'll have to take her shoes off first. They're simple black heels, but the straps around the ankles is what gets me. I make a mental note to request those for another time—along with the tequila.

With her shoes tossed aside, she glances up, fighting back a smile, as she deliberately takes her time with the button on her pants. After she lifts her hips and slides the fabric to the floor, she eases her body back to the center of the bed. My patience begins to wane, but my self-restraint is rewarded with the vision in front of me—

Leah, in nothing but panties and a bra, lying on my bed with her long hair fanned out around her like a goddess.

I squeeze my biceps in a weak attempt to ground the urge to hurl myself at her, instead directing my focus on this perfect girl before me. Her hands are splayed low over her stomach, attempting to hide what little she can. I wait for a minute, longer than I'd like, giving her the time she needs to build up the courage to drop them to her side. She's ridiculous to hide this body. She's the most gorgeous thing I've ever seen.

As if she can read my thoughts, her arms fall away— her version of a green light. I grip each ankle and spread her legs before my hands travel up her smooth skin. The second my palms make light contact with her thighs, she inhales a deep breath. I continue on my path, putting one knee to the bed and then the other, watching my hands travel higher until my thumbs scrape under the sides of her matching panties.

I'm in perfect alignment over the silver lace that runs low across her stomach. Her fingers grasp at the comforter and her hips rise ever-so slightly off the bed. If that's an invitation, I won't say no.

I brace an arm on either side of her waist, bending to kiss a line down her stomach until my lips feel the scratch of the lace. I hold steady, letting my breath heat her skin while testing her desire for me to go further. I peek up, and when there's no signal to stop, I continue my descent until I'm right where I want to be.

When I place one long, hard kiss over the sheer fabric, her knees trap me at the same time her fingers dive through my hair. She pulls me up for a wild kiss, not hesitating to tangle her tongue with mine, as I grind against her and we moan in sync.

Her confidence continues to grow as her hand travels down my stomach. When she arrives at her destination, she begins to stroke over the fabric. Between the sight of her below me and the feel of her hand sliding over me, it's just too much.

I push her hand aside, gliding my lips down her neck and leaving a trail of heated breaths that cause her skin to prickle. I tug at the straps of her bra, freeing a breast and taking her nipple in my mouth. I suck hard until a soft cry escapes her throat and her hands frantically grab at my hair. I tug the other cup down and do the same, hoping for the same reaction. When I feel the sting at my scalp, I lose another ounce of control. Forcing myself from her grip, I rise up onto my forearms and grind into her once, then twice, painfully waiting for permission.

"Please tell me you have a condom," she pants as her hands slide lower, digging her nails into my ass.

I break away, unable to get to my nightstand fast enough, throwing open the drawer and struggling for a second too long as I try to rip one free from the strip. I tear it open and step between her legs, freezing at the sight before me.

Her panties are gone as she tosses her bra off the bed. I'm expecting her to hide herself again, but she surprises me in the best way. With her eyes locked on mine, she takes a visible breath and lifts one arm up alongside her head, her eyes shooting to my briefs when my dick twitches in anticipation. She looks back up to me before raising her other arm. An offering. I want to tell her how amazing she is, what I know this means for a girl like her, but I don't want to break the moment. Right now, our silence is speaking for us, and it's the sweetest thing I've ever heard.

Ridding myself of my boxers, I roll on the condom and make my way over her outstretched body, kissing a trail up her stomach and over her chest as I go, until my fingers entwine with hers and her legs wrap around me. Every instinct in my body is telling me to go hard and fast. But this isn't about me. It's about her and, more importantly, what I want this to mean for us.

I enter achingly slow, pressing my cheek to hers, so the only sound we hear is each other's steady breaths. When I'm all the way in, I still as a groan from deep within me escapes my chest. She grips my fingers tighter and turns to kiss me, sucking on my tongue and nipping at my lip, making it tough to fight the need to thrust inside her. I'm convinced this is the hardest thing I've ever done.

She digs her heels into my thighs and expels a pained breath of her own. "Move, Heath. Please move."

Thank fuck.

I release her hands, rushing one of mine down until it's grabbing her ass and pulling her to me. She doesn't hesitate to clasp on to my back and dig in, the bite of pain from her nails only causing me to drive harder.

She lets out a stifled moan and then another. On the third, I know she's holding back. So, I do the only thing I can do in this moment. I stop, still inside her. She looks at me, brows tense in concern.

"You're safe with me, Leah. Always know that. Scream if you want to scream, scratch if you want to scratch. But don't hold back on me. Ever."

Her eyes widen at my words, so I repeat the most important one, *"Ever."*

I don't give her a chance to overthink what I said. Instead, I kiss her hard, moving again and not letting up. I know I've gotten through to her when she pulls her knees up and digs her nails into my ass, harder than before.

I rise up onto my knees, lifting her hips and driving into her deeper. She grabs her breasts and squeezes as she throws her head back and begins to come. Watching her touch herself, hearing her truly let herself go—it's the single best moment of my life. I come harder and longer than I have before, in a way I didn't even know was possible. I've never lost myself to a girl before.

And, with this girl, I'm not just lost. I'm *gone*.

EIGHTEEN

Leah

I wanted to meet with Eli first, alone, so I could have a chance to talk to him about the whole thinking-there's-still-a-chance thing, but Heath wouldn't have it. That's what I've come to think of it as. Eli doesn't have romantic feelings for me. If he did, he wouldn't have sat back and quietly been my friend for so many years. And, if he truly cares for me—as a friend—then he should have let me have a chance with someone who could make me happy.

So, here we are, sitting in Heath's condo, waiting for Eli to show up. Well, Heath's sitting. I'm pacing, fluffing pillows and wiping down the counters for the third time. I even considered opening a bottle of wine, just a sip or two to take the edge off, but surprisingly, I can't find a drop of alcohol in this place.

At the knock on the door, I rush over to it before Heath can even get up. Eli takes a few steps in, and I cave, crushing him with a hug.

He squeezes me back just as tightly. "I'm sorry," he whispers in my ear.

"Me, too."

"Ahem."

We separate and turn toward Heath. He's standing with his chin raised and arms crossed at his chest, glaring at Eli. I open my eyes wide and stare, trying to communicate with him a reminder of what we agreed to this morning. *No hurting Eli.* But he never looks at me.

"You're a dick."

"I know, man. I'm sorry." Eli steps away from me, head hung low.

I hold my breath as he walks closer to Heath. They face off for the briefest moment before reaching out and gripping one another in a one-armed man hug, each finishing with two strong pats to the other's back.

"Have you guys eaten lunch?" Eli asks as he takes a seat at the far end of the sofa.

"No. What should we get? Pizza? Mexican? Who's playing today? Did you hear Williams got traded?" Heath asks as he takes a seat opposite Eli.

"Seriously? That sucks. I could go for Mexican. Lee, does that sound good to you?" I'm watching the two of them, stunned silent. "Lee?" Eli says.

"What just happened?" I look from them, over to the spot where they hugged, then back again in total confusion.

"What do you mean?" Heath reaches a hand out for me to join him.

"It's done? Just like that? We're all friends again?"

"Yeah, Lee . . . relax." Eli clears his throat and smiles his sweet, kind smile. "We're all friends again."

Heath continues to hold his hand out.

Guys are weird.

I shake my head and breathe a deep sigh of relief because the drama is over, and more importantly, no blood was shed.

I don't take Heath's hand but move to the seat next to him, close but not touching. I'm still leery of shoving our relationship in Eli's face. Not one for subtlety, Heath pulls me tight to his side as he and Eli begin to shout and grumble at the game playing on the TV. With the warmth of Heath's body against my own, his fingers trailing along my hip, I relax. We're finally all where we're meant to be.

Heath leaves to meet the delivery guy, and the second the door closes behind him, Eli slides in next to me, mindful to leave a few inches between us.

"I'm so sorry, Lee."

"Stop apologizing. I feel like an idiot. You're my best friend, Eli, and I keep thinking I should've known how you felt, but why didn't you ever tell me?"

"This is all on me. I've never been friends with a girl the way I am with you and I made it into something it wasn't. I love spending time with you and I feel protective over you, but I think I confused that with it meaning something more. Does that make sense?"

I grip his hand as we both exhale in relief. "Yes. It makes total sense. But are you sure you're okay with all of this?"

"All of this?"

I motion to the condo. "Heath and me. Together."

He smiles flatly in understanding. "I've just spent weeks without my two best friends, and I'd be lying if I said I wasn't miserable. Without you guys, I realized pretty quickly that, if together is the only way I can get you both, then I'll take it. But, Lee, you need to know something about Heath. I love him like a brother—"

"I would never hurt him, Eli."

"That's not what I'm worried about." He takes a deep breath, and I brace. "I said some terrible things to you that day. But what I said about Heath, even though I was mad, is the truth. He's never been in a real relationship. He's never cared for anyone more than he cares about himself. And, as good as I know you would be for him, I'm not sure he'll be the same for you."

"I know enough of his history, Eli. But he deserves a chance, and until he proves to me otherwise, I'm going to give it to him. You should, too."

He squeezes my hand. "I will, but I won't be responsible for what I might do to him if he hurts you."

"I can promise you, it will never come to that."

His mouth flattens in doubt.

"If or when this thing between us ends, we'll handle it like adults. But, for now, I like him, Eli. A lot. And, for the first time ever, I want a chance to see where this can go. So, are we good?"

He moves in, his arms wrapping around my shoulders, and I hug him back.

"Yeah, we're good."

"Good. Then, there's only one thing left to do."

"What's that?"

"Find *you* a girlfriend."

He sits back as a nervous laugh escapes and runs his palms over his thighs. "Actually, my sisters may have set me up on a date"—he pauses—"or two recently."

"Eli!" I give him a playful jab in the shoulder. "And?"

"And not much came of them, but I have another date this weekend with a girl I've been talking to lately. She seems pretty cool but it's nothing serious."

116

He's blushing like a teenage girl, and I love it.

Bouncing in my seat, I rattle off the questions I usually reserve for Connor, "What's her name? Where'd you meet her? Where's she from? What does she do? How old is she? Does she have a criminal record? Any hairy moles I shouldn't stare at?"

Laughing, he raises his hands in defense to my bombardment of questions. "I'll answer your first question. Her name is Lindsey." As I open my mouth to beg for more, he covers it with his hand. "And that's all you're getting for now."

I pout behind his fingers, but he only smiles at my disappointment.

The door opens, and a second later, Heath walks into the room, two plastic bags hanging from his hands. I leave Eli and go to help, opening containers and grabbing drinks.

Hidden by the refrigerator door, Heath whispers, "Did I give you enough time?"

"It was perfect. Thank you." I give him a quick kiss.

Seriously, what a thoughtful guy. Eli has nothing to worry about.

"We've only been official for a month, Lee. I wasn't going to introduce her to my friends until I thought it might be going somewhere," Eli says as he steals one of my grapes and pops it into his mouth. We're hanging out at Heath's before meeting Eli's new girlfriend for dinner tonight.

"And is it? Going somewhere?" I take a grape and push the bowl toward him, across the kitchen island.

117

"If you had asked me that question when we first met a couple of months ago, I'd have said no way. But, now, yeah. It's good. I really like her."

A dreamy look washes over his face causing flashbacks of protective mama-bear feelings over Connor to come rushing back to me. "Why? What happened when you first met?"

Eli doesn't miss my concern, and his tone turns pleading. "Can we save this conversation for another time? I want you to come to dinner with an open mind."

His answer gives away nothing, but I decide not to push it.

"Fine. But, one day, you *will* sit down and spill all the details."

"I promise." He meets my stare before eating another grape.

I want to like Lindsey. I really do. Because I want Eli to be as happy as I am. But I'll decide for myself when we meet her in a few hours.

"Hey, Princess, grab me a towel!" Heath shouts from the depths of his bedroom.

"I thought you hate when people call you that?" Eli asks.

I raise a shoulder and smile as I rise from my stool. "Turns out, it's not as bad as I thought."

"So, you'll be fine with me calling you that from now on?" He raises an eyebrow in jest.

I get in his face and lower my voice. "Don't even think about it, *Elijah Francine*." I pull away and move toward the hall.

"Hey, my grandmother was a lovely woman! It's not my fault my mom thought she'd never have a girl."

We both laugh as he walks to the door.

"I forgot to tell you." I take a few steps back to the room as he speaks. "I left you tickets for next week's game at Will Call. Although I don't know why you're going. You hate football."

"Correction—I don't hate it. It just bores me out of my ever-loving mind. They are two very different things."

He rolls his eyes. "Whatever. I should get going though. Lindsey asked me to come by early. She's really nervous about meeting you guys."

I swat my hand through the air. "Tell her she's got nothing to worry about."

"Trust me, I did at least a hundred times. But I get it. It's hard enough to meet your boyfriend's best friend, but when there's two of them . . ."

I shake my head as a chastising tsk escapes my lips. "So, you haven't told her everything about your *other* best friend?" I point to myself.

He puffs out a breath. "Not yet. I want to make sure we're in a good place before I throw that at her."

"Well, let me know if I can help in any way. I want good things for you, Eli, and if she is what you want, then I'll support you in any way I can."

He walks over and wraps me in a warm hug. "Love you, Lee."

"Love you, too."

"Leah!" Heath shouts again.

Eli pulls away. "I'll let myself out. See you tonight."

I don't wait for the door to close as I hustle down the hall, grabbing a towel from the linen closet on my way. I hear the water running and walk in to find the rain shower pouring down over his back. When I go to set his towel on the small teak bench, I see one is already there.

"Hey, you already have a towel." I turn to find him standing in the shower, wearing nothing but a wicked smile.

"Do I?" he asks before raising his face to the water.

I try to maintain focus above his shoulders. Not the glistening body below them.

Who am I kidding? I sneak a quick glance, which turns into a long one.

"My eyes are up here, Princess." He runs his hands over his soapy hair. "And the towel isn't for me," he taunts.

"Oh." The soapy sight of him has stolen my ability to speak.

I've seen him naked more times than I can count now but usually in bed. Not like this, behind the full glass doors of the shower, where I can admire him, examine every line and ridge. It's like he's an exhibit at a fine art show. Or a caged animal.

I scream as I'm literally pulled from my thoughts, getting soaked in a matter of seconds by the wide stream overhead.

"Please tell me Eli is gone."

I've lost the ability to speak, instead choosing to run my hands over his hot, slick skin, watching with intense awe as my fingers glide through the soap bubbles on his chest. His hands lift my face up to his, and his tongue traces my lips.

"Is. He. Gone?" Fiery eyes look down on me.

I'm about to answer when he steps me back against the tiled wall and pushes his naked body against my fully clothed one.

I manage to pump soap into my hands then rub them everywhere I can reach. The feel of his lean, strong body is one of my favorite things in this world, but add soap and water, and I've found my newest fixation.

He releases the button of my khaki shorts and I continue my exploration until he peels my tank top up and over my head and I step out of my shorts and panties. With one hand at my back, he pops open the hook of my bra with practiced ease.

"Has it been long enough?" he asks, kissing my neck, his fingers wasting no time in sliding between my legs.

It's been over a week since I went on the pill and we both got tested.

He slips two fingers inside me and swirls his thumb, hitting the spot.

"Yes," I answer as I buck against the tiled wall and dig my fingers in his hair. I don't even know what I'm saying yes to right now, Eli or the pill, but fortunately, it's the right answer to both questions.

As he continues his pace between my legs, his other hand glides up my arm until his palm wraps high at my neck, angling my face to his. I'm pinned in place as his mouth takes mine and we kiss like we're in a race, furious and rough. Our teeth clash, and our chests heave. I scrape my fingers down over his shoulders, dragging a rough path to his hips and smiling when I earn a nip to my lips in reward.

The hand at my neck travels with the water, over my breast and finally to my stomach where he rests his wide palm for a long beat—his way of silently directing me not to move. His body shifts as he kneels before me and plants a trail of cool kisses across my stomach. The water from overhead is hitting his back as steam builds up around us, but it doesn't hinder the sight of him as he lifts my leg and guides it over his shoulder.

With my back pressed against the smooth tiles and his mouth between my legs, I tug on his hair, close my eyes, and let him take me to a place I never knew before Heath.

One hand comes around my backside, pulling me forward, while his other hand pushes my thigh wide, not stopping until my hands slap against the tiles, and my satisfied groans bounce off the fogged glass walls.

He finds my breasts without haste, squeezing and pinching, as he rises to his feet and my breaths begin to even out. He looms over me, eyes dark and hungry and I have no doubt what they're saying. *It's my turn.* I skim a finger down from his waist and wrap my hand around him, stroking firm and fast. But when I attempt to lead him forward, to where I need him most, his head turns in a slight shake. Instead of giving me what I want, he turns me to face the wall and reaches overhead for the wand as water begins to fire out from its chrome head.

When I look back at him, questioning, his answer is laced with a sly grin as he slips the wand into my hand and guides it down. His tan hand covers my own until the stream makes contact between my legs, and I involuntarily jolt back against him.

"Leave it there," he says in my ear.

Braced against the wall by nothing more than a forearm, my palm flat on the tile, I do as I am told. When I lose his body heat at my back, a quick glimpse over my shoulder tells me he's still close. Very close. And very much watching me.

Before I begin to think too much, he's behind me, one hand gripping my shoulder while his other is secured tightly on my hip, and he enters slowly from behind. A strained, "Fuck," travels from his lips as he moves in deeper and quickens his pace.

Just when I thought being with him couldn't get better, the spray from the wand and the force of his thrusts takes me there, harder and faster than any time before. I catch my breath, enjoying his low, guttural groans as he finishes. We stay connected as he pushes aside my wet hair and slides his lips across my shoulder.

I turn, facing him, and take advantage to study every element of his face. The straight line of his nose. The three small freckles above his right brow. The short, fine scar that runs just below his chin. When I spot a second faint white line at his jaw, I lean in and kiss it.

He bends in for a kiss, this one slow and smooth, like a relaxing, easy day at the beach. I can have it all with this man. From the hot and fast to the steady and gentle.

"Move in with me."

My mind bounces back to reality. We stand motionless. The only sound is the water pouring around us as he plants light kisses across my cheek and down my neck.

"Move in with me," he repeats, his mouth now sweeping across my own.

My head is spinning. The naïve girl in me wants to clap and cheer and giggle like a fool while the young woman in me wants to analyze and debate if we're really ready for this.

As if he senses my internal war, he braces his forearms on the shower wall, trapping me in and demanding my full attention, his blue eyes dark in the haze of mist. "I want to come home to you every day and wake up to you every morning. I want your clothes in my closet and your body in my bed. I want to cook dinners with you and take Sunday naps with you. I want you to fill this place with whatever makes you happy, makes it ours." He exhales a nervous breath. "Move in with me, Leah. Please."

An uncontrollable smile spreads across my face, and all the what-ifs and *I don't know*s float away with the steam. "Yes, Heath, I will move in with you."

He smiles back in relief. It's the gorgeous, carefree smile I'm convinced he only shares with me.

"Good, because I was ready to trap you here until you said yes."

I eye the sprayer and whisper shyly, "I'd actually be okay with that."

"If you liked that, Princess, then I've got some really fun things to show you."

When my eyes widen, his laughter bounces around us.

My experience was limited before Heath, and it showed. So, when he told me that day that I could trust him, I fought against my fears and did just that. I trust him completely—with my body and, more importantly, my heart. And, every day I spend with him, I'm so thankful that I let go and took a chance. Whatever is to come for us, I'm confident we'll see it through together.

NINETEEN

Heath

"So, how many kids are in your class?" Leah asks Lindsey.

We're meeting her for the first time, and I was so relieved to see that, although she's good-looking, she's not Leah 2.0. Lindsey is a few inches taller with dark brown eyes and matching hair that rests on her shoulders along with a narrow face and a wide, toothy smile, almost like she's got a couple of teeth too many.

I haven't decided what I think of her yet. Sure, she's a kindergarten teacher, but that doesn't necessarily mean she's nice and sweet. One of the craziest girls I ever hooked up with was a pediatric nurse. By day, she was tending to sick kids, but by night, she had a fetish for kitchen gadgets. I'll never look at a spatula the same way again.

"Twenty, but I have an aide for part of the day."

She and Leah continue talking. They seem to be hitting it off, which I'm sure is a big relief to Eli.

Although I'd love to be there when he decides to tell her the truth about his past with Leah.

I shake away the thought. I like to stay in a total state of denial when it comes to the two of them ever being together. In my mind, it never happened. In fact, I've taken it one step further and convinced myself that Leah was a virgin when we met.

"It's still early. Why don't we walk over to Duke's? There's a band playing tonight that's supposed to be decent." Eli proposes the question to the table, but he only has eyes for Lindsey as he speaks.

With her eyes locked back on his, it seems the feeling is mutual.

The band won't start for another hour, so a DJ is pumping music through the space as the bar slowly begins to fill. We're at a table in the back, talking and getting to know Lindsey better.

First thing to know about Lindsey is, the girl likes her wine. She even managed to talk Leah into a glass, and I can count on one hand how many times I've seen her drink more than a sip or two. Good. I'm glad. Leah deserves to let loose a little bit.

I take a drink of my tonic and lime as I survey the room. "*Fucking hell.*" The words fall out from under my breath before I can stop them. Unfortunately, not quiet enough.

Leah moves her hand to my thigh with a questioning glance as I turn my back on the last person I want to see.

"*Hee-eeth.*"

Damn it. Fucking Laurie Cantano.

"*Hee-eeth.*"

I hate how she always makes my name into two syllables.

I grab Leah's hand on my thigh and squeeze, a pre-apology for whatever this bitch is about to bring. Even though I can feel Laurie at my side, I don't turn.

"Laurie," Eli states flatly.

"Oh, hi, *E-lie.*"

Jesus. Did she always talk this way, and I never noticed? Probably. Communication wasn't really our thing.

When she gets nothing from me, she moves her arm across my back and around my shoulder, attempting to turn me in her direction. I shake her off and twist toward her as little as necessary, still unwilling to release Leah's hand.

"Laurie." I match Eli's tone. I catch her looking down at my hand that is gripping Leah's.

"I just thought I'd come say hi. Who's your friend?" She jerks her chin toward Leah. "Is she the reason I haven't heard from you?" Her muddy-brown hair is frizzier than usual, and she's wearing a tight, sleeveless shirt cut with a deep-V that reveals the top of her bra, along with shorts that barely cover her ass.

What was I ever thinking?

"We're in the middle of a conversation here. Do you mind?"

And, just like that, she's the crazy Laurie I remember from high school.

She leans into my face and screeches, "Actually, yes, I do mind. When you fuck a girl and say you're going to call her, then you need to *actually call her.*" Her voice ascends as she enunciates the last few words just in case the other side of the room can't hear her.

Leah's body goes rigid next to mine before she attempts to pull away from me, but I refuse to let her go.

Luckily, Eli tries to defuse the situation. "Laurie, we're just trying to have a nice night here. As you can see, Heath has moved on. So, let's just be adults about it and go our separate ways."

I silently thank Eli. Anything I might have said would not have come out that diplomatic. I'm relieved when she seems to listen to him and turns to leave.

Just as my spine softens and I loosen my grip on Leah, Laurie lunges past me, shoving a finger an inch from Leah's face. "You might be a cute little priss, but don't fool yourself. He'll get tired of you and come back to me. He always does."

I'm off my stool, tendrils of anger flaring up my neck and down my arms as I wrap my hand around Laurie's finger, twisting it up and away from Leah. When Laurie lets out a yelp, I throw her hand to the side and hiss in her face, "Fuck. Off. Whore."

"Enough, Heath," Eli says sternly from his seat.

But I hold my scowl. She has the audacity to look at me like an injured puppy before finally walking away.

We're done here. I don't even bother to sit. Instead, I hold my hand out to Leah.

"We're leaving?"

Is she kidding me right now? I scorch her with a look that asks just that.

"Heath, sit down." She pulls my stool next to her and pats the top. "Please."

She waits patiently. Finally, at the sight of her small smile and outstretched hand, I give in and sit. I focus only on my drink as she takes my hand under the table and weaves our fingers together. The weight of her stare grows heavy around us, but I can't bring myself to face her just yet.

"I need a drink. Come to the bar with me?" Eli asks Lindsey.

And, a moment later, they're gone.

"Look at me, Heath." Leah's grip on my hand tightens, and when I finally turn to her, she's wearing a compassionate smile. "We all have a bedpost. Yours just has a few more notches than others."

Regret burns in my chest at ever letting someone who wasn't her touch me. She is fresh air and calm seas and the brightest star in the sky. Everything I'll never be for her. Remorse tears through me over every Laurie who came before her, along with every drug and every drink. Self-doubt grabs ahold of me, jamming an endless stream of fear and anxiety down my throat. Eventually, she'll figure out she's too good for me, and she'll leave me. It's just a matter of time.

"Don't. Whatever you're thinking, just stop." She pulls my chin toward her and places a solid, pointed kiss on my lips before angling back. "I know more about you than you realize, Heath. Eli likes to share. A lot. Some of our best nights in college revolved around stories of the two of you as teenagers. Your past makes you who you are. And I wouldn't change one thing about you."

Despite the sincerity of her words, I eye her in disbelief.

"You still don't believe me? What about the time when you were seeing two girls behind each other's backs? When they found out, you continued to tell one that you broke up with the other until they both confronted you and slapped you across the face in the cafeteria. Or how about the college student your dad hired to tutor you in math, and she ended up teaching you a whole lot more than Geometry? And let's not forget about your friend's mom." She leans in until we're nose-to-nose, her hand burning a path up my thigh and her lips achingly close to my own. "Actually, I should write them all thank-you notes. Because, without all of that experience, you'd never have learned my favorite move. You know which one, right?"

My muscles tense as her fingers swirl in teasing circles high on my thigh.

"The one where I'm on top, and you slide your fingers down . . ."

I clutch her hand from my leg at the same time as we rise from our seats. Not wasting any time, we weave through the crowd, toward the door, every muscle in me resisting the primal urge to throw her over my shoulder and carry her home.

"Shouldn't we tell Eli and Lindsey we're leaving?" she asks through a fit of giggles as we hustle down the street.

I don't slow down to answer.

"Does this mean I'm getting *the move*?" Her continuous laughter floats through the air.

I quicken my pace and smirk back at her.

This girl is my game changer. Everything she is, is everything I never knew I needed. I don't know how I ever survived without her. I don't know what I'd do if I ever lost her.

And, yes, of course she's getting *the move*. I'd give this girl anything.

TWENTY

Leah

"I got them a plant. Do you think she's a plant person? I never thought to ask." I fuss with a twisted leaf before reaching for the housewarming card.

"It's fine. It's a plant. Who doesn't like plants?" Heath responds from the sofa.

"Us, for one."

It's true. There's not one plant in the condo, mostly because I have the blackest of black thumbs, and Heath couldn't care less either way. He meant it when he said I could fill the place however I like.

"Do you think they're making a mistake? I mean, moving in together is a big deal, and they've only been dating six months."

"What are you worried about?" He tilts his head back to me from his seat on the sofa.

I walk over and straddle his lap, my pale-yellow sundress floating out around me as my phone pings from the kitchen with a new text. I ignore it, already certain it's Burger texting me for the fifth time today.

"I like Lindsey. Really." I watch my hands run up and over his shoulders and then back down again. "It's just not like Eli to do anything so rash, like buying a house *and* asking his girlfriend to move in with him. Don't you think?"

"We didn't exactly wait around to move in together, so who are we to judge? Besides, you said before, if Eli's happy, then you're happy."

A soft huff escapes my lips.

"Want to know what I really think?" he asks as my fingers continue their perusal of the soft cotton of his T-shirt.

"What's that?"

He grasps my forearms. "I think you're so used to Eli running all of his decisions by you that you can't handle him going to someone else for a change."

He places a warm kiss on the inside of each wrist before lowering them to my sides, slightly behind my back, and holding them firmly in place. His eyes darken, and I swallow.

"I meant it when I said that I like Lindsey. She's good for him," I whisper.

"I believe you. Because I know how much you care about Eli. And that's one of my favorite things about you. You care about everyone in a way that I never knew a person could. When we first met, I thought it was an act. I didn't trust anything about you. But, between your beauty and your kindness, you made a believer out of a piece of shit like me. You're the best thing that has ever happened to me, Leah. And I want you to know that, one day, I'll be the same for you."

I want more than anything to touch him and kiss him and tell him what I truly feel for him with every bone in my body. But he's holding on to my hands the same way he's holding on to my heart. Tight and strong.

Our eyes are locked on one another, and I can feel my heart beating double time in my chest, every breath deeper than the last.

My head clashes with my heart, and without thought, my mouth falls open, releasing the three words that could ruin everything, "I love you."

His body stiffens under mine and his eyes widen in sharp contrast to his clamped mouth. The silence stretches, and with each passing second, my panic rises and pinches at my heart until he releases my hands and splays his own around my waist. Stroking with his thumbs, he pulls me forward and plants a kiss on the exposed skin at the base of my neck. I brace my arms on either side of him at the back of the sofa as he continues his path upward. When he's just about to take my mouth, he pushes his fingers back into my hair and whispers my name between our lips before pulling me down to him.

I dig my nails into the cushion, my returning kiss strained and hesitant, but he doesn't let up. His hands hold me in place until he feels the uncertainty in my muscles fade away as I give in to him.

When he's convinced I'm ready, my hands are led to the waist of his shorts. While I free him beneath me, I rise up onto my knees to allow him under my dress where he pulls aside my panties.

Taking a moment to break from the kiss, he speaks with his eyes the words he's not yet able to say. I soak them in, studying the black specks among his deep blues, before leaning my forehead against his and lowering myself onto him.

Strong, wide hands grip my middle and pull me down until he's deep inside me, causing him to release a shuddered, heavy breath. I slide my fingers over his muscled shoulders and begin to rock, meeting him as his hips lift. His hold on me hardens as we quicken our pace, and his lips brush against my own until, finally, his fingers wrap around the back of my head, and we kiss, deep and ragged, through his orgasm first and then mine a moment later.

We continue kissing as we slow our pace, wrapped in each other's arms, exactly where we need to be.

Although he wasn't able to say the words I had been hoping to hear, I know he'll get there. And, for now, that's all I need.

TWENTY-ONE

Heath

"Tell me you did not bring your Kindle to a football game." I tap on the hot-pink device sitting in Leah's lap.

"I didn't bring my Kindle to a football game. I brought it to a *boring* football game."

I shake my head and feign disappointment. "Had I known, I would've brought more cash."

"Why would you need more money?"

"Because, when people see you in these seats, reading instead of watching the game, you're probably going to get heckled. So, naturally, I'll have to fight them. And, because I'll totally kick their asses, I'll get arrested, and you'll need money to bail me out."

"What's so great about our seats? I'd rather be up in one of those." She points back to the line of skyboxes. "You get the dessert cart if you sit up there."

"Princess, we're sitting tenth row on the fifty-yard line. I guarantee you, everybody in those boxes wishes they were us right now."

Her eyes catch on the cluster of linebackers the size of refrigerators that gather in front of us. "You're right. These aren't such bad seats after all."

I cross my arms with a teasing grunt. "Are you seriously checking out football players while you're sitting next to me?"

"I thought you wanted me to watch the game."

She playfully bats her lashes before placing a feather-light kiss on my lips. That only makes me want more. I'll always want more from this girl.

I lean away and cover my lap with my hands before this gets embarrassing. "Maybe it's better for everyone if you read after all."

She throws her head back and laughs.

As the game begins, she tries her best to pay attention, occasionally cheering when I cheer, but most of the game, she does what she said she'd do. She reads. And I find myself watching her more than the overpaid players on the field. Her hair falls over her face like a curtain between us, and I wait in anticipation for the moment she pushes it back behind her ear. When she does, the glow of the screen rewards me with a clear view of her gray eyes and pink cheeks as she taps a finger over her pursed lips in deep concentration. My favorite though is when she closes her eyes and inhales a long, slow breath, absorbing the moment from the story like she's reading alone on the sofa instead of in a sold-out stadium of one hundred thousand fans.

The final buzzer sounds, and the crowd around us stands and shouts in victory.

"Did we win?" She closes her Kindle and looks up to the scoreboard, unable to see it because of the wall of bodies.

"Yes. And it was a great game. You should've been there." I throw her a wink.

Enclosed by the towering crowd, I take advantage and do what I've been waiting to do throughout the entire game. I bend in and kiss her. What starts off soft and affectionate quickly turns fervent and eager.

"Get a room!" is shouted from somewhere above us, causing Leah to instantly tug back and hide her face in embarrassment.

I pull her in by her neck and kiss the top of her head, laughing, and even though her hands are still covering her face, I feel her do the same.

The parking lot is so congested, she's asleep before we hit I-30. After the noise of the last few hours, there's nothing better than sitting next to her, only the sound of her breathing filling the small space. When we make it to the garage, I park the car and kill the engine, hoping to give her another minute of sleep. Her long hours at work are finally catching up to her.

I step out and come around to her side. "You're so beautiful," I whisper down to her sleeping form.

Just as I go to wake her, her phone, lying in the center console, lights up with a text from Burger.

They loved you. It's yours if you want it.

Seems I'm not the only one in love with Leah Dawson.

"Someone keeps texting you." Like I don't already know who it is.

She reads the message then immediately puts the phone away.

"Anything important?"

"Nope, just annoying work stuff." She bends over me, her mouth to my ear, as her hand warms my chest. "I'm going to shower before dinner. Want to join me?"

"No, I've got to fix a few work issues." I stay focused on my computer, but out of the corner of my eye, I don't miss her pout.

"Everything okay?"

"Yeah, someone opened an email they shouldn't have and downloaded a virus," I lie.

"That's all?"

"That's all. I'll order dinner." My attention stays on my screen.

"You're the best." She gives my shoulder a squeeze and then disappears down the hall.

When she told me she loved me, I willed the words to come out. But they just wouldn't. So, instead of my voice, I used my body to tell her how I felt. Every touch was my way of communicating to her the words I couldn't speak. I knew she was there with me, understood my silent thoughts. I saw it in her eyes. I felt it with every pulse of my heart. Until she went to clean up, and I went to the kitchen for a drink and happened to catch the first of now many texts from Burger on her phone. One had asked if she knew that Chicago was only a two-hour flight away. I didn't give it much thought at first.

Then, today, she got a call and took it out on the balcony. The call lasted less than five minutes, but when I asked her about it and she rolled her eyes, saying it was nothing, that hurt the most.

She hadn't been there with me in that moment after all. If she loved me like she said she did, then she wouldn't be keeping secrets.

A minute later, I hear the shower start, and I rush down the hall to where she leaves her workbag. Opening her laptop, I start scanning her emails. She didn't even bother to delete them.

Leah, it was so great to finally talk with you about the opportunity with our agency. I promise, you'll love Chicago, and with your experience, you'll fit right in at Milo Harnett.

Blah. Blah. Blah.

Looking forward to working with you.

I've seen enough. I close the laptop and reach into her bag. And there it is, right on top. A large white envelope with the words *Milo Harnett Advertising Agency*. Inside is a stack of brochures and printouts on restaurants, museums, and shopping with a bright orange sticky note on top that reads, *Everything there is to love about Chicago!*

She's leaving me.

I pace the room like a caged animal. *Is this how my dad felt when my mom left? Did he come home to a silent house and empty closets? Did she bother to leave a note, telling him why?*

Whatever it was, it was shitty enough that he never talks about it. But it doesn't matter because there's one thing I have that my dad didn't. A fucking clue. Like hell will I let her be the one to decide that this is over, to pack a bag and sneak out in the night to build a life without me in it.

Everything has been put back in its place when she enters the room, hair damp and face smiling. "What did you decide to order?"

"What?"

"For dinner? What did you order?"

"I got distracted and forgot. Order whatever you want."

At my shortness, she walks over and sits on the arm of the chair. "Are you sure there's nothing else going on?" she asks softly as she runs the back of her smooth hand on my cheek, the familiar scent of her vanilla lotion filling my nose.

I turn away. "I told you, just work shit."

"Do you want to talk about it?"

I shake her off.

"Okay, I'll give you some space."

The second she's gone from the room, I text an old high school buddy I used to party with. Then, before I talk myself out of it, I send a second text. I'm not going to be played like my dad was by my mom. She ruined him, and there's no way in hell I'll let that happen to me. I won't be the one to be left alone, looking the fool. She will.

Days later, I smoke a bowl, snort a couple lines of coke, and then chase that with a beer or three. Anything I can get my hands on to give me the courage to do what I'm about to do. To obliterate the best thing that's ever happened to me.

TWENTY-TWO

Leah

I walk in the door and drop my bag against the hall table as I slip my shoes off, my aching feet immediately appreciating the coolness of the floor. I've been waiting for this moment since the Senior Account Executive threw me under the bus when the client asked where we were at with their recruitment campaign. He tossed it to me, knowing perfectly well that he never once mentioned their request, leaving me to look like the inept idiot.

After today, I'm ready to ask Burger to find me something new, but here, in Dallas. That would do the double task of not only getting me away from my current boss, but also getting Burger to leave me alone about Chicago once and for all. The guy needs to learn the meaning of the word *no*. How many different times and in how many different ways can I say it?

On top of my work stress, Heath has been growing distant. I don't know what to do, but I keep trying any way I can. Like cooking nice dinners for him every night even though I'm exhausted, which he ends up barely touching. And, when we have sex, I'm convinced he's looking anywhere but at me. I've tried to talk to him, but he brushes me off or finds an excuse to leave the condo.

I go from bending over backward for my boss at work to doing the same for my boyfriend at home, and I'm about to break. I haven't felt so alone and fragile since my dad died, and it's just getting worse.

There's a single light on in the kitchen as I open the fridge, looking for something quick to eat, but there's nothing that can go directly from the shelf to my mouth. Instead, I grab a bottle of water, and just as I'm about to take the first sip, I hear an odd noise coming from down the hall.

"Heath?" I call out.

The hairs on my neck rise as I set the bottle down and inch as quietly as possible toward the source.

As I inch closer, the sound grows clearer. I consider running back to the kitchen to get a knife when I hear it again. It's low, male.

Is he . . .

Even though I live here, I'm afraid to barge in and catch him alone in a precarious position.

Just as I'm approaching the door, I hear a second sound. A moan, feminine and gravelly. The blood rushes from my head at the same time my hand finds the knob.

The door swings open and I manage a few feeble steps into the room—then time stops. A bomb could drop at my feet, and it still wouldn't decimate me the way the sight in front of me is managing to do.

Under the comforter of our bed, Heath is lying on top of a woman. Although her face is hidden in his chest, I know who the frizzy brown hair spread across my pillow belongs to.

Every muscle in my body grows rigid and cold as my chest hollows out with every grunt and groan that cracks my heart. He continues moving above her, neither of them the wiser that I'm even there.

I force out his name, my voice broken and weak, "Heath."

It's enough for him to lift his chin and turn, his unsurprised eyes locking on mine.

"Hey, Princess, you're home. I'll take care of you next. Better yet, why don't you join us?" An evil smile is planted across his face, curling up to eyes that are mere slits.

If it wasn't his body, in our home, I wouldn't believe what I was seeing. But it's real. Heath is in our bed with another woman.

I step backward, tripping over myself and bumping into the doorframe, before stumbling down the hall and bouncing from wall to wall like the metal ball of a pinball machine. My foot catches on my bag, so I clutch it to my chest and then race out to my car. I drive a block or two with no clue as to where I'm headed when the trembling begins to take over. My stomach churns, and my vision blurs, forcing me to pull into a parking lot. I stop the car with just enough time to push open the door and vomit onto the blacktop below, a sob following close behind.

My fingers fumble over my phone as the names on the screen go in and out of focus. I wipe the tears from my eyes and manage to call Eli.

I'm sitting sideways out of my car door, my head hanging low with nausea, as Lindsey answers, "Hey, Leah."

A spasm surfaces, forcing my silence.

"Leah? Is that you? Is this a butt dial?"

"Lindsey. I . . . help . . ."

"Leah? What happened? Where are you? Where's Heath?"

I look up and tell her the first thing I see, "Broadway Subs."

"We're on our way. I'll call Heath from the car."

"No. No Heath." My body shudders at the images replaying in my head. *"Oh, Lindsey."* They're the last words I get out before another wave of sobs takes hold.

I sit like this for what feels like hours before I hear the slam of a car door and footsteps draw near.

"It's okay, honey. You're okay." Eli pulls me from my seat, and my body sways, forcing me to grip his shirt for balance. "Are you hurt? Did someone hurt you?"

His hands roam my body as he speaks, looking for any signs of injury. I want to tell him not to bother because he won't find anything, but my throat is too tight to speak. He gives up his search and pulls me in, wrapping me in his arms in an attempt to ease my pain.

"Linds, call Heath. Tell him we need him *now*."

"No! No! No! Not Heath." That name brings me to my senses and I begin to frantically twist and plea into his shoulder, "Not Heath. Not Heath."

Not Heath. Not my Heath.

"Okay, I won't call Heath. I promise," he whispers in my ear as he cocoons me in his arms.

Lindsey runs her hand across my back. "Leah, you're going to be okay, honey," she reassures me from beside Eli. "Whatever it is, Eli and I are here for you."

I manage a single nod in response even though, right now, I can't see how I'll ever be okay again.

It's not long before I find myself curled up on Eli and Lindsey's sofa, the trip there a total blur. She tucks a blanket around me before taking a seat on one end of me while Eli is on my other.

The crying has stopped, replaced now with processing the *what* and the *how* of the last few hours.

I hear them whispering back and forth across my body, but I only respond when I hear one of them mention Heath's name.

"No," I say sharply, not even sure of what they were discussing.

Out of the corner of my eye, I see Eli give a jerk of his head, either in confusion or anger, but it doesn't matter. Nothing matters.

They continue mumbling until I feel Lindsey rise from the sofa and lean down to me. "Leah, honey, I'm going to the store. Can I get you anything?"

I force myself to look up at her and whisper through strands of hair that have dried to my cheek, "No, thanks."

Sympathy is in every line of her face as she pulls the hair away before walking out the door.

The second she's gone, Eli takes a seat in front of me on the coffee table and leads me to a sitting position. He warms my chilled hands in his heated ones. "What did he do?" His voice is forcibly gentle, but I know him well enough to know he's holding back.

I take a deep breath and drop my head, my face twisting at the last image I have of Heath.

Eli lets go of one of my hands to lift my chin, dragging my eyes to his. "Leah, I need you to tell me what he did."

Why? So, he can hurt Heath? Or, better yet, hate him? The damage is done. I've lost the man I loved. Who I thought might have loved me in return.

No sense in causing Eli to lose his best friend when he clearly warned me from the beginning.

My head spins with thoughts of the last few hours. *How long has this been going on? Did he ever really care about me?"* And the one thought I can't escape, *What is wrong with* me? The humiliation is taking root in my gut and growing by the second. I've never felt like such a worthless, used piece of garbage.

"Leah, *please.*" Eli has resorted to begging, and it's all because of me.

I have to give him something.

"We broke up." The three words I never imagined would cross my lips scratch at my throat. "That's all."

"Broke up? What? Why? Are you sure it's not just a fight?"

A single pained laugh escapes my scratchy throat. "Yeah, I'm sure."

"Do you want me to talk to him? Straighten this out?"

My eyes jump to his and now I'm the one begging. "No. Promise me, you won't do anything."

He sighs, defeated, and smooths back my hair. "Okay. I'll be right back."

I hear him in the kitchen, and when he comes back a minute later, it's with a glass of white wine.

"Drink this."

I hesitate to take it.

"Just one. It'll help you relax."

I take the smallest sip and appreciate the sweet coolness as it glides down my throat. Before I know it, the glass is empty.

Lindsey walks in, balancing Chinese carryout in one hand and a grocery bag in the other. "Anybody hungry? I picked up a bite to eat."

Without a word, there's a plate of food in front of me and a fresh glass of wine in my hand. I take only a few bites of rice but manage to drink another two glasses of wine.

Before I pass out from alcohol and emotional exhaustion, Lindsey lends me some pajamas and gives me a toothbrush. When I lie down in their guest room, it's with a spinning head and a shattered heart.

Eli and Lindsey have been nothing but supportive these last few days I've been staying with them.

Eli was kind enough to deal with Heath about giving us some time alone at the condo, so we're on our way to pick up my things. I was tempted to ask if Heath asked about me, but common sense prevailed.

The door to the condo swings open and I step inside, like I have done so many times before. But this time, it feels like a dream. Like that gut-wrenching day never happened and Heath is here, lying on the couch, smiling up at me after a long day at work. Instead, I'm greeted by an empty room.

Everything is in the same place I left it. The apples are towered neatly in the bowl on the counter. The remotes are lined up on the coffee table. There are no empty pizza boxes, discarded beer bottles, or dirty laundry strewn about—the typical signs of a man suffering from a broken heart.

That's because this is the home of a man who pulverizes hearts for sport.

With my head down, I walk swiftly through the bedroom to the bathroom to grab my makeup and toiletries, throwing them in a duffel before leaving just as quickly and dropping the bag by the front door.

Dreading going back for more, I hold my breath like I'm rushing through smoke, focusing on the far wall as I pass the bed and make my way through to the closet,

149

expelling a deep breath as I grab a wide armful of hanging clothes.

Just as I'm halfway across the room, items start to slip out from my arms and fall to the floor. I struggle to catch what I can, but more drop as I bend to pick up a dress tangled at my feet. This time, when I twist to pick them up, tears flood my eyes as I catch sight of the bed.

It's perfectly made, as if I had done it myself. The navy paisley comforter I bought us is on straight and even. The throw pillows are organized the way I like with the big navy ones in the back, the smaller paisley ones in the front, and the final round solid-white pillow placed directly in the center. The same pillows he always made fun of. But it's that simple round pillow, the one he always tossed around like a Frisbee, that undoes the fragile hold I have on my emotions.

I give up on trying to rescue my clothes, letting the rest fall to the floor and me along with them until I'm on my knees, crying.

He never cared. I never meant to him what I thought I did. And he had no plans of ever saying those three words back to me.

Eli's at my side, coaxing me up, as Lindsey shuffles by with an armful of clothes. When we leave the room for the last time, I close the bedroom door behind us, making it clear to my friends that it's to stay that way. Anything I may have left behind isn't worth the pain of going back for again.

Lindsey is boxing up my books. Instead of wrapping up the picture frames, she's placed them on the coffee table, presumably for me to choose the ones I'd like to take. I hand her only the ones that don't include Heath. Mixed among the frames is the pink tin. Hesitating, I finally open it and gaze down on the mass of pennies.

Each one, a wish. The same wish I've made as long as I can remember. That I would someday find a man who loved me as much as my dad loved my mom.

I walk to the kitchen and pull out the sliding garbage can. Turning the tin over, I watch the sunlight glisten off every last penny as they pour out and spread along the trash. The metal of the tin gives off a weak *clink* as it lands atop the pile of coins.

I don't consider the regret I may feel later, or the sadness at the loss of every wish I made in honor of my dad. I don't feel anything right now, and I don't care if I ever do again.

TWENTY-THREE

Heath

Even after spending the day in the field house, the music screaming in my ears and the sweat dripping from my body, it wasn't enough to quiet the noise in my head.

I walk through my condo door—expecting what exactly, I'm not sure. Until I walk in and see . . . nothing. Everything looks just as it was. Like she is still here and is going to walk around the corner any second now, with her hair piled on top of her head and wearing one of my old T-shirts. The image is lost when I turn and see the bookshelves. The ones I ordered just for her and all of her books.

She was so happy the day they were delivered. Lying on the sofa, I watched as she arranged and rearranged them at least three times. She kept asking if she was boring me, but if I'm being honest, watching her ass as she reached up high or bent down low was the furthest thing from bored a guy could be. I was just disappointed I didn't have a bowl of popcorn. So, I did the next best thing. I pulled her down to the rug and showed her just how bored I was.

She eventually decided to shelve them by color, like a full-blown rainbow right in our family room. Now that they're gone and the shelves are mostly bare, the whole space just feels gray and empty.

You did what you had to do.

I grab a protein drink from the fridge and twist off the metal cap before sliding out the garbage just far enough to toss it in. It takes a second before my brain registers the odd pinging sound and rattle that comes from the can as it slides back in. I'm about to take a large gulp when it hits me.

That noise.

My body moves in slow motion as I pull out the can, already dreading what I'm going to find. And there it is. Her pink tin, the one physical thing she cherished above all others, sitting atop a mountain of pennies. Every one a memory, a wish. And they're now mixed with junk mail and leftover takeout.

My head drops as reality sinks in. This may be my biggest fuck up yet.

TWENTY-FOUR

Leah

Staying with Eli and Lindsey has been just what I needed. Easy. They allow me my space, although I spend most of my days at work, and they don't ever dare breathe a word about *him*.

So, when Lindsey comes to sit a few feet away from me on the sofa, clears her throat as she turns toward me, I'm caught a little off guard.

"How's work?" she asks, motioning toward the laptop resting on my lap.

"Good. How's yours?" I give a tight smile because, actually, work isn't good. It's tiring, and I'm frustrated that I'm working yet another Saturday. But I don't have the energy to get into it with her, and I'm gauging that's not what she really wants to talk about anyway.

"Good."

There's a tense, unfamiliar silence between us that, under any other circumstances, I might be more concerned about. But, like most things lately, I just can't bring myself to care.

"Eli and I talked last night." She looks at me like I should understand what this means. When I don't offer her a response, she continues, "About the two of you. Actually, it was more of an argument than a conversation. Our first fight."

Her shoulders slouch, and guilt roils my gut.

"I'm trying hard to understand your *friendship*. Then and now." She pauses, and I have no choice but to sit patiently. "I guess it's hard for me because I've never stayed close with any of my exes. And you two just aren't close, you're—"

I cut her off. "Best friends. And, despite our brief attempt at a relationship, Lindsey, we'll only ever be best friends."

I watch her face as she processes my words, but I'm unable to discern if she believes me.

I know what she's thinking, what she's too nice to say. There's no way for her relationship with Eli to survive as long as another woman he's been intimate with is living under the same roof. Not to mention, one that works fourteen-hour days only to come home and drink wine until she passes out.

It's time to face the fact that I'm no good for anyone here.

I could go back to my mom's. She's been pushing for me to stay with her, but I know the woman too well. She'd corner me until I talked, which would mean admitting how ignorant and naïve I was. And she'd have zero tolerance for the nightly drinking, not understanding it's the only way I can fall asleep these days.

When we're done talking, I pick up my phone and send a text because it comes down to what's best for my best friend, and that is not having me here. So, after weeks of Eli and Lindsey caring for me like I'm a wounded animal, there's only one option left. It's time to be released out into the wild. And, by the wild, I mean, Chicago.

"You'll need to sign everywhere there is a yellow tab," Burger says as he flips page after page of the document. "So, you understand the two key components of this contract?" He's talking to me like I'm a toddler, but I don't care.

A silent head bob is all I offer.

"First, you are committing to one full year of employment, or you'll have to repay the signing bonus you'll be receiving in your first check. And, second, they can sue you if you go to any competing agency within six months after your departure."

Another head bob. He looks to Eli for confirmation before continuing.

"After you've read it through and signed every page, I'll get this right over to them. When that's done, you'll get a call from their relocation service to set up a day to move your things." Burger pushes the papers my way. "And if you put your notice in tomorrow morning like we discussed, you can expect your start date to be in three weeks."

Feeling like too much of a burden to everyone and in desperate need of a new setting, I texted Burger and asked if the job offer still stood. Fortunately for me, this new account brought them more work than they had originally anticipated, so it was just a matter of negotiating the contract, which was really just me saying yes to everything.

That's why I'm sitting at Eli's kitchen table as he takes the contract from me and begins to study every line.

I can't fool Eli, though. As much as I try for a happy front, he knows I'm not in a good place. He's nice enough not to talk about Heath in any capacity in front of me. If he's seeing him, he never mentions it. And I love him for that.

"I don't need a relocation service, Burger. I found a furnished apartment online, so I'll just have a few suitcases. It's Chicago, not a Third World nation. If I need something, there's bound to be a Target or Walgreens at every corner," I chide.

"Okay then," he ignores my attitude. "In that case, I think that's everything. You should be good to go."

Burger is all smiles, so I force a weak one of my own. This faking-happiness thing is exhausting.

Eli and I stand and walk Burger to the door. He hugs me, and I do my best to feign the same warmth.

"Leah, thank you. I'm only telling you this because we're friends, but I really needed this. Whatever happens, just make sure you don't bail before ninety days. That's when I get my commission."

"No worries there, Burger. Not only will I make it ninety days, but I might never come back."

I throw a fake laugh his way, at the same time I feel Eli tense up beside me. He eventually needs to learn the truth. Because I would leave right now with only the clothes on my back if it meant I could get as far away from here as possible. Besides the stress I put on Eli and Lindsey's relationship, there are too many reminders of Heath and what a pathetic fool I am.

I can't get to Chicago fast enough.

TWENTY-FIVE

Heath

"I'm having trouble transferring all the photos to our new laptop. Do you think you can come by and take a look at it?" Eli asks as he sinks his shot.

"Just call me. I'll walk you through it."

"It's not like I don't know how to transfer files, dude. But only half of the pictures show up when I try, and if I lose them, Lindsey is going to kill me."

I dribble around him and shoot, missing the net by a solid two feet. "I told you, I'll walk you through it," I respond, not bothering to hide the annoyance in my voice.

I rebound the ball and come back in for another shot, dribbling around him until I realize he's not covering me. He's not even trying.

"She's not staying with us anymore."

I ignore him.

"I know that's what you're worried about. Seeing Leah. But she's not there. She actually . . . took a job in Chicago."

Like I didn't already know.

I shoot again. And miss.

"You ever going to talk about it?"

"Talk about what?" I ask flippantly as I jog after the ball.

"You know exactly what."

I pass the ball to him, but he lets it bounce past, his focus tight on me.

"Don't be an ass. Are you going to tell me what happened? Because she won't. I think she's too worried that you and I won't be friends anymore. And that tells me one thing. You seriously fucked-up."

"Wow. Thanks for that vote of confidence. I hate to pop your perfect Leah bubble, but I'm not the one to blame here. She left me." *I just ended things before she could.*

"You're full of shit. You forget, I know you better than you know yourself."

"No, I don't forget, Eli. I don't forget anything."

Almost everyone has left the office when I hear a knock at my door. It's Jose, one of my IT staff.

"Hey, Heath. Another late night?"

I look at the time. It's no later than any other night for me. "Did you get my email about the upgrades to the server for next week?"

"Yeah, I did." He hesitates, sliding his hands in his pockets.

"Can I help you with something then?"

160

"I'm meeting friends down the street. You should come with."

"Thanks, but I've got a few things to finish up here."

"C'mon. Don't you think you've earned a break?" He pushes.

Taking a break means allowing thoughts of Leah to leak in.

"My girlfriend's best friend will be there. She's not hard to look at, dude."

"Thanks, Jose, but I'm good."

"So," he hesitates. "You're dating someone?"

"Nope. Nothing like that. Just . . . the way it is right now."

"Well, if you change your mind, we'll be down the street," he says as he steps toward the door.

"Good to know. Thanks for the offer." I'm about to get back to my work, when he doesn't go to leave.

"What?"

"It's just, no one works the way you do, as much as you have been lately, unless they're dealing with something. And I'm guessing that something is a girl. So, the way I see it, you can either keep working sixty-hour weeks, or you can go after her."

I sit back in my chair and cross my arms over my chest. "Are you done?"

"Yep, all done. The invitation still stands though."

This time, I watch and make sure he really leaves.

"If it were only that easy," I mumble to the empty room.

But I guess I need to start somewhere. I run my hands over my face before I shout from my seat.

"Jose, hold on! I've changed my mind."

The bar is packed, filled with barely-legal millennials holding drinks with herbs sticking out from their glasses. I'm already regretting my decision to come. Moving on from Leah is not going to happen here.

I shift around Jose and his friends and step to the bar to order a tonic and lime.

"Hey, Heath, my friend!"

I turn at the sound of my name and see Leah's friend, Burger. We only met once, one night when Leah and I had gone out to see a movie, but you don't forget a guy that looks like a leprechaun. Especially an asshole-leprechaun who helped her sneak behind my back and find her a job in another fucking state. Even though we're elbow-to-elbow, I give my order to the bartender and ignore him.

"Heath, it's me, Burger. Leah's friend."

"Hey, man." I can't bring myself to call anyone Burger. Not even this piece of shit.

"Let me buy you that drink. It's the least I can do." He motions to the bartender and hands over a twenty-dollar bill before I can object. "There's a lot to celebrate tonight!" he shouts in my face with a distinct slur.

"Oh, yeah? Why is that?" I take my glass from the bartender and scan the bar, disinterested.

"My biggest payday to date. All thanks to our friend Leah." He holds his glass up in a toast, but I ignore him. "That was the longest ninety days of my life."

This idiot is drunker than I realized.

"Think you're a little confused, *my friend*. Leah's been in Chicago a lot longer than ninety days."

"You think I'd forget the date of my best bonus yet? It was exactly ninety days ago today when we sat in Eli's kitchen, and I watched her sign that contract." He raises his arm high and makes a second attempt. "Cheers to me!"

I don't acknowledge him. Instead, I'm still stuck on his words as he downs the last of the brown liquid before slamming the glass on the bar with pride.

"No, you're wrong. She left long before that," I argue.

He pulls his phone and starts tapping away, squinting at the small screen. Seconds later, he turns it to me.

"What the hell is this?"

"It's a copy of the contract. Look at the date." He holds his phone too close to my face, forcing me to grab it from his hand and increase the size of the text.

It's dated exactly ninety days from today. Just like he said.

"But that doesn't make any sense," I whisper to myself, shaking my head as I do the math in my head. The contract can't be right. I turn the screen to face him. "You've got it wrong. She left long before then."

"No, she didn't, dude. I was after her for months, but she turned me down every time. I figured it was because of you. Even the HR Manager in Chicago tried everything to change her mind. Sent her all kinds of shit, hoping to win her over. Chocolates, passes to museums and plays— you name it. But she still said no. Then, out of the blue one day, she texted and asked if the job was still available. And here we are!"

He says it all with that same stupid grin on his face, oblivious to the fact that my heart is no longer in my chest but on the dirty floor of the bar for everyone to dig their heels into as they go by.

My head is spinning, worse than any high or any bottle could produce, as I stand, stunned, while he orders another drink.

"Want something stronger this time?" he offers.

"No. I've got to go."

"What's going on, Heath?" Eli asks as I pace his kitchen.

I glance at his table and remember what Burger said. "When did she sign the contract?"

"What? Heath, what's going on?"

"Just tell me, when did she sign the contract?"

"I don't—"

"To go to Chicago! Were you or were you not with her when she signed the contract?"

"Yes. She signed it after you two broke up. We tried to talk her out of it, but she was insistent. I knew she would've signed anything he put in front of her, so I made sure to go through it, line by line."

I continue pacing as I absorb every detail, working through the timeline, convinced they have it wrong. "And when was that exactly?"

"Well, I remember it was the day after my mom's birthday, so about three months ago. The next day, she put in her notice and moved about two weeks after that. What the hell is going on?"

I turn away, scraping my scalp with my nails and pinching my eyes shut in pain. *What the hell have I done?*

TWENTY-SIX

Leah

Whatever was bending in me finally broke.

I'm lying in a strange bed, next to a strange man, my head heavy and spinning, my body used and exhausted, as I try to remember a time when I wasn't so numb and apathetic.

He's turned away from me, allowing me only to see a head of messy black hair and a muscled back with a Grim Reaper tattoo the size of a dinner plate in the center. Although this is a step up from the guy who didn't bother to hide his wedding ring.

My mouth is dry and sour as my stomach churns. I step out of bed and stumble my way down the short hall until I find the bathroom, groaning in relief at the first mouthful of water I scoop with my hands. Searching his cabinets, I hit the jackpot in the vanity below—mouthwash, and make a mental note to start carrying some in my purse. My stomach rumbles again, making it clear how pissed off it is at me for yet another night of drunken oblivion that turned into meaningless sex.

But more than the protests of my body, the sight of myself in the mirror draws bile up my throat. Ashen with a slight shade of green and eyes that are irritated and red. My lips are dry and cracking, with my tongue feeling too large for my mouth. Despite all that, I feel nothing but tepid numbness.

The only thing providing actual color on my face is the sooty black of my mascara smudged in a line down one cheek and a zigzag smear down the other, à la Harry Potter, albeit without the wands and bravery. Because, even in my foggy state, I know this is the weakest of ways to deal with things. But why struggle through rational thoughts when it's so much easier to drink until I'm on the verge of blacking out and losing what's left of myself in a stranger's touch?

Besides a job, these months in Chicago have given me something else. Perspective. I know now that love made me blind. Blind to who Heath really was. Blind to the fact that I no longer know who I am. What I do know, however, is that love is pain. And, if something hurts that bad, it was never good in the first place.

I return to the room and gather up my clothes, putting on only what is essential, and then try to locate my purse and phone. The sight of them on the floor next to the coffee table conjures up fragmented memories of another night I'd soon rather forget.

Relieved he doesn't wake up and we don't have to go through the awkward good-bye I've come to loathe, I wait outside for the Uber driver as an alarm from my phone pierces through my skull. One-hour notice till I leave for the airport. I bang my head back on the brick of the Grim Reaper's house in frustration over its meaning. I have to go home.

I shuffle down the hall of my apartment to the bathroom, eager to wash away last night's regrets, before I have to turn right back around and head out the door. I hate the idea of going home. Every place is tied to some memory of Heath—and worse, my stupidity. If it wasn't for the surprise birthday party Eli put together for Lindsey, I'd never make the trip. Add to the fact that he booked me a nonrefundable, round-trip, guilt-trip ticket, and I couldn't find a way to say no.

If everything goes as planned, I'll be there and back in just over twenty-four hours. I can do this.

The party is a ladies'-only event at Eli and Lindsey's house.

"Lindsey, the patio looks great. You did an amazing job with the flowers."

"Thanks, Leah. My mom and I have been working out here for the last month. Now, I know why she was so eager to help." She smiles as she motions to the crowd with her champagne flute.

"Eli really pulled it off. I'm honestly impressed that there's real food here. I was half-expecting pizza rolls and mini hot dogs."

We laugh as she clinks her flute glass to my wine glass.

"You and me both. I'm just glad you're here to be a part of it." Her laughter dies, and her voice turns serious. "Eli's been worried about you."

"Why would Eli ever be worried about me?" I down the last of my wine before she can answer.

She watches with a weak smile. "He's not heard from you as much as he's used to."

"He's got you to talk to." I bump my arm with hers. "Besides, he knows how much I work. I have a lot more responsibility at this job and I need to prove myself so the agency will keep me on if they ever lose the client. That's all it is." I force a toothy smile in her direction before grabbing the bottle of wine and refilling my glass.

The party drags on at a pace only a grandmother would respect, but fortunately, I have my mom to make it a little more bearable.

"You're not eating?" My mom holds up a plate of finger sandwiches, each adorned with small icing rosettes in various shades of pastel.

The food, although pretty to look at, doesn't interest me.

I lean in and whisper, "Everything on the table has mayonnaise or dressing on it. You know I don't eat that."

"There's a giant bowl of fruit salad. At least eat that. You've lost weight. You're looking too thin. And, for God's sake, Leah, slow down on the wine."

My nostrils flare at her judgment.

After a moment of strained silence, she asks, "Are you going to sleep at home tonight or here?"

"Why do you ask?"

"Because I'm leaving the party soon, and I just wanted to know."

"Eli already offered to take me to the airport in the morning, so I'll stay here. Why are you leaving so early though? Lindsey hasn't even opened her gifts."

She leans in, eyes wide. "I have a date."

I meet her lean, safely holding my wine to my chest. "Do tell."

"I'll tell you something when there's actually something to tell."

She gives me a lighthearted wink, and I roll my eyes in return.

"Are you getting excited for your trip next month? I still can't believe you picked an Alaskan cruise over the Caribbean." I'm about to take a sip but lower my glass when I feel her eyes judging me.

"I've seen plenty of beaches, but how many people can say they've seen a glacier?"

"That's true. How early are you and Sheila flying out?"

"We'll be leaving for the airport at five in the morning. Oh, and don't forget; cell reception might not be the best on the ship, but I'll be checking email every day."

"Mom, relax. You're going away for ten days. I'll be fine. Now, Connor, on the other hand—"

"What?" she asks, panicked. "Why should I worry about Connor? What aren't you telling me?"

I lift a hand to my cocked hip. "Just kidding, Mom. Trying to deflect."

"Very funny. One day, you'll see for yourself, young lady, when you have kids of your own. You never stop worrying. Never."

I roll my eyes and give in to my wine, ignoring the concern on her face.

"And, when I get back, I thought I'd pay you a visit. I'm excited to see Chicago."

I choke on the wine and begin to pat my chest. "For how long?"

"Relax. Just for the weekend. I need some time with my girl." She wraps her arm around my shoulders, her body warming me from the inside out.

"I'd like that."

With the gifts opened and the hour turning late, the remaining older guests make their way home, leaving just Lindsey, me, Eli's sisters, and a handful of Lindsey's girlfriends to enjoy a girls' night in.

We dim the lights and turn up the music. I don't know if it's the nice buzz I've got going or the change in mood, but all I know is, I'm ready to take it up a notch. I open up a new bottle of wine and begin dancing my way from guest to guest, filling their glasses before they get the chance to wave me off. When that bottle is gone, I open another, making sure to top off my own in the process.

The other ladies and I are all giggling as they tell hilarious stories from their past with Lindsey. Each one ends their turn with a toast to the birthday girl before moving on to the next person in our impromptu game.

I'm bent over, laughing in hysterics as Lindsey's friend next to me speaks. Thankfully, Sienna is there to catch me when it's just too much and I slide off my stool. Finally, it's my turn. I attempt to climb the stool but quickly give up, opting for the sofa instead.

Standing with my legs spread for balance across the wide cushions, and ignoring the wine that spills at my feet, I revel in the attention and begin my speech. "When I met Lindsey, I knew before Eli did that she was special. He has been my best friend for so long, I can't remember a life without him in it. He's like the brother I never got the opportunity to dress up in my clothes or tattle on. So, when he first told me he'd met someone, I could hear something in his voice. This girl was different. It didn't take long for him to see that for himself. But, for the record, I knew it first."

They laugh briefly as I turn my attention to Lindsey.

"Lindsey, he looks at you like you are his reason for being, and he is a better man because you are in his life. May he always put you first and treat you like the beautiful queen we know you to be." I face the group. "May we all find our own Eli one day. Happy birthday, Lindsey!" I raise my glass as the other women cheer and follow suit.

I take a few large sips and begin my finale. "But let's get real, ladies. They're not all like Eli. Am I right?"

Cheers erupt louder, fueling this newfound fire inside me.

"I'm talking about the ones who lead you on, tell you what you want to hear until you give them those three *pitiful* words. Then, when they've finally got you all wrapped up in them, they turn on you, sucking every bit of laughter and happiness from your soul. They steal your confidence, your smile, while smashing your ability to love and trust before leaving you breathless and bare, like trash on the street. Fucking empty, making it impossible for anyone to fill you up ever again." I raise my glass as a few voices drunkenly encourage me on. "Enjoy the ride up, my friends. Because the ride down will fucking *decimate* you."

I finish off the contents of my glass, making sure to throw my head back and get every drop.

As the cheering dies down and the next guest begins their story, Sienna tugs at my arm. "Wow, that was a showstopper." Her tone is dry as she grabs me by both forearms and helps me down from the sofa. "A little off topic, but no one can deny you sure do have a way with words. Maybe you could turn that last part into a tagline for one of your ad campaigns."

I stumble into her.

"Just tellin' it like it is, girlfriend."

I catch Sienna looking over my shoulder as she gives a slight shake to her head. When I try to look, she jerks me forward and guides me down the hall to the guest room, far away from the people behind us who showed up just in time to enjoy my toast.

TWENTY-SEVEN

Heath

"She's out cold, but I got her to take some aspirin and drink a big glass of water before she passed out," Sienna tells Eli and Lindsey. She won't make eye contact with me even though I'm standing right next to her brother.

"Does she always drink that much?" Lindsey asks us.

"No. I've barely seen her a little buzzed, let alone whatever that was." Eli motions to the spot she just held on his sofa, trying to make sense of what we all witnessed.

When we opened the door, I never would have known it was Leah standing up on the sofa. Her frame was noticeably thinner, and her hair was longer and blonder than I'd ever seen it. I convinced myself it wasn't her until she spoke, and all doubt disappeared. Now, her words play on a loop in my head, every syllable like a barb to my chest. Each one well deserved but painful nonetheless.

As the remaining guests gather their things and say their good-byes, I take advantage and sneak to the guest bedroom. Between the light from the hall and the streetlight streaming through the bedroom window, I'm able to see Leah clearly. She's lying on her side, facing the door, her hands near her face with the fingertips of her top hand resting gently on the palm of her bottom hand. Despite what I witnessed tonight, she seems so at peace. I can't stop myself from walking to the bed for a closer look.

I push aside the little bit of hair covering her face, knowing full well that I have no right to touch her. But my body has a mind of its own, and I give in without a fight. Sitting on the edge of the bed, I ever-so lightly brush the backs of my fingers against her smooth cheek. I haven't touched her in so long, but it's just as good as I remember.

I'm startled as a warm hand slides over my thigh at the same time a faint sigh escapes her lips. This one simple touch makes me want things I can't have. To climb in next to her, hold her to my chest, and sleep while wrapped around her, like nothing ever happened. To wish it all away.

I force myself to slide out from under her touch, fighting to ignore the coolness that's left behind. With my hands shoved in my pockets, I watch her chest rise and fall with each slow breath.

My selfishness has finally caught up to me in a way I don't know how to fix. I want to make this better, but no amount of pennies can wish away the damage I've done.

TWENTY-EIGHT

Leah

"Denise, do you have any Advil? I'm out." Frustrated, I toss the empty bottle in the garbage with one hand while clutching my stomach with the other.

She appears at my side. "Didn't I see you take some this morning?"

"That was a few hours ago. And these cramps are killing me. I've never had them so bad."

"Maybe you should go home. You look awful. And I think you've lost more weight. Have you considered that this might be something more than cramps?"

I'm starting to worry that she's right. I've already thrown up once in the employee bathroom this morning.

"No, I can't go home. We're presenting the RFP on the Wellson campaign in two hours. I just need something for the pain to get me through."

"Even if I did have some, I don't think that's the answer. I've been watching you pop them like candy for the last couple of days, and they're not helping. In fact, you're slowly getting worse. We need to seriously think about getting you to the ER."

"I don't need the ER. I just need my period to come, so these damn cramps will go away." I bend over in my seat, my arms wrapped around my middle. "Will you do me a favor and see if one of the ladies in the billing department has a heating pad I can borrow? I know for sure that Sibyl has one."

She huffs, irritated. "Fine, but as soon as our meeting is over, I'm taking you to the hospital. You're so pale right now, you're practically translucent. I don't like it, Leah."

"Okay, whatever you say. Just please get me the heating pad."

Her arms crossed over her chest, she grinds her jaw, clearly aggravated with me, before giving in and leaving to get me the heating pad. A thought hits me that the ladies there might have Advil as well.

I rise to shout the request. "Denise, while you're there—"

But I stand too quickly, and blinding pain shoots across my abdomen as wetness and warmth rush down my legs. I reach unsuccessfully for my desk as my knees buckle.

"Oh my God, Leah!" Denise is back at my side as a fresh round of pain seizes my middle, and my body collapses, my head bouncing off the smooth marble floor. "Somebody, call nine-one-one!"

I wrap my arms around my stomach, dizzy with pain from head to toe, as I fight back the panic that winds around my spine.

"Call my mom, Dee. I need my mom."

It's the last thing I remember before everything goes black.

My head throbs to a constant beat while every limb aches in protest to even the smallest attempt at movement. Opening my eyes is harder than it should be. I manage to pry them just a sliver, and I'm met with blinding white light.

What the hell?

My hand jerks to cover my eyes, causing a hard punch of pain to my gut as my moan echoes around the room.

"Crap. Let me kill the lights." The voice is familiar. A second later, I hear it again. "It's okay, Lee. You can open your eyes now."

I tilt my pounding head toward the voice and cautiously try again. When I get my eyes mostly open, it takes another minute for me to focus. Although the lights are off, there's enough sunlight coming through the window to help me assess my surroundings. A thin, pale blue gown covers my chest, leading over to a clear tube taped to my arm, as my fingers tug at a scratchy white blanket that lays over my body. A warm hand slides into my own as I gradually begin to make out the features of my guest.

"Eli?" I croak.

"Shh. It's okay. You're okay." There's a forced assurance to his words.

It registers that his other hand is holding an ice pack to my head. When I look from our joined hands, up his arm, then to his face, I see the bleary and somber eyes of my best friend.

"Eli?" I ask again, unable to hide my rising panic. Pain rattles my skull as I attempt to twist my head in an effort to survey the room. I know I'm in the hospital, which makes sense because I feel like I was kicked by a horse. "What happened? Where's my mom?"

"You hit your head. You're in the hospital."

I know there's more. The throbbing ache in my midsection confirms it. "Eli, just tell me."

With a labored breath, he places the ice pack aside, unable to make eye contact with me while he cautiously considers his words. When he's ready, he squeezes my hand and bends his body over mine. "You had a miscarriage, Leah. The doctor said you miscarried and started hemorrhaging. I'm so sorry."

No. That makes no sense.

I shake my head in denial, stopping after only a second from the pain that rattles from ear to ear, as I try to remember everything that led up to this moment. I stare into his eyes, thoughts of what he just said spinning in my head and fogging my mind. He's clearly delusional. You have to be pregnant to have a miscarriage, and I was never pregnant.

His tone turns conciliatory. "You had an ectopic pregnancy and were bleeding internally. They had to rush you in for emergency surgery. You lost a lot of blood and . . ."

He rests his forehead on our hands and begins to shake. I manage to pull a hand free and rest it on his head, soothing him a moment before running it down and around to his face. Then, I tug at his chin until he meets my eyes.

His shine with tears as I beg for clarification, "Are you saying . . . I was pregnant?"

"Oh my God, Leah. I thought we were going to lose you. We were so close to losing you." He moves closer, kissing my temple for a long beat and then wiping away tears I wasn't even aware had run down my cheeks.

I cover my face as a weak cry builds from behind my palms. "No. No."

Eli hovers over me, speaking soft words I can't make out, as he nervously brushes my hair back from my face. But no amount of denial will hide what I know deep down. This is all really happening. Every night of drinking, combined with every blank face I've given myself to, has brought me to this moment.

"Does my mom know?" I drop my hands just below my eyes and wait, terrified, for his answer.

"Yes, she knows. I've been updating her hourly. She caught a flight from her last port and will be here soon."

I scrunch my brows in confusion.

"She was on her Alaskan cruise, remember?"

My muscles tighten, trying to hold back the tears at the thought of what my family must be going through right now.

Eli hands me a tissue. "Leah, is there anyone you want me to call?" He pauses, giving me a chance to consider. "Do you want me to call the person you're, um . . . seeing?"

That simple question shines a spotlight into the exhaustive and ugly sham of a life I've been living that I can no longer hide from. I attempt to turn away in disgrace as a fresh round of tears take hold.

"Leah, let me help you. If you don't want me to call him, then I won't. Just tell me what you want me to do." His pleading is only making my guilt worse.

"There is no one to call." The words burn in my chest.

He moves onto the bed, on top of the covers, and lies alongside me, turning me with care until we're face-to-face.

After a few deep breaths, I manage to continue, "There's no one to call because I don't know who he is."

When I dare to look into his eyes, they're strained in confusion.

"I don't know which *one* he is."

His body tightens as his confusion swiftly turns to pained understanding and humiliation pokes at me like a million hot needles.

His mouth pulls into a troubled grimace, and a deep V forms between his eyes.

"I'm sorry, Eli. I'm so sorry." I burrow into his chest, not able to witness any more of his disappointment.

He slides his arms around me and holds me tight. I continue to babble apologies, only for him to shush me again and again.

"You're okay now, honey. It'll all be okay." He repeats that one word, "Okay," over and over.

But, right now, lying in this hospital bed and admitting what got me here, it makes me question how I'll ever be okay.

With his hands spread protectively on my back and my face nestled in his chest, I inhale his familiar scent and finally settle.

When my crying stops and my breathing evens, he whispers into the silent room, "What did he do, Lee?"

I exhale long and deep, too tired and broken to protect Eli and Heath's friendship any longer. I've not only held on to the pain of Heath's betrayal, but, worse, I've allowed it to spread like a poison through every muscle that threads through me. I've embraced it and nurtured it like it is a real, living thing, only for it to continue to grow and grow. Until, eventually, it is who I've become.

I give Eli every moment, breath by painful breath, as I recount everything I felt for Heath. How I told him I loved him and how I let myself fall further than I ever had before. Everything that led up to that crushing day and every ugly day since.

At times, he grips me tighter but never utters a word, his occasional flinch or low grumble in his chest doing the speaking for him. When I'm finished, he simply kisses my head and holds me until I fall asleep.

Eli refuses to leave my side until my mom is physically in the room, so we use the time to fill in the blanks.

After I collapsed, Denise grabbed my cell phone and called my mom. When she got her voice mail, she hung up and called Eli.

Witnessing the sadness as my friend speaks, I can tell he'll forever be changed by this. One more cross I have to bear.

"I talked to Connor. He's on his way too," he states matter-of-factly as we both stare blankly at the TV. My fists clench beneath the blanket, knowing what this must be doing to my brother.

"Does Lindsey know?"

"Yes."

"No one else, Eli?"

Without a glance or second of hesitation, he answers, "No one."

I'm relieved when he doesn't offer to leave as the doctor comes in to check on me. I can't stand to be alone right now. I know I'll only drift to a dark place of self-loathing that I'm not sure I could claw my way out of.

The doctor explains in more detail what Eli has already told me. I was dealing with an ectopic pregnancy that led to the rupture of one of my fallopian tubes. The tube had to be removed, but he goes on to say that, thankfully, there are no issues with the other tube. As if that's supposed to make me feel better. Then, I come to find out that all of the ibuprofen I was taking for the pain only managed to thin my blood, causing the bleeding to worsen. Choosing alcohol over food didn't help the situation either.

Shortly after he's gone, the door to my room violently swings open, hitting the doorstop and bouncing back. Eli and I jump, his body moving protectively in front of mine, as we're met with the sound of heavy panting. Connor stands in the doorway, his chest heaving and his face as red as his shirt. His eyes are wild, like he's torn between either killing someone or curling up in the fetal position.

The second Connor's tearful eyes meet with my own, I know Eli has shared everything.

All of my shame disappears, instead replaced with intense relief that my brother is here. Physically just feet away. I've never loved him more.

He reads me like no one else. Bolting to my side and wrapping his arms around and under my body, he leans low while pulling me into his chest. I don't flinch at the pain because the relief that he's here is stronger than any painkiller.

"I'm here now, Lee Lee." His voice shakes with the nickname he hasn't used since grammar school. "I'm going to take care of you."

I know he means every word. Although Connor is just two minutes older, he will always be my big brother.

I quietly but freely cry into his shoulder, hearing his occasional hush, as his hands stroke my back. I don't know which one has a tighter grip on the other, but in the strength of my brother's arms, I know, somehow, someday, everything might just be all right.

Moving to a chair on the side of my bed, opposite Eli, Connor sits but doesn't release my hand. He is my lifeline, my connection to the person I was. A life that was clean air and warm nights. A reminder of all the goodness that has graced my life. And of the girl I once was and wish upon every penny to once again be.

The three of us watch the news and then a cooking show, followed by *Jeopardy!* with one of us occasionally whispering the answer, until my mom arrives. She's disheveled, and it's obvious she's been crying when she makes it to my bedside.

"My girl. My baby girl," she chokes out as she runs her hands over my hair and around to my cheeks before scanning the rest of my body. When she sees every appendage is accounted for, she brings her face to mine and repeatedly kisses my cheeks before resting her lips on my forehead an extra beat.

"I'm so sorry, Mom. I'm *so, so* sorry," I rasp out, ringing my arms around her back as we cry, my face buried in the matted hair hanging over her neck.

"Enough of that now, sweetheart." She lifts up and dries my tears before tending to her own. With her eyes locked tight on mine, she speaks slow and firm, "Listen to me, Leah Margaret. You are going to get through this."

I give her a weak nod, but she holds her eyes to mine. I know what she's waiting for.

"I am going to get through this," I repeat her words with stuttered conviction.

She smiles back, pride mixed with determination, giving me hope that, if she can have faith, then maybe I can, too.

Someone clears their throat from the doorway, and we all four turn toward the noise. My doctor is standing there, his hands folded at his waist.

"I'm Dr. Panou. I performed your daughter's surgery and—"

My mom whips around, cutting him off, while eyeing him up and down, "How do I know you're the best?" She stands tall, facing him with her arms crossed over her chest.

His professional, confident demeanor weakens. "Pardon?"

"Mom," I whisper-hiss.

She takes a small step closer, enunciating every word. "How do I know you're the best doctor for my daughter?"

He jolts slightly back, and if I didn't know better, I'd say he's a little afraid of Madeline Dawson. *Smart man.*

His confidence returned, he cocks an arrogant shoulder back and lifts his chin. "*Chicago Magazine* ranked me as the number two ob-gyn in all of Chicago, and I've—"

Her arms move to her hips. "Number *two*? That's all? We want—"

"Mom, stop. *Please.* They've been taking very good care of me here." My words aren't enough though. It's not until Eli nods in confirmation that she backs down.

"Mrs. Dawson, I presume? If I could speak to you and your daughter in private," Dr. Panou asks.

Connor doesn't budge, and Eli barely manages to rise from his chair.

"Everyone here is family," I state firmly.

"Very well."

Dr. Panou steps up to the foot of my bed at the same time I find the controls and raise myself up as much as I can comfortably manage.

"Now that you've recovered from the effects of the anesthesia and you have a support team in place, there are some serious issues for us to discuss. We've talked about your mild concussion. Continue to use an ice pack, but other than that, rest will be your best medicine. As far as the surgery goes, you're doing remarkably well, all things considered."

Anxiety swirls in my chest as his tone grows gentle.

"But, like I said earlier, what effect this will have on your reproductive health is yet to be determined. Along with that, I have another serious matter to discuss with you." He pauses cautiously. "You are grossly underweight with troublesome signs of malnutrition and dehydration, all leading to concerns for your mental health."

My mom grips my hand in support.

"I've arranged for our nutritionist and psychologist to visit with you, if that's all right."

My mom looks to me, waiting for approval. When I give her a weak smile and small shrug, her eyes flicker with pride, and she gives my hand another squeeze.

I turn back to him. "I would appreciate that." My voice is small, childlike.

His face warms with a genuine smile, and the tension from earlier evaporates. "Good. I'm glad to hear that because this could have turned out much, much worse, Leah." When he sees my eyes fill with tears, he moves in close. "But it didn't, and you're still here. And, more importantly, you have people who are here for you and who love you. Whatever you're struggling with, I promise you, it will get better if you accept help."

My mom brushes my hair with her fingers and looks down to me with a mixture of hope and pain at his words. Eli is focused on something on the floor while Connor steps in to lend a supportive hand to my shoulder.

Connor takes Eli to the airport shortly after the doctor's visit, leaving my mom and me alone, just the two of us, for the first time in months. She pulls a chair up alongside my bed and takes in every part of me. I know what she sees, and I'm more than ashamed. A gaunt, pale, sad version of what was once her loving, vivacious, smiling daughter. I've all but forgotten that girl. And, in this moment, I miss her as much as my mom does.

I speak honestly with her, something I haven't done since the day my heart was broken. About what really happened between Heath and me and every ugly day that followed. I cry out of embarrassment, out of shame, and out of fear for how poorly she must think of me. But my mom, being the loving woman she is, never judges or criticizes. Instead, she listens and consoles. Then, she plans.

Together, we decide it's best if I finish out the final month of my contract, while meeting with the psychologist and nutritionist recommended to me by the hospital. She will stay these next two weeks, and then Connor will fly back for the final two weeks. She said it's to make sure I'm healing properly and taking care of myself, but if we're being honest, there's also concern that I might fall back into newly acquired, and toxic, habits.

A month later, with my mom and brother by my side, we pack up the little bit I have here and head home, leaving a year's worth of mistakes behind.

TWENTY-NINE

Heath

It's still early enough that I'm able to get a small table in the far corner of the bar. I don't even know why I'm here, just that I'm restless as fuck, knowing Eli dropped everything to be with Leah in Chicago. I can't shake the way his face changed when he answered his phone and how he yelled to Lindsey to book him a flight before running to his room to pack a bag. When I tried to block him, to find out what had happened, he screamed at me to back off. So, I did. I stood behind the counter in the kitchen, out of the way but not willing to leave, hoping he'd give me something. Anything.

When he said good-bye to Lindsey with tears in her eyes that matched the strain on his face, that was when I lost it. Charging to the door before he could get there, I grabbed his sleeve. "Eli, *please.* Tell me what the hell is going on."

His jaw locked as he shook his head, before pulling Lindsey in for one last kiss and running out the door for the airport.

So, here I am, down the street from my place, sitting in a dark bar, drinking my usual tonic and lime. Frustrated and alone. And I deserve every miserable second of it.

"Hey, Heath." Lucy surprises me as she sets down her drink and takes a seat on the stool next to me.

I barely glance her way. "Hey, Luce." I fake a small smile and focus on my drink.

"Wow, you're in a great mood tonight. Want to talk about it?"

"No." I don't bother to raise my head. "Have you talked to your brother?"

"No, just Lindsey. He's in . . ." She catches herself. "Something about him being out of town."

I nod, knowingly, then stand and throw a few dollars on the table. "Actually, I think I'm going to walk home. I'll let you get back to your friends."

"I'll walk out with you. There's not much going on here." She slams back the last of her drink and stands, gripping the table as she sways into it.

As I breathe in the heavy air with my hands tucked deep in my pockets, my mind is on one thing and one thing only. Leah. I texted Eli, hoping for the slightest crumb of information, but he hasn't responded. Not that I expect him to. But that doesn't mean I'm about to stop trying.

I barely notice as Lucy continues to walk with me, her rambling on since we stepped out from the bar nothing more than white noise. When we make it to the lobby of my building, she follows in, as if this has been the plan all along. Whatever. Maybe a little conversation will distract me from all the insane scenarios running through my head of what might be happening in Chicago.

"Nice place, Heath. It actually looks like a respectable adult lives here. You're even dressing like a grown-up these days," she says with a drunken wink as she motions to my button-down shirt and slacks.

I ignore her and take a seat on the sofa, and she does the same, just a foot away. Leaning forward, head down and forearms resting on my thighs, I take a few cleansing breaths. Being home isn't any better as my imagination runs wild with a hundred what-ifs. Dragging my hands through my hair, I groan in frustration just as I feel Lucy's hand come to my shoulder. I don't want anyone's kindness right now. I don't deserve it. Even from Lucy, who's like a sister to me.

It's not until I feel her hand run over my back and her body inch closer to mine that I realize she might not feel the same way.

"Luce." I tilt back at the same time she leans in.

"Heath."

The acrid sweetness of alcohol coats her breath as her hand travels confidently over my thigh. When her lips land harshly on mine, I open my mouth in protest. She takes advantage by sealing hers to mine, her tongue pushing its way forward. I try to focus on the fact that I've got an attractive young woman willing to kiss me, whom I'm free to kiss in return—and probably much more—so I pressure myself to take this one moment. Moving into her, I bring my hand to her head and kiss her back.

Maybe this kiss will ease the ache since Leah left. But her hair under my fingers isn't as soft as Leah's. She doesn't taste like Leah either. And her body pressed tightly against mine doesn't feel like Leah. She certainly doesn't make my skin heat like Leah.

Leah. Leah. Leah.

I force my body back and jump from my seat, my hands behind my head as I catch my breath. Looking down at her, I know I've made a huge mistake. Because I don't see an attractive brunette. All I see is the young girl who cried when we hung her doll from a tree. Or the snotty teenager who told us every day how much she hated us. I only see her as a surrogate sister. That's it. I can't think of Lucy in any other way—ever.

"Heath?"

"I'm sorry, Luce. I can't . . . you and I, we're not . . ."

She stands, finding her purse and retrieving her phone before tapping at the screen.

"No, don't apologize. I get it."

"Luce, I'm sor—"

"I said, don't apologize!"

She won't look at me, keeping all her focus on her phone. When I attempt a step toward her, she moves back.

"It's fine, Heath. It's my fault. I had a little too much to drink, and, well, you're *you*." She goes back to typing.

"What does that mean?"

She's drunker than I realized, and now, I feel like a bigger ass for not seeing it.

"C'mon, Heath. Just don't right now, okay?"

"Don't what?"

"Never mind. Can we just forget this ever happened? And please don't tell my brother. That's all either of us needs." She reads a message on her phone before bringing it down to her side. "I texted a friend at the bar. She's meeting me halfway."

I reach out to her. "No, Lucy. At least let me walk you." *Please say no. Please say no.*

"No." She forces out a laugh. "I want to be alone with you right now about as much as you do with me." She throws her purse over her shoulder and walks toward the door.

Just when I think this clusterfuck is over, she turns back. "You still love her."

Every muscle in me tightens at her proclamation.

"My advice, do everything you can to win her back. Otherwise, you'll never forgive yourself for not trying." Her voice softens. "Most everything is forgivable, Heath, and everyone deserves a chance at forgiveness. Even fools like you." With that, she turns and walks out my door.

Is she right? Can I be forgiven?

I'd give Leah my deepest, darkest truths, my heaviest regrets. I'd lay every part of me out to her, at her feet, nothing left unsaid. Every raw emotion and insecurity. I'd give it all to her if I could just earn the chance.

———

I've been stalking Eli's house so long, I can't believe the neighbors haven't called the cops yet. But I couldn't care less. He never responded to my texts, and I can't take it anymore. Lindsey took pity on me enough to let me know that his flight is due to get in at four o'clock today. So, here I am, sitting out front of their place in my car. Waiting. She invited me inside, but I declined. There's no steering wheel to bang my head on in there.

Every time a car turns down the street, I sit up, alert, my hand ready on the door handle. And, every time, it's a false alarm. Just when I'm about to slouch back in defeat,

I recognize Eli's car. Flying out of my seat and across the yard, I expect him to slam the front door in my face, but instead, I get the opposite.

He pulls the car into the driveway on an angle before flinging the door open and charging toward me. I continue to move forward, not caring about what he could possibly scream at me right now, but he doesn't say a word. He lets his fists do the talking.

I don't see the first swing coming before it connects with my jaw, forcing my head to snap back and my body to lean to the side. I manage to catch myself before I make it all the way to the ground. With my hands out in defense, I only have a second before the next hit comes square in the ribs, knocking the air from my lungs and my body to its knees. I claw at the grass, willing my lungs to work when Eli lunges at me and knocks me to my back.

Straddling my chest, he fists my shirt in one hand while the other is cocked back and ready to fire. "You motherfucker!" His spit sprays my face, and my eyes close instinctively.

When I don't make an effort to fight back, he fires fast and hard into my face. My vision rattles and pain explodes as he connects with my nose, causing a thin but rapid stream of blood to gush down to my mouth and across my cheek. The pain radiating from my face and chest are trivial compared to the agony and hatred spewing from every molecule of my best friend's body.

He's shouting, calling me names, telling me he's done with me and that I'm worthless. I know he's right—about all of it. I've known for a while now. So, when I watch an arm pull back once again, I dig my fingers into the grass and dirt below me and close my eyes, bracing myself for my next round of punishment.

But it never comes.

When I dare to open my eyes, I see Lindsey in his face, crying and pleading with him to stop. It's not until she kneels down and pulls him in by his shoulders that he seems to actually hear her. She tugs him off of me and then grips him in a tight embrace. Even with pain throbbing throughout my body, I can hear the sobs coming from Eli as she leads him inside, followed by the sound of the front door closing.

I continue to lie there, my nose pounding at a rhythmic rate. The blood flowing down my face has slowed to a trickle, and despite what just happened here, the day is peaceful. No sounds of traffic or playing kids. In fact, as I lie, aching, on my back, I'm surrounded by green grass and a perfect blue sky, dotted with small white clouds. And for the first time since I can remember, I cry. Because I now know whatever happened in Chicago is far worse than anything I had imagined.

I look for images in the white shapes passing over me, as the trail of blood lessens, leaving stains in the grass below. A warm cloth wipes at my face before Lindsey slides her hand under my head and lifts. I raise my hand, motioning for her to stay back, so she does, handing me the cloth in exchange. Between my own crying and the blood that has traveled into my throat, I need a minute before I can stand. I wipe at my face and attempt the first dizzy steps toward my car.

But Lindsey surprises me. "He wants to talk to you."

I freeze. Not because I'm afraid of what he'll do to me, but because I'm terrified of finally learning the truth.

With an arm hugging a tender spot at my ribs and the other holding the cloth to my nose, I find Eli sitting at the kitchen table. One hand rests flatly under a bag of ice while the other holds a glass of clear liquid, a bottle of Grey Goose sitting, uncapped, next to it. I pull out the chair at the far end of the table, but he stops me before I can sit.

"Not there." He looks to the seat across from him as Lindsey pulls out my chair and gives me an ice pack, only leaving us when Eli promises there won't be any more bloodshed.

I don't dare speak first, but the silence is killing me. He's staring down into his glass, lost in thought. I want to shake him and force it out of him. Just get it over with because every minute that passes makes my mind wander into darker and darker places.

I pull the ice pack from my face and break the silence. "Will she be all right?"

He grinds his jaw, deciding whether or not to answer me.

"Please, whatever it is, just tell me." My voice is weak and desperate, any ounce of pride I once had long gone.

His head drops, and his shoulders shake, causing my own eyes to burn. In all our years as friends, this is an Eli I've never seen before, and his obvious pain is starting to scare the shit out of me. *If she's not okay, if this is irreparable* . . .

"Please." My voice catches, forcing me to swallow.

He lifts his head and looks to me with red eyes and wet cheeks. "She's not all right. Not even close." The words come out on a harsh whisper. "But I'll do everything I can to make sure she gets there."

I nod in appreciation. It's all I can do because I have no rights here. She's not mine. I sure as hell made sure of that. All I can do is trust in Eli that he'll do what I can't.

"Whatever she needs . . . you hear me? Do whatever it takes. Give her whatever she needs."

Christ, if she needed an organ, I'd cut it out of my body myself.

He lifts his glass, takes a generous sip, and then watches as he lowers it to the table. Speaking each word with precision, he says, "What she needs is for you to stay the fuck away from her. That's the only thing you will do for her right now." His voice carries a tone that I've never heard from him.

In a matter of a few short days, whatever happened in Chicago has changed him, hardened him in a way that will likely follow me for years to come. And that is worse than any punch to the gut.

He looks at me like he's seeing me for the first time. "How could you? How *fucking* could you, Heath?" He slams his good fist on the table and then once more. "I know what it's like to love her. But only you knew what it was like to have her love you back. And you threw that away. I trusted you to take care of her. I trusted you to treat her better than I ever could. But you didn't. Instead, you destroyed her."

We sit in pained silence until Lindsey appears at his side. He doesn't hesitate to make room on his lap and wrap her in his arms. She squeezes him in return, whispering something in his ear.

I feel like a knife has been jabbed and twisted in my chest, and I know I deserve every slice of pain. I don't know how to make it go away, but even if I did, I wouldn't want to. I want to be reminded every second of every minute of every day of what happens when I allow insecurities to rule my life.

It's taken total destruction of the people I love to see how I hurt everyone around me. I need to find a way to repair the damage I've done. Not just to Leah and Eli, but my dad as well.

I leave them without another word and drive home. I go straight to my room, open my bottom dresser drawer, and reach into the far back corner. The pink metal container is cool, as the coins jostle around inside. I place it front and center on my dresser before running my hand over the top. I know down to my bones that, if there's any chance of fixing the hurt I've caused, then there's only one place to start. At the beginning. I have to go back if there's any chance of moving forward.

It's time to clear out the skeletons. It's time to put the demons to rest. It's time to make my peace with my mother.

It's no surprise, given my history of being an asshole, that my dad and I didn't always get along. I can see now all the ways I didn't make it easy on him. But, since we've been working together, I can wholeheartedly say that not only do I like him, but I also *admire* him. He's a good man, and I'm just now seeing it.

My dad and I have been driving into the office together for some time now. He picks me up, armed with coffees made fresh by Louise, and we make the most of the little bit of time we have in the car together to catch up. There's something about being enclosed in a metal and glass box that shuts out the rest of the world, and in that space, anything goes. No judgment or criticism. Just guidance and encouragement.

It's after six p.m., and as the office quiets down, I'd typically be finishing up and checking with my dad to see if he was ready to go. But, instead, I'm staring at my computer screen, looking at the result of a little side project I've been working on.

"Wow, she still looks exactly the same. Barely a line on her face." My dad appears from behind, causing me to jump in my seat and flip my laptop shut. "It's fine, Heath. I'm actually shocked it's taken you this long."

"Apparently, she's been married eight times," I stutter, reopening my laptop.

He shakes his head, unsurprised, as he leans against the corner of my desk. "So, is she still in France?"

"Dad, I just . . ." I turn from my computer to him. "Wait, how did you know that?"

I just found out myself that she had an address listed in Marseilles. It took a little while to find her, considering the multiple changes to her last name.

"I've kept tabs on her over the years. I had to, to protect you."

"Protect me? Why would you have to protect me from someone who *left* me?"

He shuts my office door and takes a deep breath before continuing, "Heath, I've always been honest and told you your mother left. And she did, but that's not because she wanted to. It's because I told her to. She wasn't given a choice in the matter."

"No, that's not true. She left us."

"Before you get upset, let me tell you this. It was the most difficult decision I've ever had to make. But I wouldn't hesitate to do it all over again if that meant keeping you safe." He's still leaning on my desk, his hands folded casually on his lap, his features calm.

"Keep me safe? I don't understand. What could she have done that was so bad, you'd force her to leave her own child?" I roll my chair back and wait for an explanation.

Shoving his hands in his pockets, he focuses on me as he starts from the beginning. "We were so young when we married. So many hopes and dreams. Our biggest dream was having kids. Lots of kids. Or so I thought. It wasn't long until she got pregnant, and, Jesus, I was so happy. The woman I loved was pregnant with my baby. There's no better feeling." He looks down at his shoes, momentarily relishing the memory.

"That was, until I noticed her acting strangely, mostly not taking care of herself. I'd catch her drinking, and she'd brush me off, saying it was just a sip or two. Or she'd take off on a bike ride when the doctor clearly told her to avoid anything with two wheels. But it was like she was actually trying to do the opposite of what was best.

"I was working sixty-, seventy-hour weeks back then, building the practice, so I thought it was her way of gaining my attention. But, when I started finding empty wine bottles hidden in the garbage, I knew it was something more.

"Once, I even got a phone call from her, screaming and hysterical that she had been roller-skating with friends and fallen. *Fucking roller-skating.* I rushed to the hospital, and she was crying that she'd lost you before a doctor even did the ultrasound. Fortunately, they confirmed that not only was she still pregnant, but that you were also all right.

"I couldn't even give myself a chance to be relieved though because, now, I was trying to figure out what was wrong with my wife. Why did it seem like she was doing everything she could to lose you? And our dream of a family right along with it." He shakes his head at the memory.

"The doctor asked if she had a family history of mental illness, but there was nothing. So, I watched her closely and had everyone possible watching her as well. Near the end of the pregnancy, the possibility of postpartum depression became a big concern, so, a few weeks before you were delivered, she agreed to go on an antidepressant for the next few months.

"Then, you were born, and you were perfect. We doted on you like we were the first people to be given a child. Your mom, she couldn't take her eyes off of you, insisting on doing everything for you herself—to the point that I could never even change a diaper. You refused to breast-feed, so I'd get up at night to feed you, but she'd already be there. She wasn't sleeping, but you wouldn't know it because she was bouncing off the walls with energy. She said it was from too much coffee. So, I figured that you were cared for, and that was the most important thing.

"Until shortly after your first birthday. That was when you started getting sick. Odd rashes, vomiting, diarrhea, dehydration. It felt like she was constantly running you to the doctor, but they couldn't find anything wrong. She became obsessed by the idea that you had cancer, so much so that even I started to believe it.

"Together, we took you to specialist after specialist. You had more tests done on you in one month than anyone should have in a lifetime. But, other than ruling out cancer, no one could explain your symptoms.

"It wasn't until I walked in on you having a seizure on the family room rug that everything changed." He begins pacing in front of my desk, raking his hands through his hair and taking a few strong breaths.

"Dad, it's okay. Just tell me," I whisper.

"It was the strangest feeling. I'll never forget it. Something in my gut had told me to get home. To *run* home. That you needed me. I literally walked out of a meeting and ran to my car. And, when I walked in the front door and came around the corner, there you were, lying on your back with your eyes rolled back, jaw clamped shut, and every limb of your tiny body rigid and stiff. And she was just sitting there, on the sofa, casually watching you, like this was a fucking normal, everyday occurrence."

His face is twisted in agony, but when I begin to rise from my chair, he holds one finger up, asking for a moment. I sit back down and give him whatever time he needs.

"I called an ambulance and carried you outside, completely helpless. It was the worst feeling in the world, and I will never forget it for as long as I live. The seizing settled by the time the ambulance got there, but you started vomiting and foaming at the mouth on the drive to the hospital. They saw signs of poison and immediately pumped your stomach. And, sure enough, they found household cleaners in your system. She had been feeding her own baby poison. She had been intentionally making you sick! And for what? What did she get out of it? Sympathy? Attention?"

"Everyone told me to leave her. But, by then, a sense of guilt so deep had set in. We lived under the same roof. How had I not known? So, I tried to do the right thing. To get her help and stand by her side. I found her the best doctors, spent thousands and thousands of dollars, but the truth of the matter was, how could I leave you alone with her ever again? I had to worry about your safety around your own fucking mother.

"It didn't take long for the guilt to turn to anger. I knew I'd never forgive myself if I didn't get you away from her. So, I offered her a huge check and told her to take anything she wanted. And you know what? She took it. She took it all and never looked back. She didn't just leave you that day, son; she left both of us. Every hope and dream I'd had for my family was gone. With one signature, I became a full-time, single dad.

"I've examined every moment with your mother more times than I can count. Logically now, I know there was mental illness, but I can't help but think that I wasn't enough for her. That you and I weren't enough. I don't know. I don't think I'll ever know honestly. And I'm okay with that because, in the end, I got *you*. And you are all that ever mattered."

My head is spinning. I'm still in my seat, digging my fingers into my knees, as I grapple with the bomb that's just been dropped.

My dad saved my life.

He's always been there for me. In ways I couldn't even comprehend.

"I'm so sorry, Heath. We should've had this conversation a long time ago. But you have to know, I've always done what I thought was best for you. Always."

I raise my head to him, hating to see his face strain as he fights back tears. Knowing everything this man has done for me is breaking my heart. I stand and wrap my arms around my dad for probably the first time since I was five. He clutches me back, his embrace telling me one thing strong and clear. I am so lucky to have him.

We separate, and he pats me on the shoulder. "Can you tell me why this is all coming up now?"

My shoulders hunch as my fingers twist together. "I really screwed up."

"With Leah?"

"With Leah. Eli. You. Everyone who matters. All because of *her*." I glance at my computer.

"So, what are you thinking? Do you want to fly to Paris and confront her? Because, if that will help you find what you need, we can leave tomorrow."

"No. I think I'm good. I have everything I need right here."

THIRTY

Leah

What the hell is that noise?

"Mom!" My voice is hoarse as I shout with my head sandwiched between two pillows.

As the sound travels further away, my shoulders relax, and the rest of my body melts back into the bed. Just as my thoughts fade off, the sound roars back, vibrating the window above my bed.

"Damn it." I smack the bed with my hand and push myself up.

The clock says it's barely eight a.m., and the noise is definitely a lawn mower. And I know one thing for sure. Whoever is on the push end of that machine is about to feel my wrath.

I stomp down the stairs to the front door and fling it open, the early morning sun burning my retinas. As the passing lawn guy comes into focus, I don't have the patience to wait to rip him a new one, so I jump the few steps and begin my attack from behind. It's the most physical activity I've had in some time, not to mention much needed vitamin D.

"What the hell are you doing? Excuse me!"

He doesn't hear my shouts over the sound of the mower. I follow him and yell again. This time, when he still doesn't answer, I notice his earbuds and poke a finger into his shirtless, tan shoulder blade. The engine dies at the same time he turns to me.

You have got to be kidding me.

I stumble back a step.

"Heath?"

A wall instantly goes up, blocking off the old, familiar pain that washes over me like a bucket of ice water.

With my defenses armed and raised, I go for haughty. "Do you have any idea what time it is? People are sleeping!" I bring my hands to my narrow hips. Although my old running shorts are riding low, my attitude is firmly in place. "And what are you doing cutting my grass, anyway?" My eyes are hard as I point, disgusted, at his sweat-beaded chest.

He swallows and answers quietly, "You're home?"

I roll my eyes and shake my head. "Yes, Heath, I'm home." Turning to the driveway, I notice my mom's car is gone, and slap my hands to my sides. "Great. Where is my mother?" I huff under my breath and turn back to him. When I do, he's still staring at me. "What?"

"It's Saturday."

Frustrated, I fist my hands at his non-answer.

"Yes, Heath, it's Saturday."

"On Saturdays, I cut the grass, and your mom goes to the farmers market with Mrs. Emerick."

"*You* cut the grass?"

"Yeah."

"Since when?"

"I don't know. A while now?"

He's still staring at me like I'm back from the dead, and it's making me uncomfortable. I run my fingers through my hair, and they get stuck half way through in a tangle of knots. At least, now, I understand why he's staring.

"You're home." This time, it's not a question but more of a wistful declaration. "I mean, are you *home*, home or just home for a visit?"

I cross my arms over my chest, just now realizing I'm wearing a stretched-out tank top with nothing underneath. "*Home*, home." I turn my head up and away.

"Good. That's good. I know how much your mom missed you."

My jaw grinds. *Who is he to talk about my mom?*

"Well, I'd better finish up. Sorry I woke you." He drops his head and backs up a few steps away before stopping. "It's good to have you home, Leah." He walks to the mower and continues where he left off.

After he disappears around the side of the house, I storm back inside and climb back into bed, although there's no way I'm falling back asleep. Seeing Heath was not on today's itinerary. *What is on today's itinerary?* The same as the day I crawled into this bed a week ago.

Feel sorry for myself. *Check.*

Feel pathetic. *Check.*

Feel like a failure. *Check.*

I've already accomplished so much in one day. But facing Heath for the first time in more than a year? Definitely not on today's to-do list. Or tomorrow's. Or the day after that.

Lying back on the bed, I bring a pillow over my eyes and force myself to think of something other than the last five minutes. But it's worthless.

Heath.

He looked the same but somehow older. His features were softer than before, less angry than I remember. His shoulders weren't on guard, and his eyes weren't suspicious. It's a Heath I don't recognize. A Heath I don't know.

I stay in bed until the lawn mower stops and then wait another ten minutes until I'm sure he's gone. When I finally make my way to the kitchen, I'm met by my mom unloading vegetables from her bag.

"Well, there's my darling daughter. Good to see you out of bed." She continues to pull produce from her bag.

The pieces start to fall together. "This was your plan all along, wasn't it?" I pull a sweatshirt over my head before crossing my arms, irritated.

"Plan? I'm not sure what you mean." She brings a hand to her chest, feigning offense.

"You haven't bugged me once about getting out of bed this past week because you knew eventually the lawn mower would do the trick. Or, more importantly, the person pushing it."

"Lee, that's ridiculous. I always—"

"Mom, just stop."

When her features soften and sympathy fills her eyes, I know I'm right.

"Heath, Mom? Really?"

"He needed someone to talk to, Lee. As much as I know he hurt you, he needed a mother. I couldn't turn him away."

I hug myself and ask, "Did you tell him? About what happened to me?"

"Absolutely not." I squeeze tighter as she continues, "I didn't know at first, what had happened between the two of you. I just knew he needed someone to confide in, and for some reason, he picked me." Her voice softens. "He's changed a lot in the last year, Lee. I'm not saying you have to be friends with him again. But just understand that he's not the same person he was when you were together."

"Are you seriously defending him?"

"Never." She walks up and places her warm hands on my cheeks. "You are always first. You and Connor. And what he did is inexcusable. And I made that clear to him. But I also know a cry for help when I see one. And that boy wasn't just crying. He was screaming. So, I had to make the choice to either watch him slip further down the hole or reach a hand out to help. I chose to help him. If that hurts you, I'm sorry. But I'm sorrier that I didn't realize you were sliding down that same dark hole." Her eyes turn glassy, and her voice breaks. "I will never forgive myself for not being there for you. For not seeing that things were as bad as they were."

"It's not your fault, Mom. It was easy to hide when I was almost a thousand miles away."

"No, you're my daughter. My baby girl. I should've seen it. Hell, I should've *felt* it. But I didn't. And, honey, I am so sorry for that."

She's about to cry. Something I rarely see from her and definitely something I can't handle. I pull her in for a hug and rest my chin on her shoulder. She holds me, and for that brief moment, I feel a little less sorry for myself, a little less pathetic, and a little less like a failure.

"Lee?" she asks into my hair.

"Yes?"

"I love you, you know that?"

"Of course I do. I love you too."

"Good. Remember that when I say what I have to say next."

I brace myself, and she reflexively tightens her grip. "Okay."

"For both our sakes, go shower. And brush your teeth. Twice. Because, sweetheart, you smell like ass."

THIRTY-ONE

Heath

Leah is home.
She's home.

When I turned and saw her, standing in front of me for the first time in forever, I just wanted to touch her and see if she was real. Because, although she looked like my Leah, the person standing in front of me was nothing like my Leah.

She stopped being your Leah a long time ago.

This Leah was frail with her collarbones sticking out from underneath her tank top and her cheekbones harsh and defined. Her skin was pale with bony hips above legs that were stick thin.

What hurt the most though was the look in her eyes. Total hate and disgust that I never knew possible from her. There was no sign of the happy, carefree Leah I once knew.

Eli was right. I'd destroyed her.

But, despite the anger in her voice and the weakness of her body, she was still the most gorgeous girl I have ever seen. I know the sweet, trusting Leah I fell in love with is in there somewhere. And I hope more than anything that she finds her way out. And, if I were someone who believed in miracles, I'd wish for me to be the one to help her find her way.

But miracles, like second chances, are hard to come by.

I head to my room in desperate need of a shower, stopping first at my dresser to pull open the top drawer and remove the pink tin box. I look at it every day now. It's my reminder of how damaging selfishness and fear can be. And to never go back there again.

I open the lid and then reach for the penny in my pocket, adding it to the pile as I make the same silent wish I've made on every penny since the day Eli punched me in the face.

Let Leah find her happy.

THIRTY-TWO

Leah

Why do I agree to these things? Oh, yeah, because I love Eli and Lindsey.

I fuss with the ribbons on the small box and head up the walkway. They're having an impromptu barbecue with a few friends to celebrate their recent engagement, and I couldn't say no. Not that I would even want to. They've both done so much for me, and I truly couldn't be happier for them.

As far as I'm concerned, Eli is family, and Lindsey is better than anyone I could have ever picked for him. She's funny and kind, and she looks at him like he's the center of her world. And, with everything that happened in Chicago, any bitterness she may have felt toward me and my past with Eli has vanished.

My only real problem at the moment is the car that sits out front of the house. Heath's car. I know at some point I'll need to learn to coexist with him, but until then, I'm going for subtle avoidance.

I enter the house and am immediately met with the sounds of soft music and jovial conversation. Cautiously, I move toward the heart of the party, ready to divert my eyes and change my path if necessary.

"There you are." Lindsey greets me with a warm hug before gracing me with her cheerful smile. "You look wonderful, as always. Did you get some sun today?"

"I did. Thanks." Remembering why we're here, I excitedly grab her hand. "Let me see!"

Her engagement ring is a stunning round one carat diamond encircled with an outer layer of small diamonds, all set on a platinum band. I actually already saw it when Eli brought me to the jeweler for a second opinion, but seeing it on her hand only makes it more beautiful.

I lightly squeeze her fingers. "Gorgeous, Lindsey. I'm so happy for you."

Her face eases into a wistful smile. "Thanks, Leah. I'm pretty happy myself."

With an arm around my shoulders, she leads me into the family room. Eli mentioned it was going to be a small get-together, but it's more so than I expected, which is going to make avoiding *him* even harder.

As the sun goes down and the temperature cools, the group ends up outside, seated around a bonfire for s'mores and easy conversation. Heath has either sensed my need to be left alone or he's enjoying the attention of Lindsey's friends. Thankfully, I have Eli's sisters to keep me company. As if they sense my anxiety, at least one of them has stayed by my side.

It's been borderline exhausting, keeping tabs on him all night so that I'm not caught by surprise. I manage to steal a glimpse when he's not looking. Just long enough to see he's dressed in black slacks and a navy button-down shirt with the sleeves rolled to the elbows. There's been more than one moment where I could feel his eyes on me, but I've stayed vigilant to shift away when needed.

"Can we have everyone's attention, please?"

The group collectively turns to our hosts, who are standing as the fire lights up their beaming faces.

Eli looks down to his hand that's entwined with Lindsey's before beginning to speak. "We've asked you all here tonight, not only because you are our friends and family, but also because you each bring something special to our lives. And, for that reason, we'd like to ask each of you for the honor of standing up in our wedding."

Cheers ring out as we all encircle the couple. I hug Eli first and then move to Lindsey. When I step back, my heels meet someone's toes and I immediately turn to apologize.

But, when the owner of the toes turns out to be Heath, I skip the apology altogether, stepping around him and grumbling, "Excuse me," as I pass.

As soon as I see an opportunity, I say a quiet good-bye to Eli and Lindsey and then sneak, undetected, to my car.

Just as my feet travel from the roughness of the stone walk to the smoothness of the paved road, I hear steps approaching from behind me.

"Leah."

Shit.

My skin prickles as the hairs on my neck rise. *So much for subtle avoidance.*

THIRTY-THREE

Heath

This night couldn't have gone worse if I'd tried. Between Leah avoiding me like I had a skin-melting, gas-inducing virus and Lindsey's friends following me around like homeless, horny puppies, I didn't get a single chance to talk to Leah. And, now, she's leaving.

While we were together, anytime I walked into a room, her eyes always found mine, like a magnetic pull. I'd swear, she was powerless to take them off of me. Her body hummed with impatience, like she couldn't physically wait to kiss me. Like she *had* to kiss me. I felt like a king.

Now? Now, she walks out of a room when I walk in. Her eyes land on anything but mine. She smiles at everyone but me, never gifting me with a single glance. Because I know now, that's what they were.

A gift.

Every look. Every touch. Every kiss.

But I'm not giving up.

"Leah." I jump down from the front step and run across the yard, like the complete pussy I am. But I lost my last fuck a long time ago. "Leah, wait."

She throws her shoulders back before turning to me, the hatred rolling off her attempting to flatten me.

"I didn't get a chance to say hi."

She gives me nothing.

"So, how are you?"

"I'm well, thank you." Each polite syllable is crisp and cold.

She shifts her weight from foot to foot, anxious to bolt.

"What have you been up to since you've been back?"

"Are you serious right now?"

"Yeah, I was just hoping we could talk. Catch up."

The anger that stretches across every angle of her face tells me this may have been a huge mistake.

"Catch up? Okay, Heath, let's do that. Let's *catch up*."

She steps closer into my space, and I'm momentarily grateful.

Until she continues, and her words scrape my skin. "I spent the last year in Chicago, trying to scrub the image of the man I loved in bed with another woman." She raises a finger to my chest but doesn't touch me. "You took away my self-worth, my pride, and my ability to see the good in myself. But the worst part of it all is that I let you. I let you rip me apart until there was nothing left. And I hate myself for it as much as I hate you."

I stutter a few times, but no sound makes its way out.

She turns to leave when I find my voice.

I run in front of her and cut her off. "It was a mistake, Leah. I would give anything to take it back. Anything."

The laugh she releases is harsh and bitter. "Eli was right. You destroy everything you touch. Everything good in your life, you find a way to fuck it up. Then, you sit back and complain that nothing goes your way. You are an immature, selfish, spoiled brat who cares about no one but himself. "

She starts walking, and I beat her to her car, pressing my body back against her door.

"You're right. About all of it. But so much has changed since then. I've changed. I deserve your hate. I deserve every disgusted, disappointed look I get from you. And let me tell you, each one kills me. Each one is a knife to the chest. But that's okay. I will take it all from you because I will forever and always regret what I did to you. To us."

Gripping her hips, she asks faintly, "What do you want from me, Heath?"

"Just the opportunity to be in your life. However I can get it. Give me a chance."

"How many more chances can I give you to hurt me?"

"I swear to you, I will never hurt you again."

She turns away and whispers, "You're hurting me right now."

My eyes pinch in pain at her words. "What can I do to make this better? What can I give you? Tell me, and it's yours."

She looks up to the dark sky in thought. I meant it when I said that I'd give her *anything*. I'd give her my eyes if she needed them to see. I'd give her the clothes on my back and every penny I had in the bank. I'd even walk away and give her Eli and Lindsey. The only thing I can't give her is my heart. She already has it.

She finally looks back to me. "Space. You can give me space."

Relieved, I take a wide step to the side without hesitation. "I can do that. I can give you space."

She nods and then pulls open the car door.

"I'm not the same man, Leah. I'll do whatever it takes, give you as much time as you need, to prove that to you. One hour at a time, one day at a time, one month at a time—whatever it takes—until your heart tells you it's safe to trust me."

Without a second glance, she slams her door and drives away.

THIRTY-FOUR

Leah

"Hi, honey. How was your appointment?" my mom asks before I'm even all the way through the door. I've been seeing both a nutritionist and psychologist regularly since I've been home.

"Fine. She said she can see my face filling out more."

"Have you weighed yourself lately? Maybe you should do that?"

She's sitting on the sofa, her back against the armrest and her knees bent, with a book resting in her lap. I take a seat at the opposite end and mirror her position, bringing us toe-to-toe.

"Relax, Mom. When I told you I was feeling better, I meant it. Oh, and Lindsey says hi."

"That's nice. So, the appointments with Dr. Gallus are helping?"

"I think so. She definitely makes me look at things from a different perspective. All I saw before, all I felt, was the weight of my mistakes and the shame they brought with them. But she's helping me to see that they don't define me. That they're just that—mistakes."

My mom nods her head, silent, as her lips are forced shut in a slim smile.

"Actually, today was mostly about Heath. I've been thinking that maybe it would help if he and I sat down and talked. It's the right thing to do."

"What did Dr. Gallus think of that?"

"She said that it was entirely up to me, but I should be prepared that he might not say what I hope he will, what I need him to."

"Well, if you decide that's what you want to do, you know where he'll be this Saturday morning."

"Yeah, thanks for that by the way." I push my feet against hers and she pushes back.

"Hey, that's all him, Lee. When I came back from Chicago, I might have lost my mind a little on the boy. After all my crazy mama-bear shouting in the yard that first Saturday, I thought for sure I'd never see him near this house again. But then he showed up the next Saturday and every Saturday since."

We sit in silence for a few minutes before she continues, "He knows how bad he messed up, Lee."

I avoid her eyes.

"And, no, I'm not taking his side. What he did to you was . . . deplorable. But I truly believe he knows that now. And I think he's working hard, just like you, not to be that person again."

Bright and early, the lawn mower starts. My Saturday morning alarm clock. With my mom at the farmers market, I know I've got about an hour before he leaves.

So, I get dressed, brush my teeth, and pull my hair into a messy bun on top of my head before I go to the kitchen to have the necessary servings of protein my nutritionist planned out for me. When I hear the engine of the lawn mower die, I slip on my flip-flops and head outside.

Other than that first Saturday morning when I charged at him like a lunatic, I've never once ventured outside until I was sure he was long gone. But I've decided that today is the day. I'm going to extend an olive branch. For the sake of Eli, for the sake of our families and friends, but most importantly, for myself.

I feel the heat of the day already brewing as I swing open the door and walk out onto the grass just as he comes around the house, his shirt hanging from his hand.

"Heath?"

At the sight of me, he jerks to a stop. "Hi, Leah." His voice is unsure as he nervously wipes at his forehead with his shirt.

We stand in silence, just feet apart. His hair is shorter than I've ever seen it, and he's wearing his old black basketball shorts that he used to shoot around in. As he wrings his shirt in his hands, I break the uncomfortable silence.

"Thirsty?"

"Sorry?"

"Are you thirsty? You look like you could use a drink." I throw a thumb over my shoulder, motioning back toward the house.

"Sure. That'd be great."

I turn and head back inside, holding the door for him as he slides his shirt on. "Sweet tea?"

"Sure."

He stands on the opposite side of the counter as I grab the pitcher from the fridge. I pour us each a glass and lean back against the sink and watch him quickly down half of his tea. I can't get over how different he looks. Not just his hair, but his whole demeanor, too. The way he holds himself. The arrogance and attitude I remember from so long ago don't seem to be such a strong part of him anymore. There's a shyness about him that's endearing yet humbling at the same time.

"How have you been?" I force myself to look at him.

Dr. Gallus said eye contact was important to keep me present and give me a better gauge on what he was saying and how he really felt when he said it.

"Good. Yeah, good. You?"

"Good."

We each take a sip, needing to fill the silence. His gaze moves downward, but I maintain my stare.

"I found my mom," he says to the floor.

Eyes wide, I stop and pull my glass away from my lips. "Seriously?"

He shrugs. "Yeah. It was just something I needed to do."

"Did you actually see her, talk to her?"

"No. There's no need. My dad and I have been talking a lot. He's been answering my questions, and, well, it's . . . good. I don't need her in my life to be happy, to be a good man." His focus is stuck on the liquid in his glass as he swipes his thumb across the condensation. "And I understand now that the people I care about aren't going to leave me like she did."

Pride swirls with regret. I'm so proud of him for seeing what everyone else already knew, even if we had to go through what we did for him to realize this.

He sets his glass on the counter and then looks to me, speaking low, "Leah, you have to know—"

"It's okay, Heath. You don't have to." I wave him away. This is beginning to feel like too much.

"Yes, actually, I do. You were the best thing that has ever happened to me. What we had—" He shakes his head as his face twists in pain. "I am so sorry, Leah. I will never forgive myself. Never."

The tears I've been fighting back break free, forcing me to turn away. When I feel him come toward me, I hold out an arm, afraid he'll touch me. I still need more answers, but this is all I'm strong enough for right now. He stops, respecting my space, before handing me a napkin.

I dry my face and turn back to him. We're mere inches apart, looking into each other's eyes.

"We've both made mistakes, Heath. As much as they've hurt us, we can only learn from them and move on. You *are* a good man, and I'm so glad you're able to see that now, to see what the rest of us see in you. And I need you to know that I forgive you."

With that, his head drops as he covers his face with one hand, the other on his hip. I give in and step to him, lightly wrapping my arms around him. I'm about to let go, worried I crossed a line, when his arms do the same. He sucks in a long, shuddering breath against my hair.

We stay like that, lost in our thoughts and each other's warmth, until he pulls back to look down at me. "Are you okay?"

With a small smile, I answer honestly, "Yeah, I'm okay."

He doesn't hide his hefty sigh of relief. "Good. That's all that matters." He steps out of my space and heads for the door. Just as he's about to close it behind him, he stops. "See you next Saturday, Leah."

"Yeah, see you next Saturday, Heath."

"Eli, will you please start the grill for me? Leah, grab the kabobs from the fridge," my mom orders.

"What can I do, Mrs. Dawson?" Lindsey asks.

"You can toss the salad and update me on the latest wedding drama," my mom says with a wink.

Stepping to the fridge, Lindsey doesn't hesitate to start. "Did I tell you guys about the band the wedding planner suggested?" She looks from me to my mom. "She showed me a playlist that includes oldies, like Duran Duran and some guy named Pat Benatar. If I've never heard of him, I'm sure our guests haven't," she says with an incredulous huff.

My disbelieving eyes flash to my mom's, knowing Lindsey is talking about one of my mom's favorite *female* artists. "Those kabobs aren't going to cook themselves," I announce before sneaking out the patio door and breathe a sigh of relief. Lindsey's great, but her endless wedding dilemmas may be the death of me.

"I know that look," Eli says as he takes the plate. "That's the look of someone ready to go cross-eyed with wedding woes."

"Eli, you know I love Lindsey, but—"

"But this wedding can't get here soon enough?"

"No, it's just—oh, screw it. I can't wait for it to be over. I'm sorry, but it's all Lindsey can talk about, and I just don't see what the big deal is with ribbon colors or what flowers are in season."

Eli nods knowingly toward the grill. "I hear ya, sister. And we still have six months to go."

"Remind me, please, when the time comes, to elope."

He raises his tongs in agreement as I move to his side, watching him lay the food out on the grates of the grill.

"How are you doing? No one ever seems to ask the groom that question."

He doesn't hesitate. "I'm actually really good, Lee. I look at Lindsey, and I just can't wait to be married to her. I can't wait to call her my wife."

The smile he gives me about breaks his face with happiness. And, when you see someone that full, you just can't help but share in their joy.

I lift up onto my toes and kiss him on the cheek. "I'm so happy for you. You're an amazing friend, and you're going to make an incredible husband. Love you, Eli."

He closes the grill and turns to me. "Love you, too, Lee. And I'm so proud of you, you know that?"

My throat tightens. It's still difficult to think about how far I fell, but I know how fortunate I am to have good people who helped me through it. What Heath had done was wrong and hurtful on so many levels, but it was my own response to his betrayal that had been most damaging. Because, when it comes down to it, it was a breakup, plain and simple. They happen across the globe every day. With the guidance of my doctors and my family's support, I've learned I can't control the actions of others, but I can control my reaction to them without losing myself in the process.

"Eli, I never thanked you for everything you did for me. I put you through so much, and you never gave up on me. Saying thank you doesn't seem like enough."

He wraps me in a strong hug that I quickly return.

Rocking us from side to side, he says in my ear, "I've seen the bridesmaid dresses. Let's call it even."

We both laugh as he checks on dinner.

"So, how did your coffee date go yesterday? Are you going to be a plus-two for the wedding?"

"That's a big, fat no," I mumble.

"Ooh, tell me. Is this better than the guy who took you to his grandmother's funeral? Or the guy who got matching haircuts with his dog? Or how about the guy who wouldn't swim in a pool because he was afraid of sharks? And let's not forget about the guy who cried about his ex-girlfriend because she'd dumped him for his dad!" He's holding the barbecue tongs high in the air, proud of himself for remembering every awful first date I've shared with him.

"Ugh. Don't remind me." I swat the memories away as he tends to the grill. "No, this guy started off strong. Good-looking, has his own electrical business, and owns his own home."

"So?"

"So, he actually had the gall to tell me how many women he'd had sex with."

"Whoa. Seriously? How many?"

I give him a playful jab in the arm. "The best part was that he'd documented every sexual encounter—down to times, locations, positions, and overall ratings. He had the book with him to prove it."

"He carries it with him?"

"Yep, because, as he said, 'You never know when an opportunity will arise.'" I suggestively raise my eyebrows up and down, just like my date did to me.

Eli's laughter starts out slow, growing till it barrels into a full-blown belly laugh and tears. That makes me start to laugh until we're both bent over, holding our stomachs.

"Oh, Lee, as much as I want you to meet a great guy, I am loving these stories. You should write a book."

"I have been actually."

He looks at me, surprised, still catching his breath.

"Journaling. It's part of my therapy. I'm really enjoying it even if it's just a couple of paragraphs a day."

He smiles with pride.

I take advantage of the brief silence and ask what's been weighing heavily on my mind, "So, the wedding. Who is Heath bringing?"

"No one." When I scrunch my face in doubt, he repeats himself, "I'm serious. It's just him."

"Hmm."

"He mentioned you guys were talking. Is he behaving himself? Or do I need to beat his ass again?"

"No, he's fine. Wait, beat his . . . what?"

He shuts his eyes slowly and expels a long, exaggerated breath.

"Eli?" When he doesn't answer, my voice turns stern. "Eli!"

"Okay, relax. Geesh." He holds his hands up in surrender and then spills out his next words. "He was waiting for me when I got home from Chicago."

My shoulders lock. "Please tell me you didn't say anything," I whisper.

He gives me a pointed look. "Hell no. You've got to understand, Lee. When I came back from Chicago, I was physically and emotionally exhausted, and when I saw him in front of my house, I completely lost it and beat the shit out of him. I punched my best friend in the face." He drops his head, wincing in pain at the thought.

I rub his shoulder. "Oh, Eli."

"And I would do it again. What he did to you . . ." He shakes his head before continuing. "I was worried at first, but after seeing him with you, I honestly thought that he'd be good for you, Lee. You have to believe me. I never imagined he'd hurt you the way he did. But I want you to know, the reason he's in my wedding, in my life in any way, is because of what's happened to him since. Losing you did something to him. He's not the same selfish asshole he always was. He goes to work, puts in long hours, and then comes home. If we get together, we meet up at his dad's to play basketball and watch movies. No drinking, no drugs." He hesitates. "No girls."

Although it's none of my business, I can't deny how relieved I am to hear all of that.

Eli's voice drops. "Lindsey said he had been sitting in front of our house for hours, waiting for me to get home that day. He didn't even know what had happened to you, but he was sick about it all the same. And, when I hit him, he never even tried to defend himself. He just lay there and took every hit, like he thought he deserved them."

We stand in silence, and I watch Eli mindlessly move the food around on the grill.

"So, you know that we've been talking a little bit more, on Saturdays when he comes by to cut the grass."

Eli nods.

"Being able to have a normal conversation with him, it helps. But hearing you say he's changed for the better . . . I needed to hear that. I want what's best for him, Eli. What happened between us is done, and I just want him to be happy."

"And that's why you'll always be too good for any guy out there, Lee. Don't ever forget that."

THIRTY-FIVE

Heath

"Does Lindsey want a bow tie or regular tie?" I ask Eli as I hold up one of each.

"She said she didn't care. It's up to me."

When I don't respond, he turns my direction, not missing my doubtful stare. "What? That's what she said."

I shake my head and put the bow tie away.

"Give me a break, dude. It's the one thing I have a say in."

"Then, say regular tie, *please*." I hand it to him.

He finishes straightening his lapels, and wraps the tie around his neck, focusing on his own reflection. I take a seat on one of the store's deep leather chairs and watch as he struggles with his knot.

"I saw her this morning. We didn't talk much, but she looked good. Happier," I say, changing the subject.

He smooths out the ebony silk that runs down his chest and looks at me through his reflection in the mirror. "She's dating."

My eyes wince at his words. That is not what I was expecting him to say. I have to will my voice to work. To say the right thing. "Well, that's great. Really."

Eli doesn't miss my discomfort. "There's no one serious. Just coffee dates. She's taking it slow."

I nod.

"But, Heath, it's not going to take long for some guy to lock on to how amazing she is. And, when he does . . ."

I nod again—this time, in painful understanding. "Good. I'm glad."

He stares, assessing how truthful I really am.

"I mean it. I want to see her happy as much as you do."

Suddenly restless, I rise from my seat in need of a diversion from the weight that's taken up residence on my chest. I start rifling mindlessly through a rack of sports coats.

"Like I said, they're just coffee dates. She's not bringing anyone to the wedding."

I continue to feign interest in the sea of navy and black in front of me.

"For what it's worth, she asked about you."

My body betrays me and twists to face Eli.

"Relax, it was awhile back. Anyway, she just asked what you'd been up to and"—he pauses—"if you were going to bring anyone to the wedding."

The pressure in my chest lightens as my heartbeat doubles. Even though we've become friendly, she continues to hold me at arm's length. But this is more than I've been given in months. And, when you're desperate for the slightest opening, you wedge your toes in and don't dare budge.

"Before you start analyzing it, Heath, it doesn't mean anything, okay? It's more that she's made her peace with everything that went on between the two of you, and she's ready to move on."

I don't speak, instead anxiously moving my attention to a stack of shirts.

God, I'm so glad I said no to Lucy. When she asked me to go to the wedding together as friends, I knew what she really meant and didn't hesitate to tell her no. She took it well, but I didn't like hurting her. I've done enough of that to the people I care about already.

Eli continues, "The important thing is, the old Leah is coming back. She's put on weight, she seems to be in a good place, and she says she really likes her new job."

"She got a new job?" I tamp down the hurt that she didn't tell me herself, but it's her right to share with me what she wants to.

"Yeah, marketing director for the local library. She's even talking about buying a house."

I turn back. "Really? Good for her." And I mean it.

From the little bit that we talk each week, I've seen for myself that she's looking healthier, lighter. But moving out of her mom's house and getting her own place? That's huge.

"If she needs a realtor, let her know I've got a number."

"I will, but I think she and her mom are already supposed to see a couple of houses this weekend. She wants to stay around her mom, but that area has gotten expensive. Looks like she'll have to settle for a small lot and a fixer-upper. But she's excited. It will give her and her mom something to do together."

I think back to when she was helping me look at condos and how cute she was, talking about cabinet space and window treatments. What I'd give to experience that again, but knowing that this time it was all for her.

When we leave, I talk Eli into buying both ties. Who is he kidding?

"Do you have to use the bathroom?" Leah asks Eli.

"No."

"Then, stop fidgeting, or I'll stick you with the pin," she mumbles as she tugs on his lapel, a pin clasped tightly between her lips. She struggles to hold the boutonniere straight as she inserts the first pin. "No wonder your mom had trouble with this thing. It weighs five pounds."

Eli's wedding day is finally here. *Thank God.* I think it's safe to say we're all tired of hearing about eco-friendly confetti and gluten-free dinner options. Let's not forget the month-long debate over brussels sprouts versus green beans. At least we got out of doing a choreographed dance. I told Eli that's where I drew the line.

"Lindsey wanted it big, so it'd show in the pictures," he says with all seriousness.

Leah pauses a second to glance at me. I'm leaning against the wall, arms crossed, the same position I've been in since Eli texted her for help. She's always beautiful, but today, with a copper glow to her skin and her dark blond hair falling in waves down the low back of the strapless dress, I'm thankful for any excuse to stare at her.

"There. That extra pin should do it. Hopefully, you won't stick her when you go in for the kiss." She pats him on the shoulder before turning to leave the small back room of the church.

"Hey, Leah. Hold on a sec. I want to talk to you, both of you."

She steps back, coming in next to me, so we're side by side in front of Eli. So close, I can see a light dusting of gold shimmer along her bare shoulder.

"I just want you to know how much it means to me that you're both here. You are two of the most important people in my life, and I wouldn't be the man I am today without your friendship. I'm so proud of you for moving past everything that's happened. For a while, I was sure I'd lose you, but I didn't, and that has nothing to do with me and everything to do with the two of you. And, more than anything, I know that, one day, you'll each find someone to make you as happy as Lindsey makes me."

Leah wraps an arm around him on one side while I grip the shoulder on his opposite side, giving him a solid pat as Leah gives him a kiss on the cheek.

"Well," she says. "Now that we got that out of the way, let's go get you married."

With me on Eli's left and Leah on his right, we head out the back room and prepare to do just that.

As the first bridesmaid begins her walk down the aisle, Eli begins to cry. I don't know how he's going to make it through the ceremony. I bow my head to hide the short laugh that escapes, and Eli shoots me the side eye.

"Do you need a tissue, Nancy?" I whisper as I bump his arm with my own.

He leans back and whispers something in response, but I don't hear it. Because every one of my senses is tuned in to one thing and one thing only. The stunning woman walking down the aisle. Leah. She's smiling brightly with her head held high as she locks eyes with Eli and sees, even from a distance, the tears that fill his eyes.

She covers her mouth before a laugh can escape as she approaches her spot with the other bridesmaids.

I watch her mouth to him, *I love you*, and catch him do the same in return.

I swallow, forcing down the harsh reality that I'll never hear those words from her again.

As she takes her place and turns toward the guests, she catches my stare. I panic, but just as I expect her to look away, she tilts her chin toward Eli, who pulls the handkerchief from his pocket and wipes his eyes. She shakes her head and brings a hand to her chest, fighting to hold back her laughter, all the while keeping her focus on me. My smile and growing laughter only spur her on until the two of us are standing in front of more than a hundred guests, bent at the waists and laughing hysterically.

Eli is still wiping at his eyes as our laughter spreads to the guests seated in the first few rows. As the crowd settles, Eli takes a visible deep breath and squares his shoulders when the string quartet changes songs, Lindsey's cue to appear at the end of the aisle. Everything about Eli changes as he takes in his bride-to-be.

I'm so happy for my friend. He deserves every ounce of what this day is about to bring.

The music flows across the high ceiling of the church, and Lindsey takes the first steps into this new chapter of their lives.

———

Eli and Lindsey just reappeared after vanishing since their first dance. I don't want to know where they were because I'm sure it involved a coat closet. Good for them.

The band begins a new song, and I recognize it in the first few beats—Eric Clapton's "Wonderful Tonight." I take a deep breath and wipe my clammy palms on my jacket.

Just do it. Worst she can say is no.

I cross the room and interrupt the conversation she's having with Eli's sisters.

With the lightest touch, I place my hand on her wrist. "Dance with me?"

When the smile she was wearing a moment ago disappears, I brace myself for rejection.

She considers my offer for a few painful seconds, then, with a hesitant smile, she finally answers, "Sure."

I want more than anything to tangle my fingers around hers and lead her to the dance floor, wrap my arms around her body, and spend the next few hours swaying the night away. But I know that's just a dream, and I'm thankful to have this one small gift she's giving me.

Without a word, we take the standard slow-dance position. Her right hand is out to our sides and folded over my left hand as her left hand is lightly holding my upper arm. My right hand rests softly on her hip. It's the same pose she took with Eli's uncle, but I couldn't care less.

We start to step in a comfortable rhythm, as if we've done this a thousand times before, and halfway through the song, I feel her body relax into mine. With her warmth radiating around me, my eyes close on their own as I press my cheek to her temple, our bodies continuing to rock to the slow beat of the song. From head to toe, every part of her fits perfectly into every part of me, just like I remember. I savor every second.

As the song hits the final few notes and the rapid techno beats of the next song begins, Leah pulls away and wipes at her face before turning and weaving her way through the crowd that's now overtaking the dance floor. I follow her every twist and turn through guests and tables, finally catching up with her as she swiftly turns to the right and exits out to the gardens.

"Leah, stop. What's the matter?"

It's not until we're in the darkened silence, surrounded by a wall of tall shrubs, that she stops. When she turns to me, the moonlight glistens against the tears streaming down her face.

"Don't you feel it, Heath?" Her voice isn't much more than a pained whisper.

"Feel it?"

"Yes, *feel* it." The hurt in her voice matches the pain in her eyes.

I'm missing something here, and if I don't figure it out soon, I'm going to lose the momentum we've made in the last few months. But I'm too late.

"Oh my God. You don't, do you?" Wiping at her face, she shakes her head and whispers under her breath, "I am such an idiot."

She storms off, farther into the maze of trees and shrubs, but I finally grab her arm, holding her in place.

"Leah, please, tell me what I'm missing." I grudgingly drop her arm. "Tell me, so I can make it better."

Her shoulders rise and fall in defeat as she points toward the hum of the reception. "That should be us in there. *We* should be having our first dance. *We* should be buying our first house. *We* should be talking about our honeymoon and babies . . . but we're not."

Her words are a twist of the knife that has been settled in my heart since the day I threw everything away.

I want nothing more than to fall to my knees and tell her the truth. That I still love her. That I never stopped. That I live every day with remorse.

"I can't make you feel something that's not there," she mumbles to herself more than me.

I take one step toward her as she protectively takes one step back.

Just tell her how you feel. Say it.

"Leah—"

She cuts me off, shoulders hunched and eyes pleading, "Why, Heath? We lost so much. We lost everything. You've told me you're sorry, but you never told me *why*."

I dig the heels of my hands into my eyes and answer honestly, "I thought you were leaving me. I read your emails and saw the paperwork in your bag. You were going to leave. So, I—"

Her voice low, she cuts me off, "So, you left me before I could leave you." Her hands rise to her hips as she looks away and shakes her head. "I would never have left you, Heath. *Never.* You were all I wanted, all I saw. You were the beginning of every day and the best part of every night. You were my present and my future." She takes a ragged breath. "And we lost it all. Do you know what that did to me? How far I fell? I almost . . . I didn't just lose my boyfriend. I lost one of my best friends. And it's been so damn hard to be your friend since then. But I'm trying. Because I need it, and I think you need it, too." She swipes away tears and throws her shoulders back with fresh confidence.

Her honesty spurs me on to reveal some truths of my own. "Sometimes, I want to go back to that first kiss and erase the moment along with all the others that led up to that day. No matter how perfect they were along the way.

So that you'd never have to experience the pain I put you through. Do you ever want that, too?"

She doesn't hesitate. "Never. I will always cherish that kiss and hold it close for what it was at the time. The beginning of something I thought was the best. No matter how long it lasted."

She surprises me, enclosing me in an embrace that rocks me back on my heels as she burrows her face into the crook of my neck. Willing the last of her pain away, I place my hand on her head and take a moment to appreciate the familiar silkiness before lifting her chin and holding her eyes to mine. There's one more thing I need to admit before I let her go.

"Do you know, I make wishes on pennies now because of you?"

Her head gives the slightest shake.

"And every single one is a wish for you. That you're happy and you find that happiness in whatever form it takes even if that doesn't include me. I can never say I'm sorry enough times to fix what I did, Leah, but knowing you're living a good life might just help."

With a smile laced with heartbreak, a reminder of who I am to her now, she brushes her cheek against mine and brings her lips to my ear.

"I've already forgiven you, Heath. You just need to forgive yourself now." She places a soft kiss on my jaw before stepping out of my hold. The tightness in her face has disappeared, and a sense of peace has taken over as she turns and walks back into the reception.

THIRTY-SIX

Leah

One foot in front of the other. Keep going. You're almost there.

A large exhale of air leaves my chest when I make it to the ladies' room, before quickly locking the stall door and slumping back against it. I shouldn't have done that. I shouldn't have pushed my feelings on Heath. But, the way we were dancing, how it brought me right back to our nights when I was in his arms, I thought for sure he was feeling what I was feeling. But, if there's anything I've learned, I can't control how anyone else acts. And he's acting like a man buried in guilt. I've worked so hard and come so far, but what good is that if he can't move forward as well?

I can still feel his chest against mine and how his muscles tensed when I wrapped my arms around him. He felt lean and strong, more so than I remember, and I wanted so badly for that moment to mean something other than what it really was. A final good-bye to what we once had been.

It hurts more than I can say that he didn't feel the loss that I did, that we should be the ones in the wedding gown and tuxedo. But at least we're at a place where we can be friends. Because Eli will always be a part of our lives, the one constant thread keeping us connected.

At the sink, I clean up my smudged makeup and square my shoulders before heading back out to the reception to find my mom. She spots me at the same time I spot her. I must not be hiding my emotions as well as I thought because she takes one look at me and excuses herself from her conversation.

She places a hand on my cheek, scanning my face for any clues. "Leah, everything okay, honey?"

"It will be," I answer honestly. "Heath and I talked."

"And how are you feeling?" she asks.

"Pretty great, actually." A warm sense of relief washes over me as the truth of those words fully resonate. I feel like I hiked through a never-ending forest full of bristles and pines, and after countless scrapes and bruises, I finally made it through to the other side.

"There you are, Lee." Connor appears between Mom and me. "I want a dance with my two favorite ladies!"

He puts his elbows out to the sides, waiting for us to latch on. We do so with full smiles on our faces and head out to the crowded dance floor. The three of us let go without a care in the world, bopping our hips together and waving our hands in the air. We dance all through this song and the next, each of us knowing Dad is looking down on us and enjoying the show. Connor eventually leaves us to grab a drink at the bar with Eli's sisters while Mom and I wave and continue to wiggle and shake.

We're just about to head to the bar when the first few beats of the next song pump through the room, causing us both to break out into full-blown belly laughs and rush back to our spots. There's no way we're sitting out on a Pat Benatar song.

I'm giving him two more minutes, and then I'm leaving.

I take a sip of my hot tea and watch the door. At least, it was hot twenty minutes ago when he was supposed to be here. Too bad. I've been wondering what this guy's story is. Maybe he knits sweaters from cat hair or collects life-size blow-up dolls.

"Are you Leah?"

I turn to the voice and look him over before answering. He's fairly tall, maybe six feet, and clean-cut with dirty-blond hair and brown eyes that angle downward just enough to give him that sweet puppy-dog look. He's wearing a white oxford shirt under a turquoise V-neck sweater and dark jeans.

Deciding he doesn't look like a serial killer, I extend my hand. "Hi, you must be Campbell."

His smile is broad as he shakes my hand and takes the seat across from me.

"I'm sorry I'm late. We had an emergency patient come in, and it was a little more complicated than we had expected."

"Emergency? Oh my gosh, of course. I hope they're doing okay."

"Yeah, we got the toy out, and as long as there's no infection, he should recover completely."

"A child swallowed a toy? That's terrible!"

His smile is shy. "No, I'm not a doctor. I'm actually a resident in veterinary school. A family brought their golden retriever puppy in after he swallowed their kid's foam ball, and the head vet and I had to do emergency surgery on the little guy. I'm sorry. I thought you knew I was studying to be a vet. It's in my bio."

"I must have missed it. Honestly, it seems like most people lie on their profiles anyway, so I don't do much more than glance at them. It's not like someone is actually going to admit to being an ax murderer or a clown collector."

He laughs, and I can't help but think how nice a laugh it is. It's not deep and harsh or annoying and barky. It's the kind of laugh that makes you want to join in.

When he steps away to grab his coffee order, I hide my phone under the table and sneak a text to Eli with a thumbs-up emoji. Anything else, and he would have been ready to converge on the coffee shop and pretend to be my estranged husband, begging me to take him back, while Lindsey barged in behind him with a pillow under her top, hitting Eli over the head with her purse and shouting at him for leaving her pregnant and barefoot. I'm a little disappointed that didn't get to play out, but if the first two minutes are anything to go on, this might actually be the first promising date I've had since I joined the dating site.

I get an immediate response from Eli and laugh to myself when I see it's a long line of emojis in response. Everything from clapping hands to party horns and red hearts.

Campbell comes back, coffee in hand, and we spend the next hour talking.

He earned a degree in art, but after he graduated and couldn't find a job, he started working part-time at a vet's office. He liked it so much, and they liked him just as well, so much so that they've supported him through vet school. He's due to graduate, and will be taking all the licensing exams in a few months. He's also six years older than me, something else I should have taken note of on his bio. Not that it matters, but the longer we talk, I definitely get the sense that a relationship and marriage are where his head is at.

We leave the coffee shop and go our separate ways. Campbell waits all of an hour to call and ask me out on an official date. I can't hide the smile in my voice when I say yes to dinner this Saturday.

"This is a big moment, Lee. We need to celebrate," Eli shouts. "It's the first time anyone has been awarded the rare and coveted second date."

I lean over and jokingly punch him in the arm as he sits at the other end of the sofa. "You're an ass."

"What did Eli do now?" Lindsey asks as she enters their family room and sees Eli rubbing his arm.

"Nothing. He's giving me a hard time about my date with Campbell."

"You mean, Soup Boy," he says, fighting a smile. "You know, like Campbell Soup?"

I roll my eyes. "Yes, I get it. And, no, you will not be calling him Soup Boy. Understood?"

When he doesn't answer immediately, Lindsey gives him a teasing smack to his head as I deliver my death glare.

He flinches and rubs at his head. "Fine. I won't call him Soup Boy," he whines.

"Who aren't we calling Soup Boy?" Heath asks, wearing a smile, as he enters the room.

My stomach doesn't hesitate to drop at the imminent awkwardness.

"Leah's new boyfriend. His name is Campbell, and I'm not allowed to call him Soup Boy. Can you believe how mean she is to me?"

Heath's face falls when Eli uses the word *boyfriend*.

We were going to have to get past this at some point. I just wasn't ready for it to be today.

"Campbell? Really, Leah? You're making it too easy for us with that one." Heath throws me a wink as he pulls a drink from the fridge.

My spine relaxes. He took that better than I could have hoped.

I'm still getting used to this new *us*. Ever since the wedding, he's been treating me differently, like an actual friend—making jokes and talking about everyday random things. It's nice but weird. Very weird actually. This new friendship is going to take some getting used to. But, if Heath can make an effort, I can, too.

"You guys are terrible," I say as I throw a pretzel at Eli.

It bounces off his head and onto his lap. He picks it up and eats it, grinning smugly.

"Leah, look at any good houses lately?" Lindsey asks.

"Nothing, unfortunately. Everything is over my budget or requires so much work, I can't afford the renovations. But my realtor just emailed me this morning about a listing that's coming on the market this Saturday. Want to come check it out with me?"

"I can't. Eli and I have plans with my parents."

"I'll go with you." Heath says from the kitchen.

"You want to look at a house with me?" I fail at hiding my genuine surprise.

"Sure. Why not? You did it for me. I'll be returning the favor." He shrugs casually.

"Okay, if you're sure. Just be prepared, this isn't like when we looked at condos. Anything I can afford isn't exactly in move-in condition."

He lifts his drink in the air, as if delivering an oath. "Well, consider it my job to help you see the possibilities."

"All right, then. I'll get you the address."

Without warning, Lindsey jumps from her spot and hustles to the powder room, as if her life depended on it. When we hear retching echoing off the walls of the small room, we all move swiftly.

Eli gets to her first, kneeling beside her and brushing her hair back away from her face as she continues to heave. I get a cup of water and a dampened washcloth ready to go. When she sits back on her heels and looks up, she's pale and sweaty.

Eli takes the washcloth from me and wipes her face. "That came out of nowhere. You good now?"

She nods as he helps her stand, and she takes the water, rinsing her mouth out in the sink. Heath and I back out into the hallway, and all three of us continue to closely monitor her.

Eli is feeling her forehead, her neck, her hands—anything to try to get a gauge on her sudden sickness. "Let's get you to the sofa. Do you think it's something you ate?"

She shakes him off.

"Do you need some tea? Crackers? A blanket?" He continues.

She looks up at him, still pale but now smiling. "I think . . . I think I need a pregnancy test."

THIRTY-SEVEN

Heath

Holy shit, Eli's going to be a dad.

"Congrats, man. That's awesome."

"Take another test. Leah, go back to the store. We need more tests." Eli pulls on his hair as he rocks back and forth on the sofa.

My initial surprise is wearing off, but his is going to take a bit longer. *Am I a shitty friend if I start recording this?*

"Eli, three was enough. And each one said the same. Congrats, Daddy!" Leah hugs him, but he doesn't hug her back.

He's in total shock, and he's managed to look paler than Lindsey did not long ago in the bathroom.

Leah's doing this cute little dance, swinging her hips, and singing, "We're having a baby," over and over again.

But I don't care about the words. Her smile and genuine giddiness over the news is all I can focus on. Whatever happened in Chicago seems to be behind her.

This new guy probably has something to do with it as well.

She continues to move around the room until she makes her way back to Eli and Lindsey. Eli stares blankly as Leah and Lindsey hug tightly. Lindsey only lasts a minute before a new wave of nausea hits, and she takes a seat next to Eli.

Since he's still lost in his own thoughts, I have to smack him on the shoulder and look to Lindsey. It only takes him a second to come out of the fog and pull her onto his lap, rubbing her back and whispering in her ear.

I suddenly feel like I'm intruding on their private moment. When I look at Leah, a shadow of sadness takes over where excitement just was.

I step into her space and whisper, "Want to grab a coffee?"

"Sure." She moves in to give our friends a quick hug as I wait for her at the door.

As the door closes behind us, I ask, "So, the place on the corner?"

"Oh, you were serious? I thought you were just looking for an excuse to give them some privacy."

"I was. But, if you've got something going on"—*with Chicken Noodle Soup Boy*—"then we can just meet up on Saturday."

When I say Saturday, it's like a bell has gone off. She had already forgotten.

"Yeah, can we just meet up Saturday? Do you mind?"

"Not at all. Just text me if you still want me to tag along. If not, no big deal. Really."

"Okay, thanks." She raises her hand in a short goodbye before getting in her car and pulling away.

Well, so much for that. But what did I expect? I put her on the spot, and she's too nice to say no. Besides, why would she want to spend time with me when she can spend it with Cream of Celery?

————————————

It's Friday night, and I'm doing some work from home, two laptops running in front of me, but I'm unable to focus. I haven't heard from Leah about the house tomorrow, so it looks like another weekend of hanging out at my dad's.

I start searching for houses and what I think Leah's price range might be. She's right; for the area she wants, there are only a few options, and even those are so bad, they'll probably be sold for the land.

As I scroll through listings, I come across one that resembles Leah's mom's house but larger. Same Cape Cod style, but this one has a full wraparound porch and what could possibly be a third level. It's on half an acre, and from the photos, it looks recently updated.

She'd love this.

Then, I see the price, easily four times what I'm guessing she can spend.

I flip through the photos, inspecting every room. This isn't just a house. It's a home—meant for kids, dogs, barbeques, family. Kind of like the house I grew up in. I may not have siblings, but, growing up, our house was always busy with family parties and Saturday night sleepovers. Everything Eli and Lindsey have ahead of them.

It comes at me like a braided rush of fear, anxiety, and *hope.* For the first time in my life, the thought of being tied to someone and everything that goes along with that—babies, bills, holidays, weddings, funerals—doesn't scare the shit out of me the way it used to. In fact, watching them as they rode alternating waves of fear and excitement, that all they could do was hold each other, just spotlights that growing, burrowing feeling. There is a hole in my life. A hole I've been unable to fill since I lost Leah.

As if she knows what I'm thinking, my phone buzzes next to me with a text. It's from Leah.

First house is at 9 a.m. Meet me at my mom's by 8:45.

I respond.

I'll bring the lattes.

Seconds later, my phone vibrates.

Deal. Wear your hazmat suit. ;)

I'm at Leah's mom's fifteen minutes early.

I've actually been in the neighborhood longer than that, but I know she's not a morning person. I hung out at the coffee shop as long as I could until I couldn't take it anymore. This will be the first time we're out alone since we were an *us*, and I've never been more afraid of screwing something up than I am this day. But I've already done the stupidest thing in my life and survived that. Now it's time to do the hardest thing by being her friend.

When I knock on the door, lattes in hand, I expect her to answer barely awake in her pajamas. But, instead, she's dressed in dark skinny jeans and a red-and-white-striped T-shirt. Her hair is up in a long, swirling ponytail, and she's wearing the gold hoops I gave her when we first started dating. She'd had a similar pair but lost one. She hadn't made a big deal of it at the time because she said they were cheap, but I went out the next day and bought her new ones, eighteen karat. This led to an argument over me spending too much money on her, which led to making up on the sofa.

When I think she's caught me staring, my arm launches forward with her coffee. "Where's your mom? I thought I'd say hi."

"You know her. Up and out early. She said something about a hair appointment. Apparently, she's not the only one with a date tonight." She freezes as realization hits. "I'm sorry, Heath. I—"

I wave it off. "Don't worry about it. Really." *Shit.* I've been fighting the thought of her going out with Bean with Bacon since I heard the dreaded word *boyfriend.* "Should we get going? We don't want anyone buying the house out from under you."

"Yeah, sure. Actually, my realtor has a few houses for me to look at if you have the time."

"Of course. Whatever you need." I catch a whiff of her perfume. It's different from what she used to wear. Citrus, maybe? I lean in closer and sniff again.

Stop it. A friend doesn't try to smell another friend's perfume. Or check out her legs in those jeans. Or notice her tight . . . Be a good friend. Be. A. Good. Friend.

I force my eyes away and lead us to my car.

"What is that smell?" she whispers, adorably, since there's no one around to hear us.

We each have our hands over our face, as if that will actually clear away the stench. It's not working.

"Probably just some old food left behind," I answer. *My damn luck it'll be a body.*

The smell grows stronger as we stop at the beginning of the hallway, our mouths pinched tight waiting for the other to chicken out. But curiosity gets the best of us, and we continue on toward the source.

"Breathe through your mouth," I offer. She nods in appreciation before pinching her nose and following me into the hall.

The house is small with three bedrooms and one bathroom. The first door we come to is the bathroom, complete with a mustard-yellow sink and matching toilet.

"Oh my God, Heath. Have you ever seen anything so ugly?" She's motioning to the sink and toilet, two fingers still pinching her nose, as she reaches over and opens the cabinet door on the vanity. "Ah!" she shrieks.

She jumps back into my chest, and my arms instinctively encase her body, turning her away from the threat. I move her to the hallway and go back to the bathroom. Whatever scared her has yet to make a sound, but the one thing neither of us can miss is the potent odor. When I bend over and discover the source, I slam the cabinet door shut, grab her hand, and pull her down the hall and out the front door.

We're each inhaling exaggerated deep breaths of fresh air as the realtor hangs up her cell phone and approaches.

"So, what did you—"

"There's something dead in the bathroom. Possibly skunks, but it's too decomposed to tell for sure."

Both women bring their hands to their faces in shock.

"Oh my goodness. I'll call the seller's realtor right now."

"You do that. We'll meet you at the next house."

The woman starts tapping at her phone as I lead Leah to the car, shaking my head in disgust.

The second I'm seated, Leah looks over to me, saddened. "Do you really think it was skunks?"

My shoulders rise and fall. "Whatever it was, it's been there for a while."

She nods flatly.

Just as I think this day is over before it started, she startles me and raises her hands out between us, flapping them like she's trying to shake something off, while breaking out into full-blown laughter.

"Holy shit, that was disgusting!" She takes a few deep breaths of stifling, stagnant air. "Open the windows. Hurry! I need air. Fresh air!"

I do as I'm told as my own laughter rolls over me. As soon as I get both of our windows down, we each lean our heads out and take long, cleansing breaths. As we drive to the next house she continues to tilt her head out the window, her ponytail whipping in the wind and her beaming face turned to the sky. Seeing her smiling and color filling her cheeks, it's almost too much. I watch as long as I can before I'm forced to turn my attention back to the road.

Pulling herself back in and resting her head on the seat, she turns to me, eyes as wide as her smile. "I've seen some bad houses, but that one wins the prize."

I focus on the road, barely able to force a smile in agreement. That's because I can feel her staring at me, and she has yet to turn away. Her eyes sear my skin more than the blazing sun shining down on us. Resting my elbow on the open window ledge and laying my head in my hand, I give my hair a tug in a poor attempt to keep my shit together.

The next three houses are equally small and dated, although fortunately without anything dead lurking in any dark corners. Each one is in need of expensive repairs.

We're pulling away from the last house when she starts to show signs of defeat.

Out of nowhere, she sits up in excitement, grabbing my knee without thought. "Look at that," she whispers, entranced. "That's beautiful."

When I follow her eyes, I see it. The house with the wraparound porch that I found on the Internet. It's just like the picture, except with one difference. The realtor's sign posted in the front yard now has a SOLD sticker stuck diagonally over the front of it.

I stop, watching her take in every nuance of the house. She tucks a stray hair behind her ear as she stares out the window, but all I can do is take in her.

My stomach chooses that moment to rumble loud enough for her to hear.

"Want to grab lunch?" I ask.

"Sure. Oh, wait. I'd better not. I'm . . . going out for dinner tonight."

Fuck.

"Oh, yeah. Forget I asked."

"No, I'm sorry. The least I can do is feed you after the morning we had. Rain check?"

"Absolutely."

THIRTY-EIGHT

Leah

"No. Nope. Not happening. Go change." Connor points toward the hall before I barely get a chance to enter the room. He's home for the weekend, although he never really said why.

"Why? What's wrong with this outfit?"

"That skirt is too short. That's what's wrong. Who takes a girl to an outdoor concert on a first date anyway? Is he trying to get out of paying for a meal?"

"You are such a pain, you know that? He's packing us everything we need for a picnic dinner."

"And you think you're going to sit on the ground in that skirt? Put something else on, Lee."

"Will you stop? He's bringing chairs. No one is sitting on the ground. Besides, the skirt is fine. Deal with it."

"When is Beef Barley picking you up anyway?"

"Have you been talking to Eli?"

His silent smirk is my answer.

"He's not picking me up. I'm meeting him there."

Connor crosses his arms over his chest and narrows his eyes. "I'm liking this guy less and less."

"It was my idea, Con. I still haven't ruled out the possibility that he's a belly-button-fuzz-collecting sociopath."

The truth is, Campbell wanted to not only pick me up for the concert, but also spend the entire day with me. He thought we could start at the arboretum and then head over to a new farm-to-table restaurant for lunch, followed by a walk through an art fair before the concert at night.

I might have told a small white lie and used my brother's visit as an excuse for only being able to swing the concert. It wasn't entirely untrue. We did catch up over bowls of cereal before I left to go house-hunting with Heath.

"Campbell, this is quite the spread. I was picturing fried chicken and potato salad, but you really outdid yourself. Thank you."

We're seated side by side in camping chairs, a large hunter-green blanket spread out below us and a low table covered in a red-and-white-checkered cloth in front of us. It's loaded with everything from an antipasto platter and pastry-wrapped asparagus to fruit kabobs, Cobb salad in mason jars, and mini-cheesecakes.

I'll have to get the name of his caterer.

"Thanks. Because we didn't get together this afternoon, it gave me time to work on this." He motions to the table in front of us.

"Wait, you made all of this?"

"Yeah. Why? You don't like it? They sell food here if you'd like something else."

"No, it's amazing. I just assumed you ordered it from somewhere. It's all so pretty. I almost feel bad about eating it."

Although I'm impressed, this is all becoming too much, too soon. He hasn't stopped watching me, like he's looking for some sort of validation, so I grab a fruit kabob and pull off a piece of melon. Of course, it's perfectly ripe, just like everything else seems to be with this guy. From his perfectly pressed oxford shirt, folded perfectly up his tan arms, to his perfectly pressed khaki shorts and perfectly styled hair and perfectly white teeth, this guy is too—

"How are you single?" The words escape me before I can stop them.

"What?"

"I mean, do you secretly like to eat drywall or something? There must be something wrong with you."

"Drywall?" He's laughing now.

He thinks I'm kidding. Well, maybe I am about the drywall, but so far, this guy is the complete package.

"Actually, I was with someone for five years, but we broke up a few months ago."

"Oh." I'm such an idiot. "I'm sorry, Campbell. That's a long time."

"It's fine. Really. A lot can change over five years. While I was trying to decide what was next for me, she seemed to have her life all figured out. It turns out, what we wanted just didn't fit together anymore, so we went our separate ways."

"That's very mature of you both. Are you still friends?"

"Yeah, but she travels a lot for her job, and I'm busy with school and the vet's office, so we rarely talk anymore. It's just the natural course of things, I guess. I mean, how weird would it be to be close with your ex after you started dating someone new?"

It hits me that I can't imagine not seeing Heath anymore all because I'm involved with someone else. And that goes for Eli, too. Even after everything, or maybe because of it. The three of us are a package deal.

"Leah?"

I look into his kind eyes as he pulls me from my thoughts.

"I asked if you'd recently dated anyone seriously."

"Oh, sorry. No, not for a while. I've had a lot of strange first dates lately though, but that's been it." I've never considered having to tell someone about my relationship with Heath and everything that's happened since. The thought terrifies me.

Campbell's hand strokes my arm, and I stiffen.

"I think they're starting. Maybe we should make a plate before the lights dim."

As if on cue, the lights strung high among the gathering trees start to flash, signaling the concert is about to begin, before going out entirely a few minutes later.

We sit in the darkness, the only light coming from candles on our table and those of the tables surrounding us, when he reaches over and pulls my hand from my lap and holds it in his own.

"Is this all right?"

I can barely hear him over the music, so I just nod in response. It's the first time I've held another man's hand since Heath, and it just feels . . . foreign. After all this time, I can still feel the difference between the two. My hand doesn't feel as small in his as it did with Heath. And he doesn't give my fingers the occasional squeeze the way Heath always did.

I turn my thoughts away from Heath and focus on enjoying this incredible date with a smart, polite, caring man. A date any girl would be thrilled to be on.

A text flashes on my phone, saving me from my thoughts. I slide my hand from his to grab it off the table and see it's my realtor. Just as I was ready to take a break from house-hunting, she says there's a house that's been reduced, and they need to sell it fast. We confirm a time for early tomorrow morning.

Campbell reaches to take my hand again, but I excuse myself to use the restroom. Once there, I text Heath.

Free tomorrow morning?

Fortunately, I get a quick response.

Sure. Another house?

Yeah. Realtor thinks this is THE ONE.

Then, let's get you a house.

Easy now. We don't know what lurks inside.

Aren't you on a date right now?

Yes.

That exciting, huh?

Very funny.

261

Send me the time, Princess.
I'll pick you up with your usual
skinny vanilla.

Thanks. You're the best.

I go back to my seat, a genuine smile gracing my features for the first time since my date with Campbell began.

During intermission, he does most of the talking—everything from school to his love of animals, his parents, travel, and food. I'm sure there is more than even that, but after a while, his words fade into white noise. I can't grasp on to any of it. Nothing is drawing me in for more. Here I am, with a chance at a fresh start, but my thoughts are somewhere else. But where, I struggle to work out.

With the night over and the leftovers packed up, Campbell and I are leaning against my car. He's holding my hand again, something I'm realizing he really likes to do, and I can tell he's thinking about what I'm thinking about. The good-night kiss.

Even after all of my mistakes in Chicago, I somehow feel like this will be my first real kiss since Heath. I knew it was going to happen sooner or later. I just need to suck it up and get it over with. Besides, I'm sure Heath has kissed plenty of women since me. My stomach does an odd clench at the thought.

Campbell tugs on my hand, drawing my focus back to him. "Did you have a good night? Because I did."

A flash of guilt rides over me with the realization that I've been only half-present tonight.

I smile, hoping to cover it up. "It was a wonderful night. Thank you. I think it's the best date I've been on in a long time."

He steps in front of me, my back still planted to the car, as he takes my other hand and sets his feet on either side of mine. "I hope to get the chance to give you many more."

He leans in and brushes his lips across my own before pulling back, giving me a moment to get my bearings about me. I take a shallow breath and will my tense muscles to relax as he brings his mouth back to mine—this time, with far less trepidation. With our hands still connected, he kisses me like the man I've gotten to know over the course of the night. Gently, with care and compassion.

As he breaks the kiss, all I can think is, like everything else about him, this kiss is nice. And nice is good. Nice is easy. Nice is comfortable. Nice might not make my toes curl and my breath quicken, but nice is predictable, and more importantly, nice is safe.

THIRTY-NINE

Heath

Always for you.
I immediately hit backspace, remembering not only that's not who we are, but also that she was probably sitting next to Minestrone as she was texting me. Which means, she was just sending a simple, average text that she'd send to any friend.

Who cares? She texted me—*me*—while she was out with him.

The thought fills me with a new energy that I was certain had faded after two hours on the court. I jump up from the sofa and take the few steps to the glass doors. I start the music, grab a ball, and go in for a layup. Then, another. But it's not enough.

I roll the ball to the side and start running sprints the length of the court. I push myself harder each time, fueling my body with thoughts that she stopped to think of me while she was on her date. It doesn't matter that it was about a house. She could've waited until she got home or not even texted at all. But she did, and that's all that counts.

———————————

The house is a modest redbrick ranch with three bedrooms and two baths. The realtor told us the husband had already relocated while his wife and new baby stayed behind to sell the house. They were all set to close when the buyer never showed to the closing. So, last night, in a panic, they dropped the price, and here we are.

We barely make it through the door when I see Leah's hand rise to her chest, and her eyes widen. She likes it. With a nine-foot ceiling and glistening hardwood floor, it's easy to see why. It's deceivingly more spacious than it appears from the outside.

To the left of the narrow foyer is a small living room painted in a light beige with a white-washed brick fireplace at the far wall. We walk past that room and into an eat-in kitchen that looks to have been remodeled in the last ten years or so. The cabinets are white with matching white appliances. I know I've been looking at too many houses with her when my first thought is how much better it would look with stainless steel. *I wonder if she'd let me buy them for her housewarming.*

Unlike the other homes, the realtor hasn't left her side. I'm sure she's expecting Leah to put an offer in and wants to get it done as soon as she can. It wouldn't surprise me if she's carrying the contract in her purse.

The kitchen is open on one side to a decent-sized family room with a vaulted ceiling. On the other side is a dining room that connects to the living room and painted in the same beige. A simple brass fixture hangs in the center of the room.

I watch Leah glance from wall to wall, room to room, and think of nothing other than holding her hand, bickering with her over paint colors and furniture placement. Like any of that matters. As if I wouldn't give in to her every vision and desire. Just to see her smile. And to know that I was the one who put it there.

The realtor leads us down a long hall where we take a quick look at the first bedroom, then the master, which has a small and dated bathroom, and finally the third bedroom. Unlike the first two bedrooms, Leah freezes in the doorway, just peeking her head in. I come up from behind her, expecting to see the deal-breaker, but all I see is pink. Every wall is painted a bright cotton-candy pink, each finished with a stenciled floral design that runs along the top. Against the far wall is a white crib, and in the corner is a white rocking chair.

"Jesus. How many coats do you think it'll take to cover *that?*"

She doesn't answer me, just continues to stare a moment longer before turning away.

We walk through once more, making note of the closets and attic space and the fenced-in yard. Overall, there's no question. This house is better than anything we've seen so far even if it is at the top of her price range.

She asks the realtor to give us a minute. As soon as we're alone, she turns to me.

"What do you think?" she whispers.

"I think it's great. You should make an offer."

She's looking for a voice of reason, and I'm determined to be just that.

She nods, looking like she's lost.

I bring my hands to her shoulders and lean down to her. "Hey, what's going on in that head of yours?"

Her thoughts spill out. "It's a house, Heath. A real house. With real bills and real problems. It just makes me nervous; that's all."

"Whoa, take a breath. You haven't even put an offer in yet."

She nods as she wrings her hands.

"Can you see yourself living here? More importantly, can you see yourself being happy here?"

"I can. I really can. I think I'd paint the family room white and get a gray sofa and maybe put a big, oversized chair with an ottoman in the corner by the window so I can sit and read. And I saw a table and chairs set online that would fit perfectly in the kitchen. And I'm sure Connor would come home and help me put in a new vanity in the master bath. And I would paint the spare bedrooms something neutral and eventually get a couple of beds for friends to stay over. And, in the yard—"

"Slow down, Princess. Let's get that offer written up before someone else gets the same idea." I turn her body toward the front door and teasingly march her to the front where she waves the realtor back inside.

Twelve hours and some negotiating later, the house is hers.

FORTY

Leah

I squeeze the keys in my hand, relishing the small prick of pain, before opening my palm and taking a full minute to examine every ridge of the two pieces of metal before me. As of this moment, I am officially a homeowner. Like, I can do whatever I want, however I want, whenever I want, all in the privacy of my own home, homeowner. Dance naked in the kitchen? Yep. Drink milk straight from the gallon? You betcha. Wear my dirty shoes on the carpet? Yes, indeedy. Will I ever actually do any of those things? Absolutely not. But the important thing is, I could if I ever wanted to.

Right now, what I really want to do is start painting. Eli and Lindsey are shopping for me today, picking up some new light fixtures I have on hold as well as stopping at a furniture store to text me pictures of sofas and anything else they think I'd like. Heath is coming over this morning to help me paint, but I'm too excited to wait for him.

It's only six in the morning, but I get dressed and make myself a cup of coffee before driving the short mile to my new home.

My goal for today is to get the family room painted.

Last night, after the closing, Eli helped me drop off the paint, drop cloths, and ladder, so I'll do as much as I can before it gets too high. Heath said he had what we needed to reach the highest parts, so that is a huge relief. Then, my mom is coming over later this afternoon to paint the pink room.

When I took her through the house after my offer was accepted, it didn't get past her how much anxiety that room caused me. It's a painful reminder of what I went through. I was almost a mom. Almost. But I'm not, and that's okay.

I pull up to the house—*my house*—and reach for my shiny new key chain, a gift from Lindsey. It's a giant crystal heart on a short silver chain, and it means so much more than something that simply holds my keys.

I enter the front door with my bag slung over my shoulder and move from room to room, opening blinds and letting the early morning sun soak up the space. Every room is a new beginning, open to endless possibilities and countless memories to be made.

I stand in the middle of the master bedroom, picturing how my furniture will fit. At the doorway of the next bedroom, I make a mental list of what this room will need.

But, as I step into the pink room, my happiness and excitement stall. That's because, although the crib and rocking chair are gone, my pain still lingers. I apply the skills I learned in therapy to fight against the memories. That weak girl back in Chicago, so full of self-loathing and spite, only able to dull the pain with alcohol and random men. I try to shake it off because I know better now—I really do—but the guilt is rising, and these pink walls are screaming at me like a constant reminder of every reprehensible moment from my past.

I turn on my heel and step swiftly down the hall to the family room where I tuck a drop cloth under my arm and grab a paintbrush and a gallon of paint before heading back to the bedroom. I fold out the drop cloth and set up my wireless speaker. Turning the volume to full blast, I'm thankful the air-conditioning is on, so I don't disturb my neighbors. With a newfound determination, I push myself forward and focus only on the white. *A fresh start.*

As I dip the brush over and over again, working my way around the edges of each wall, silent tears start to build. Every now and then, I raise a shoulder up to wipe them off, but I push through it. Just as I'm finishing up the last of the trim, I feel someone moving behind me. When I spin around, there's Heath with a second gallon of paint in his hand. He raises a brow, his way of asking me if I'm all right, so I give one solid nod in response. We couldn't have a conversation right now if we wanted to. The music is too loud. But, even if it wasn't, he knows me well enough to know that he should just leave me be right now.

He works alongside me but not close enough to ever step into my space. Thankfully, he never once asks about the slow flow of my tears that continue as we work. It's just what I need without ever realizing how much I needed it.

When the second coat is finished and every inch of the room is white, Heath turns off the speaker and steps up beside me in the center of the room. We silently critique our work.

"Would you look at that? A clean slate."

My cheeks now dry and my demons put to rest, I take in our work before walking to the door. "C'mon, I'll order us a pizza."

Because, for the slate to be truly clean, there's still one thing left I need to do.

FORTY-ONE

Heath

I let myself in the house when Leah didn't answer the bell. The second I opened the door, the music pounding from down the hall told me why. I expected to see her singing into her paintbrush and moving her body to the beat, but what I walked into was anything but that.

When I saw her tears, instinct made me want to turn the music off and go to her, prepared to rip the limbs off the person responsible. But, as I watched from the doorway, I knew this was different from any other time I've seen her cry. She wasn't shuddering or shaking but instead working through something. What, I still don't know, but whatever it is, I realize somehow, it's best to just let her find her way through to the other side. So, I grabbed some paint and worked silently close-by.

By the time we finished, her tears had dried up, and she slipped on a content smile. With every stroke of the brush, whatever weight she'd been holding on to fell away in the span of the last few hours.

"Sorry there's nothing to sit on," she says as she pushes the pizza box my way, a slice hanging from her other hand.

The pizza is hot and greasy and tastes like the best damn thing I've had in a really long time. Or maybe it's just that good because of the company. I don't bother hiding the fact that I'm staring at her as we sit on opposite sides of the box in the middle of her dining room floor.

"Thanks for helping me paint," she says.

"That's what friends are for."

She's picking at a pepperoni, unable to look at me.

"You know what else friends are for?"

My question shifts her attention to me.

"Listening." When I don't get a response, I try again. "Talk to me, Leah." It comes out on a whispered plea.

Her eyes scrunch up tight at my words, her emotions at war, most likely deciding if she should trust me with the final piece she's been keeping from me. But, after the last couple of hours of watching her wipe away her tears, I need to know, no matter how much it's going to hurt.

"Lee," I beg.

Her face drops to her lap as she sets her slice on the cardboard. "What I have to tell you . . . you'll never look at me the same again."

"You can trust me."

After a moment's pause, she does. "My year in Chicago, it's still hard to believe it all really happened."

I set my half-eaten slice down, my appetite abandoned, and steel my emotions for what's about to come.

"That day I . . . found you, well, it did something to me. It turned me into a different person. Someone I didn't recognize. Or even like. I started drinking. And, when I went to Chicago with no one to lean on, that person only became uglier, colder. I hated the person I saw in the mirror.

"The drinking got worse. Soon, it became every day—from the minute I walked in the door after work until the time I passed out. Sometimes, I made it to my bed. Sometimes, the sofa. Once I even woke up on the floor. But the alcohol didn't help. It didn't ease the pain of that day. I could still see you with her. And I never felt more worthless."

She's picking at a splatter of dried paint on her shirt, and I have to fight with myself to stay back when all I want to do is hold her and tell her, again, how sorry I am and how amazingly brave I think she is.

She takes a deep breath and rubs her hands back and forth on her cheeks, preparing herself for what she has to say next. "I started going out to drink. And I started . . . meeting people."

She lifts her eyes to mine, making sure I understand her meaning. But she doesn't need to because the audible groan of pain that rumbles up my chest is enough to tell her what a shock to the heart that is.

"I finally found a way, for a little while at least, to numb the pain. To erase the image of that day from my mind."

I drop my head to my lap and pull at my hair with my hands. The thought of her being with strange men tears me up. I want to beat the shit out of anyone who touched her.

"I was barely eating, working sixty hours a week, and drinking every night. It started to take a toll on my body, but I didn't stop. Finally, I didn't have a choice."

This is it. I force myself to look at her. She deserves that much. But, when she goes quiet, I think she's changed her mind. Then, she says something that will forever crack my chest and stab my heart.

"I got pregnant."

It's an invisible punch to the gut. My lungs momentarily seize and my muscles tighten like stone. I'm hoping there's some small chance in a deep, dark corner of hell that she's anything but serious, but when she wipes away a single tear, I know she is.

"No." My throat is closed so tight, I don't know if any sound even came out.

But she's not done. When I feel her in front of me, pulling my hands and holding them in her own, I know there's more.

Our bodies connect, her knees pressing against my own, as our heads are both lowered to our laps. We silently watch our fingers wind together like they are acting of their own free will. I try to think of what she needs right now, and the only answer I have is me. My attention. My support. My love. I tug on her hands, and she raises her glassy eyes to mine. With a squeeze, I promise those three things.

"I thought I had cramps, that I was getting my period. But it never came. And the pain only got worse. One minute, I was hunched over at work, and the next thing I knew, I was waking up in a hospital bed. I had started hemorrhaging. Because of an ectopic pregnancy."

I feel the tears hit our hands, and I'm not sure if they are hers or mine.

"That's when Eli came. He jumped on a plane and stayed by my side until my mom and brother got there." She pauses. "I'm sorry I told him what happened with us. I never wanted to come between the two of you. You have to know that."

My brows crease in confusion as my hands clench and every muscle in my body fights the urge to pull her close and squeeze her in my arms. When she slides herself onto my lap, I give in and do just that, the feel of her against my chest momentarily knocking the air from my lungs.

I push back her hair. "You're apologizing to me? Don't ever apologize to me, Leah. After everything I did to you. Everything I put you through. I don't deserve your apology, and I definitely don't deserve your friendship."

"That's not true. You are a good person, Heath Braeburn. A very good person who made some mistakes, just like the rest of us."

Her arms wrap around me as her cheek meets my own. I hold her in return and think of all the ways I would protect her if she were mine. I don't know how long we stay like that, her sitting in my lap on the dining room floor of her empty house, but I soak up every minute.

Finally, her warm lips move across my ear. "Clean slate?"

"Yeah. Clean slate."

FORTY-TWO

Leah

"Leah, where do you want this box? It's marked *Crap*."

"Anything marked *Crap* goes in the dining room. Thanks, Campbell!" I shout as I run out the door to grab another load from the truck. Heath and Eli rented it for the day as my housewarming gift. I pass them as they each carry an end of my new sofa. "That goes in the family room, under the window," I shout.

I turn when I hear the crunch of tires just behind me on the street. "Nice of you to show up and help, considering that's why you're home and all."

Since I bought the house, Connor said that he'd be there to help with the move, but somehow, he got in yesterday, and this is the first I've seen of him.

He walks up beside me, and we each take a box from the truck.

"Sorry, Lee. I had something I had to take care of this morning."

"Yeah, right. What's her name?" I tease.

Considering I've known him since his first breath, I know all of his tells. He looks up at the ceiling when he's lying, at the floor when he's in trouble, and scratches at the back of his head when he's frustrated. Right now, he can't stop scratching.

As my eyes widen in understanding, he makes a rush for the door.

"Are you serious? Connor, get back here! Who is she? How long has this been going on? Does Mom know? When can we meet her? What's her name? How did you two meet?"

With the box in his arms, he turns on me. "There's nothing to tell," he growls.

"Aw, c'mon. You can trust me. What's the big deal?"

"I said, there's nothing to tell. Leave it alone."

"Geesh, okay. Fine. She can't be that great if you're keeping her a secret."

He jerks forward, and I follow.

"Can I just say one more thing though?" When he doesn't answer, I take that as a yes. "You're one of the good ones, Con. And, if she can't see that, whoever she is, she's not worth it. Move on."

Connor has never kept his girlfriends a secret before, and trust me, there have been plenty of them. But, for him to do so now, it can only mean one of two things. He's realized he's being played . . . or he's in love.

I enter the kitchen, deep in thought over who my brother could be all tied up over. Just as I set down the heavy box and wiggle out the numbness in my arms, Campbell comes around the corner and surprises me with a quick kiss to the lips.

"What was that for?" I ask with an uncomfortable giggle.

"Just happy for you; that's all." He smiles and heads out to the truck.

I hear a sound from my other side and find Heath and Eli watching me.

"Things with Clam Chowder look like they're getting a little serious," Eli prods.

"I don't know about that. We're taking it slow."

"Somebody had better tell him that," Heath mumbles before he turns and walks out of the front door.

Eli and I watch Heath from out the window until he's at the truck with Campbell.

"You know he misses you, don't you?"

"I wish I could believe that."

We stand in silence, both of us continuing to stare out to the truck.

"How serious are you about this guy?"

I sigh. "I don't know. I mean, he's nice. Thoughtful. Polite."

"Polite? That's the best you've got?" he asks, crossing his arms and raising a doubtful brow.

"He always calls when he says he's going to. And he asks me before he makes other plans. He even brings my mom flowers."

"I didn't realize you were dating my grandpa."

I roll my eyes and start to work on the boxes on the counter, opening one and fishing around aimlessly. "How's Lindsey feeling? Still getting sick?"

"Don't change the subject. What are you doing with this guy, Lee? Because, let me tell you, if you were trying to find the most boring guy ever, you did it."

"What's wrong with boring? Boring is . . ."

"Safe. Face it. You're with him because he's safe. Sweetheart, I get it. I do. But this guy only wants one thing. A wife."

"That's ridiculous. Why would you ever say that?"

"He's older, solid job path, and I caught him staring into each room like he was making plans for them. He's all about taking that next step." His head swings to me as a thought hits him. "He's the anti-Heath. You're dating the anti-Heath."

"Okay, now you're just being ridiculous," I huff as I throw a spatula back into the box.

"Am I? I dare you to ask him about kids. The more detailed his answer, the more he's looking to settle down. You know I'm right. Any guy not ready for that shit will run the second a woman says the word *baby*. Look at Heath. Since Lindsey's been pregnant, he keeps a constant ten-foot radius from her at all times, like she's contagious or something."

"That's not true at all."

But we both know he's right.

"You didn't answer me. How is Lindsey?"

Thankfully, he lets the subject go. "You can ask her yourself. She's coming by with lunch."

"Well, I'm glad to see you two got over your initial freak-out."

"Can you blame me? We weren't exactly trying for a honeymoon baby. I still can't believe it."

"What did you think was going to happen when you had sex in the Jacuzzi every night?"

"She told you that?"

My smirk gives him my answer.

"I figured the heat and water would nix any chance of *that* ever happening."

"Oh, my sweet, sweet Eli. Give yourself more credit, my friend. You've got some determined little swimmers there."

"Little swimmers?" Campbell asks from behind us.

Eli tilts his head ever-so slightly toward Campbell, and I respond with the lightest shake of my own. Now is not the time.

But Eli thinks otherwise.

"Yeah, Leah and I were just talking about babies." Eli smiles at me before continuing, "I was saying it would've been nice to wait a while longer, enjoy married life with just the two of us, and then talk about having a family after a few years. What are your thoughts on the subject, Campbell?"

Campbell doesn't hesitate. "I think it's great you're pregnant. The sooner you start, the more you can have. Am I right?" The excitement in his voice rises near the end as he looks back and forth between Eli and me.

"You make an excellent point, Campbell. What do you suppose is a good number for a family?" Eli leans against the counter, enthralled.

Just like Eli said, Campbell's answer is immediate. "At least four kids. Or six. I've always thought you should keep it even. That way, no one is the odd man out."

Six?

Eli looks at me smugly before continuing, "Another fabulous point. We should probably start thinking about names, too. Any suggestions?"

"Well, I always imagined, if I had a daughter, I'd name her after my grandmother, Dolores."

I choke on his words as Eli taps his foot against mine in victory. Campbell's smile is hopeful. But I can't bring myself to feign one in return. I'm too busy trying to keep my breakfast down. I gradually manage a flat smile as I step past him and out through the patio door. I need air. Lots of it. But what I really need is to figure out how to end things with Split Pea and Ham before he starts merging our bank accounts.

FORTY-THREE

Heath

"How's it going?" I have to force out the words when Campbell comes up beside me at the truck.

"Have you ever been in love, Heath?"

"L-love?" *Yes, and I still am.*

"Because, I mean, I thought I knew what love felt like, but this is different. This *girl* is different. She wants the same things I want. I mean, I think so at least. She's not high drama or high maintenance. She doesn't care what brand something is or how much it costs. She likes kids and animals and has great friends."

He thinks he's in love?

Jesus, all I did was ask the guy how it was going.

I almost drop the box I'm holding but manage to get it back on the truck bed before I do.

I had no idea they'd gotten so serious, so fast.

Eli was right. It didn't take long for someone to see how incredible Leah is.

Watching him lean in to kiss her, like he'd done it a hundred times before, was too much to handle. I'm just thankful her back was to me.

I would jump through a million hoops and walk through fire if that was what it took to make her smile. I know I'm fucked when I want her happiness more than my own, and that includes watching her fall in love with another man. It's what she deserves. But it hurts like hell all the same.

"Yeah, great friends," I mumble.

He takes a box from the truck and heads up the walkway, not before giving me a pat on the shoulder. He may have even called me "Bud" at some point.

He enters the house, comfortable and confident, like he belongs here. While I want more than anything for her to have everything good that comes her way, all I can think about is this guy sharing it with her. His shoes by the door and his clothes in her closet. Him watching movies and hosting barbecues with her. Building a life with her.

I can already feel the friendship we've reconstructed slipping away.

Gravel spits out beneath the tires of a truck pulling up close behind me. I immediately recognize the logo on the side and walk to the driver.

"Delivery for Leah Dawson," The driver says as he holds out a clipboard.

"Yeah, I'll sign for her." I sign then walk with him to the back of the truck where he slides up the door and positions the ramp.

"It's all gassed up and ready to go," he says as he makes his way inside.

Great, just in time for Broccoli Cheese to take it for a spin.

He wheels the gleaming red lawn mower down from the truck.

"Here's all the paperwork on it. It's a nice one, and it looks like she got the extended warranty, so tell her to call us if there are any problems."

"I'll make sure to do that." I stare blindly down at the papers as he gets in his truck and drives away.

"What is this?"

I turn toward Leah's voice as she comes up next to me.

"Heath?"

"Happy housewarming, Princess." I step aside to give her a full view.

"You bought me a lawn mower? But the truck rental was my gift."

I shrug a shoulder.

"Heath, this is really nice. Too nice. You shouldn't have."

She's silent as she runs her hand over the handle and pulls the lever before walking around it like it's a new car.

"Heath . . ."

"He already left. No sending it back now." I dig a hand in my pocket and force a smile.

"Thank you, Heath. It's beautiful." Even though she lets out a small laugh, she looks almost sad. "Is it weird that I just called a lawn mower beautiful?"

"No, it just means you're a responsible, home-owning adult."

"Do you know what else it means?"

"What's that?"

"It means that I'll need you to come over next Saturday to show me how the heck to work this thing."

I don't dare tell her that was my hope all along. "I'd be happy to." *Although I'm sure Golden Mushroom will beat me to it.* "I'm really happy for you, Leah. Not just the house, but . . . everything. You should be really proud of yourself."

She tries to hide her blush, but she can't get anything past me.

"I've come a long way. We both have."

Our silence is interrupted by Campbell. "Wow, now, that's a lawn mower. I can't wait to give it a try. I can be your personal lawn boy." He wraps an arm around her shoulders and smiles down at her.

"You'll need this then." I hand him the paperwork and walk away.

"Why the hell am I assembling a crib *I* paid for?" I ask Eli as I dump out a package of nuts and bolts on the floor, searching through them for the piece I need.

"Because they wanted an extra hundred dollars for assembly. And you were already paying enough for the furniture."

"A hundred bucks? That's it? I would've paid five times that to avoid this shit."

"Will you shut up? We're making memories. One day, I'll tell little Eli Junior about the time his dad and Uncle Numbnuts spent the day putting his first bed together."

"Eli Junior? Are you serious? Don't curse the kid with that name. And how do you know it's going to be a boy anyway?"

"Because I just know; that's how. Call it a father's intuition."

"Yeah, right. You're doomed to end up like your dad, covered in glitter and surrounded by hormonal girls."

"Not happening, dude. I won't let it."

"You're an idiot. You do know how this works, right? You can't just wish something to be true. If that were the case, I'd . . ." I catch myself and shut up.

"You'd what?"

"Nothing. Where is piece C2? This is bullshit. I'm calling my dad's handyman and paying him the hundred bucks to put this bastard together." I'm lifting and sliding parts and pieces, not even sure what I'm looking for.

"Is it hard to see her with someone else? Even after all this time?"

I ignore him, instead turning my focus to the page of directions in my lap.

"Maybe you should try dating someone else. How long has it been?"

He knows exactly how long it's been.

"She's in a good place now, Heath. She's healthy, she has her own home, a job she likes, and she's dating a decent guy. You know as well as I do, she wants the same for you."

I continue to ignore him.

"I think she's starting to worry about you."

That gets my attention.

"I watch her watch you, like she's trying to piece together what you need, how she can help you."

My eyes narrow in doubt. This is all news to me. I've never once caught her looking my way.

"You know, it's been a big year for me. I married the love of my life, and in just a few months, she's going to have my baby. But, as good as all of that is, one of the best parts is that I got my two best friends back. For a while there, I never thought it would happen. I thought I'd lost you and Leah forever. But you both came back to me. And I just need to tell you how thankful I am for that. I know it wasn't easy. And it still isn't. I can see how badly you want her back, but I also know you'll never do anything about it because you think she deserves better."

Having a baby has turned him soft. I'm about to tell him this much, but, unfortunately, he's not finished. "Have you stopped to think that maybe that could be you? *This* you? The guy who takes his job seriously, doesn't smoke pot or drink, exercises, and never misses a Sunday breakfast with his dad?"

"Even if I did agree with you, she's with him now. He's good for her."

"Oh, come on. We both know that guy is boring as hell. Is she happy? Sure. But is she *happy*? I think we know the answer to that. She doesn't love this guy. Not even close. The only time she's ever been in love was when she was with you. And I could say the same for you. So, the question is, what are you going to do about it?"

"She let me back into her life. That's more than I could ever ask for."

"Well, maybe it's time to ask for more."

That's where he's wrong. She'd never take that chance again.

"Have you seen my phone?" I search under bags of bolts and pages of instructions until I spot it.

"So, you're going to call her?"

"Not a chance."

"Then, who are you calling?"

"Someone to take care of this mess. Otherwise, I'll be telling Junior the story of how close I came to killing his dad that time we put his crib together."

FORTY-FOUR

Leah

"How was your date last night?" I ask my mom as we wind through the aisles of the baby store looking for Lindsey's shower gift.

"Let's just say, there won't be a second."

"Oh no. What happened this time?"

"It started out fine. We went to that nice sushi place I'd told you about. Everything was going well until he unwrapped his chopsticks."

I stop the cart and give her my full attention. "And?"

"And he tucked them under his top lip, then tried to sing The Beatles' song, 'I Am the Walrus.'"

"Seriously?" I laugh.

"Like a goddamn heart attack," she deadpans.

"Well, points to him for liking The Beatles at least, right?" I ask, and hand her Lindsey's registry. "What's with us Dawson women rarely making it to the second date? Are we too picky?"

"There's nothing wrong with being picky. A person should never settle when it comes to finding a partner. How about you, hon? Have you thought about getting out there again now that you're single?"

"Ugh, no. I'm still recovering from breaking up with Campbell." I shake my head and continue to push the cart down the aisle.

"I'm sorry, Lee. That's never an easy thing to do."

"He cried, Mom. For two straight hours. All I kept thinking was: How much longer is this going to last because I really need a sandwich?" I shake my head at the memory. "I'm an awful person."

"You are not an awful person, Lee, you hear me? But it's your own fault for doing it at your house. Next time you break a boy's heart, make sure you're somewhere you can get in your car and leave. That'll teach you." She glances over as we both stop in front of a long line of strollers.

"I would have, but I honestly wasn't expecting to do it right then. I walked in on him measuring one of my spare bedrooms. He said he was going to surprise me with a desk, but I knew deep down that the desk was for him. I think he was slowly planning to move in with me, and I knew if I didn't do it then, I'd wake up one day to find his underwear in my laundry and his car in my garage. I should've never let it go on for as long as it did."

"I knew he wasn't the one."

"What do you mean? You loved Campbell. You were always saying what a nice guy he was."

"He was a nice guy, but he wasn't the *right* nice guy." Her voice eases. "Did you ever tell him about what happened in Chicago?"

"No." I reach for a stroller and begin to slide it back and forth.

"And why is that?"

I hesitate.

"Because you didn't feel like you could. Maybe you couldn't trust him? Maybe you thought it'd scare him off? Whatever your reasons were, you kept something important from him. When the right person comes along, you won't feel that way. You'll know."

The people who matter most in my life already know. I can't imagine sharing that with anyone else.

"Do your friends know about Campbell?"

"I told Lindsey last night, which means Eli knows."

"And Heath?"

"It hasn't come up."

She stops and turns to me, arms crossed. "Uh-huh."

"Mom, don't. It's taken Heath and I a long time to get to where we're at now."

"And where is that?"

"We're friends. Good friends." And that's the truth.

If we didn't have Eli as our anchor, we might have never made it to this point. But, after a lot of life lessons, we did just that, and that's all that matters.

"Here's the stroller she wants," I say, changing the subject.

Together, we lift the large box and angle it into the cart.

"Let's check out and grab some lunch." My mom starts to push the cart toward the registers.

"You don't want to look at anything else?" I ask. "You love little baby clothes. Especially baby girl clothes." I tug the cart toward the sea of pink.

"No, not today. I'm pretty hungry."

When she attempts to continue on, I stop the cart. "It's okay, Mom. It doesn't bother me to be here.

Honest." When she doesn't say anything, I repeat myself, "Seriously, I'm good."

In the middle of the stroller aisle of a baby superstore on a busy Saturday afternoon, my mom hugs me tightly. "I know you are, honey. I'm so proud of you."

"Thanks, Mom." I take a second to relish her hold before pulling back. "Now, come on. I saw sparkly baby tutus and little rainbow leg warmers that we absolutely have to check out."

I dig my phone from the bottom of my purse as Pat Benatar sings about being invincible. "Hey, Eli."

"Leah, thank God!"

"What is it? Is Lindsey okay?"

"She's fine. But we came home from her doctor's appointment, and the garage won't open. For some reason, the power is out on our entire block, and neither of us has a key."

Eli had one spare key, and when Heath and I argued over who should have it, we played Rock, Paper, Scissors. I picked rock. Heath picked paper.

"I can't help you. You gave Heath the spare, remember?"

"Yes, and trust me, I'm totally regretting it right now."

"So, call Heath."

"I have, and he's not answering. I left him a voicemail, but I don't know how long we can wait. Can you go to his place and get it?"

I haven't been to Heath's condo since I packed up my things, and have no plans of ever going back. Eli knows this.

"Please, Lee. Lindsey's in the car with the air-conditioning running, but she's exhausted, and she would really like to lie down. I know it's asking a lot, but I need you to do this."

Lindsey's in the final weeks of her pregnancy and swelling up like a bloated whale. I can't sit by and let her suffer more than she already is.

"Of course. Will she be okay until I can get there?"

"Yeah. I'll take her for ice cream and French fries."

I laugh because that's been her favorite thing to eat these last few months.

"Sounds good. I just need the codes to get into Heath's place."

"They're still the same. He never changed them."

"It's been a long time. Refresh my memory," I lie.

Heath's building has keyless entry, and I still remember the code to the main door as well as the door to his place.

I take an early lunch from work and go on a drive I never imagined taking again.

Get in, and get out.

I turn the handle and let the door swing open before taking a step in. "Hello?" I call into the empty foyer.

Inside, I'm met by the same narrow table that sits against the foyer wall. The one I always set my keys on and my bag below.

I move in farther and call out again.

No answer.

When I enter the family room, I see nothing has changed. The same furniture, the same decor. I slowly spin around and see the same for the kitchen. The only thing out is a bowl of fruit on the counter. Heath would never put out a bowl of fruit. It must have come from someone else.

I'm tempted to investigate for more signs of a girlfriend, but I push the urge aside and do what needs to get done. Eli said to check for the key in Heath's top desk drawer of his office, so I head toward the hall.

Behind the desk, I find the key right where he said it would be. I know I should get out of here and over to Eli as fast as possible, but as I peer down the hall, toward the open master bedroom door, I can't help but wonder. My mind is screaming at me to go left, but my body wills me to go right.

I go right.

I peek into the room and notice the only change is new bedding. Everything else is the same, in its original place. The room itself is organized and clutter-free, except for a large but basic cardboard box with bright yellow mailing tape sitting off in the corner.

It's what's across the room though, tucked into the frame of the dresser mirror, that draws me in. I take two steps in and freeze. I should not be doing this. This is Heath's private space. But I ignore common sense and cross the room. So much for getting in and out.

I pull the picture away and run my thumb over the image as I'm taken to a moment I all but forgot.

We were lying warm and comfortable, wrapped up in each other on his sofa, when he said he wanted to get a drink. But he didn't come back with a drink. He came back with a black velvet box. And in that box, were the gold hoop earrings he gave me to replace the ones I had lost. It was also the day I knew I was falling in love with him.

I casually took a selfie of us on the sofa, but there was nothing casual about it. That day meant everything to me, and I needed a picture to capture that feeling of new love. My first love. I never wanted to forget how it felt to be consumed in a way I never had been before. How insanely happy I was in that moment.

I remember he wouldn't smile, instead making all kinds of funny faces just to mess with me. It wasn't until he got up on an elbow and tickled me in the ribs, causing me to scream out in laughter, that I managed to take this picture. My head is thrown back, my smile bigger than I knew possible, as I was begging him to stop. And he's looking down on me, wearing a sexy grin, that, had I seen it through my hysterics, it would have stopped my squirming cold.

As I put the picture back in its place, I catch myself smiling at the memory.

"Did you find the key?" a voice says from the doorway.

I squeal and spin around, bumping into the dresser. "Heath, I'm so sorry. I didn't mean to be nosy. When I saw the door was open—"

"It's okay, Leah."

"No, I was snooping. I had no business coming in here. I'm sorry."

"Really, it's no big deal." He takes a single step closer.

The two of us stand silently in Heath's bedroom— me, clenching my hands at my waist and him with his hands tucked in his pockets. The memories made in this room swirl around us.

Finally, he breaks the silence. "I heard you and Tomato Soup broke up."

"Yeah. It just . . ." But I stall there, glancing back at the photo.

"Since you're here, I have something I've been meaning to give you." He walks to his dresser, turns his back to me, and opens the top drawer.

When he faces me, my eyes burn as his arms extend out.

"You kept that? But . . ."

"Yeah, I had to go through the trash, but I think I got them all." He moves an inch closer, encouraging me to take it.

I cross the short distance and take the pink tin from his hands, our fingers brushing against each other as I pull away. I don't miss the tingle his touch leaves behind as I stare down at what has been one of my biggest regrets—and biggest lessons—throughout all of this.

"I hope you don't mind, but I've added a few."

My eyes widen up at his. "You were serious about that?" Smiling, I remember his comment the night of the wedding.

"Of course."

"And you made wishes on them?" The words sneak out before I can stop them.

He locks eyes with me, answering without hesitation, "Every single one."

I hold the cool tin to my chest, the coins tumbling inside. "Thank you, Heath."

He leans a hip against the dresser and gives a shy nod of his head.

"Well, I should get going. Ice cream and fries can hold Lindsey off for only so long."

"Of course." His hands are back in his pockets as he follows me out.

Just as I'm about to leave, I turn back to him, the tin safely at my side. I look down to it then back up to him. "And Heath, thank you. This means a lot to me."

He nods as I walk out the door.

Outside, I barely register the bush I brush against when I step out into the blazing heat.

Heath and I—that's done. Dead and buried. So, why do I feel this way? Like something dormant is coming back to life. Something familiar, but new all the same. The question is, what do I do about it?

FORTY-FIVE

Heath

Leah *smiled.*

As I watched her from the doorway of my room, it was the first thing I saw. The only thing. A genuine smile sparked by a memory, a time in our lives that I now know means as much to her as it does to me.

When she walked out my door she left me with one thing. *Hope.*

FORTY-SIX

Leah

"God, my back hurts." Lindsey moans as she paces the room and attempts to rub at her spine.

"Again?" Eli asks as he stops her and begins to knead at her back. "Maybe we should call the doctor."

"No, just keep doing that. That's perfect." She sighs.

Lindsey's due date is still a week away, but with the scene playing out in front of me, I'm starting to doubt that she'll make it that long. Heath looks over at me, presumably thinking the same thing but with far more fear.

I slide over next to him and whisper, "Relax. It's not going to happen right in the middle of the room."

"Maybe we should take her to the hospital?" Heath asks the group.

Lindsey breaks away from Eli and starts pacing again. Eli, his face pinched tight with worry, is left standing there, helpless, looking to be in as much pain as Lindsey.

"I don't want to go to the hospital. They'll just tell me to turn around and go home." Lindsey huffs as she stops a moment to brace herself against a chair and take a few deep breaths. "At yesterday's appointment the doctor said there was no progress"—she releases a long, slow exhale before resuming her steps—"and most first pregnancies go the full term."

She jerks to a stop in the center of the room when water begins to trickle from under her sundress. Wide-eyed, she freezes as we all focus breathless on the puddle forming at her feet.

The drips quickly turn into a steady stream when Heath announces, "I think *that* counts as progress. Now, can we go to the hospital?"

FORTY-SEVEN

Heath

"It's a girl! We have a daughter!" Eli shouts through happy tears.

Leah rushes him, wrapping her arms around his middle in a strong hug.

"And Lindsey?" I ask.

"Perfect. They're both perfect." He releases Leah and then turns to me for a hug.

I thought he looked happy on his wedding day, but this version of the man in front of me is something profoundly different.

"C'mon, come meet my daughter."

We enter, and exuberant chaos and family file into every corner of the room.

"Wow, who *isn't* here?" Leah asks as she makes her way through the crowd of family.

Lindsey looks overjoyed but exhausted from her bed. Leah leans down to Lindsey for a hug and then heads straight for Eli's mom, who's holding the tiniest pink bundle. Eli's sisters surround her, and the group doesn't think twice about making room for Leah.

I, on the other hand, haven't left the safety of the doorway.

I watch Leah as she softly runs her fingers over a dark tuft of hair on the sleeping baby's head. The baby lets out a soft cry, causing all the women to sigh and smile.

"Pretty amazing, huh?" My dad surprises me from behind.

"Dad, what are you doing here?"

"Eli texted me. Besides, why wouldn't I be here? He's family."

We're interrupted by a new body pushing her way into the room. Leah's mom. With a quick hello to the two of us she weaves her way through to Lindsey and Eli before shuffling in beside Leah.

It's like a live production playing out in front of me. Eli is sitting beside Lindsey, talking, kissing, while intermittently scanning the room for the baby. When he sees her being passed safely to Sienna's arms, he turns back to his wife and kisses her again, their smiles saying everything for them.

Leah is shoulder-to-shoulder with Sienna, the baby's tiny hand wrapped tightly around Leah's finger. She pulls away from the baby's grasp, only to slide her hands underneath the bundle, lifting her up and bringing her close to her own chest.

She's holding the baby like she's done this a thousand times before. With a light sway of her hips, she turns, and I'm able to get a better look. The baby's dark blue eyes are open and focused solely on Leah. Leah's talking to her, animated and smiling. When the baby's eyes widen in response, Leah throws her head back in laughter and catches my stare. She doesn't hesitate to walk to me, tucking herself in at my side.

"Isn't she amazing?" Leah tilts the baby up but continues to only have eyes for the little one in her arms. "Put your arms out."

Startled, I don't answer or move.

"Heath, it's all right. I'm right here. Put your arms out."

I do as I was told, imitating her pose as best I can, and brace myself to take the weight of the baby, shocked when she seems to weigh barely an ounce. She's the first baby I've ever held in my life, and I panic at the thought of doing anything that could hurt her.

"There you go. Just bring her head up a little." Leah gives a light tug on my arm until I'm in the right position. "Look at that; you're a natural." She smiles at me with pride and then places her finger back in the baby's tiny palm.

With the three of us squeezed in tight, I look from the baby's skinny fingers wrapped around the tip of Leah's pinkie to the content warmth spread throughout Leah's face. Anxiety and panic mixed with an odd sense of urgency courses through every inch of me. I see it now. No, *I feel it.* A roaring desire for this to be my life. My reality. And I want this with Leah. I understand now what she was feeling at the wedding.

This should be us.

When her eyes rise to mine her smile fades and a worried frown takes its place. "What is it?"

It's at that moment Eli swoops in and carefully takes his daughter from my arms before returning to Lindsey's bedside. Leah eyes me warily, but I feign attention on Eli, all the while trying to calm my frazzled nerves.

"Everyone, we have a name!"

The room quiets in anticipation.

"We've decided to name her after Lindsey's grandmother, Charlotte, but we're calling her Charlie."

Everyone erupts in cheers, causing the baby to startle and release a tired cry.

Leah excitedly turns back to me as she gives my arm a light squeeze, and at the same time, a tightness seizes my chest.

"It's perfect. She looks like a Charlie. Don't you think?"

I swallow hard and nod, trying not to focus on the walls that are closing in on me.

"Hey, are you okay? You don't look so good all of a sudden."

"Hot," I cough out. "It's just really hot in here."

The back of her hand presses against my forehead. "Let's get you some air."

Leah makes her way through the tight crowd where she kisses Charlie's small head, Lindsey's cheek, and then turns to Eli for a long hug. Watching the three of them, the feeling charges through me again. *This should be us.* Leah should be lying in this bed, holding our baby, living this same moment and everything that goes along with it. The happiness. The family. The love.

But it's not us.

I can't get out of this room fast enough.

FORTY-EIGHT

Leah

Heath rushes toward the exit like his ass is on fire. Or he's about to be sick. Either way, I quicken my steps and keep close to his side. Something happened to him in that hospital room, and it seems to be following him outside.

The sun has set, but the air stirs warm and dry. Under the fluorescent lights of the parking lot, I give his arm a strong tug and shout for him to stop. His strides are replaced by long paces as he pulls on his hair and mutters nonsense under his breath.

He stops momentarily, taking in my face, taking in all of me, like he's caught between a breakdown and a breakthrough and only I hold the key to his relief. He's so weak in this moment, so fragile, but I don't know what to do for him. Only that I'm not going to leave him until he works it out.

When he resumes his pacing, I use my body as a roadblock and grab him by the shoulders.

"Talk to me, Heath" I order. "What happened in there?"

Light bounces off his face, casting a glassy shine and darkening of his blue eyes. When he glances away, I grip him tighter, urging him back to me. He rubs frantically at the back of his neck and expels a nervous breath. I release my hold and wait patiently.

"I feel it." The words tumble out, pain laced throughout each one.

My body locks tight with immediate understanding.

"I get it now. I feel it. Fuck, I feel *all* of it. That should be us, Leah." He wildly swings an arm toward the building. "That should be you in that bed, holding *our* baby, with me by your side. But it's not. It's not, because of me!"

He's frustrated and scared and upset, dragging his hands over his face, mumbling nonsense, yet all I can do is . . . smile.

He resumes his rant, his voice growing louder and more frustrated with each step, as my heart swells by the second. "*We* should be bickering about whose turn it is to do the dishes. *We* should be taking vacations together. *We* should be sharing a medicine cabinet . . ."

I'm standing, hands on my hips, my smile widening by the second as he rambles on.

"You're smiling? How can you smile right now?"

"Say it again, Heath."

"Say what?"

"You know." I step close and grip his forearms before lifting to my toes. "Say it again." My smile holds as I wait.

I watch his Adam's apple bob.

"I feel it," he whispers. *"I fucking feel it."*

I shake my head and smile.

310

"Well, it's about time."

A warm breeze swirls around us, like a band pulling us close, sweeping away all the remaining dust from our past. I reach for his face and kiss him on closed firm lips, catching him by surprise.

He breaks the kiss, eyes wide, and anxious. "Tell me that means you feel it, too."

"I never stopped."

FORTY-NINE

Leah

It's been a few days since that night at the hospital and we've been taking our time getting reacquainted. I watch out my front window as Heath walks up my driveway with a large box in his arms, the same box with the yellow tape I saw in his room that day I went for the key. When I let him in, he bends in for a quick kiss before rushing down the hall to my bedroom. When the door shuts behind him, I shake my head and go back to checking Instagram and drinking my sweet tea in the kitchen. Whatever he's up to, I'll find out soon enough.

The sound of Heath clearing his throat lifts my attention. Except it's not Heath standing in the doorway of my kitchen. It's Han Solo.

Dressed in a white collarless shirt and dark vest, a toy gun strapped to his thigh over dark pants, he slides the large box onto the counter. I push aside my drink as he begins to pull out one package after another, laying them out on the table in front of me.

Fred and Wilma Flintstone.
Bacon and eggs.
Gangster and flapper.
Peter Pan and Tinker Bell.
Superman and Wonder Woman.
Prince Charming and Cinderella.

He continues to pull more costumes from the box, but I can't make out what they are because my eyes are burning with tears of understanding.

"This should get us through the next ten or so Halloweens."

I suck in both lips and fight against the ugly cry as I grab one of the clear vinyl packages. All I can make out is that it's green, so it's either Peter Pan or Tinker Bell. He takes it from my hands and pulls me up from my chair, wrapping his arms around my back.

"You went out and bought all of these?"

"Actually, I've been collecting them for a while."

I somehow manage to laugh and cry at the same time, causing an odd, painful hiccupping sob to rise up as my face falls into his chest. The vest smells like vinyl, and the shirt scratches my cheek, but it couldn't be more perfect.

He brushes my hair from my face and brings my eyes to his. Eyes that are filled with a newfound reverence and maturity.

"Leah, I've learned so much in the time we've been apart. How amazing it is to live a life with you in it, and the pain of living one without. And I know now what it means to be a good man. At least, I'm figuring it out. But none of that matters if I can't be a good man for *you*. And I swear, Leah, I will be a good man for you.

"I can't promise that I won't ever screw up or piss you off, but I will never hurt you. Never. Because I also know how valuable second chances are, how valuable you

314

are to me, and I will work every day to make sure you feel that."

He takes an extended breath. "I love you, Leah."

My head gives the slightest tilt back in surprise, but he doesn't miss it.

"Yeah, I said it." A small laugh plays behind his words. "*I love you*. Sometimes, I hated myself more than I loved you, but I never stopped loving you. Even when you were a thousand miles away or with another man. I loved you through it all, and it's time you know it. So deal with it, Princess."

Even with the sexy smirk and cocky raised brow, I believe every word.

"You don't have to say the words back to me. Take all the time you need. I'll wait. As long as I know . . ."

But I've heard enough. He needs me as much as I need him. Everything he's promising me, I want to give him the same in return.

I wrap my hands around the back of his head and cut him off with my kiss. I kiss him with a strength that comes from deep within me. It surges through every vein, leaving no doubt that he is mine. He has always been mine.

It's when I pull back, wiping my tears from his vest, that I notice one costume I missed earlier. The white Princess Leia dress. I can't help but be a little disappointed.

He notices and dips his face to mine. "Something wrong, Princess?"

"It's just . . . I'm surprised to see Leia's white dress. I would have pegged you as a gold-bikini kind of guy."

With a devilish smile, he reaches into the box once more, revealing a gold bikini top that dangles from his hand. "I saved the best for last."

I cup his jaw in my hands and sigh, "I love you."
"I know."

EPILOGUE

Leah

Heath filled the last crack, tended to every fading wound, and sewed together the final tear in my damaged heart. And, in the process, we both learned what love was. How to love ourselves and how to love others in return.

But we wouldn't be where we are now if I didn't work on myself first, to become the kind of person I wanted in my own life. And I'm so thankful that Heath did the same.

"Um, Heath, you just drove by our street."

"Really? I didn't notice." He's fighting a smile.

"Heath—" I say in warning.

"Give me a minute." He flashes a sly wink before pulling the car over. "Here we are."

We're sitting in front of the large house we've driven by a hundred times before. The one with the wraparound porch I've always liked.

"Joan called me this morning. She's been keeping an eye on this house for me, and, well, it just went on the market."

I sit, silent and still.

"What do you think? It's the house you've always wanted." He wraps his hand around mine, his eyes smiling until he sees mine aren't mirroring his. "I know we've only been married a few months and that you love your house—*our* house—but we don't know when we'll get this chance again, if ever."

He wants this. I can see the hopefulness in his eyes. But I know my husband, and I know he wants this simply because he's trying to make me happy.

I was hoping to do this tonight as I sat in his lap on the sofa, but here goes. "Your dad and I have been talking."

He doesn't bother to mask the concern on his face, so I move a comforting hand to his thigh.

"You know how he's added a few new lawyers to the practice?"

He nods.

"And you mentioned he's been coming in later and leaving earlier?"

Another nod.

I slide my hand back and forth in hopes of calming his growing anxiety. "He's ready to retire and, well, wants to sell the house and downsize. But, before he does, he'd like to offer it to us first."

Heath is now the one sitting silent and still.

"What do you think?"

He points out the window. "But you like *this* house. You've always said so."

"You're right. I do like this house. But there's a difference between 'like' and 'love,' and what I *love* is the idea of raising our kids in the same home you grew up in. Watching you play basketball with them in the field house or singing 'Happy Birthday' to them in the same dining room."

"What about your mom? If we lived here, we'd still be only a mile or so away from her."

"There's no denying how much I love my mom, but we've been living close to her these last two years. And a little bit of a drive means she won't be able to make her usual 'pop-in' visits." I tug teasingly on his hand. "Or have you already forgotten how she almost caught us the other day?"

He looks at the house and then back to me, ignoring my playfulness. "Are you sure that's what you really want?"

"From the first day I walked through the door of your dad's house, I saw it for what it was always intended for, family. When I picture our babies sleeping in your old room, or watching you read to them in front of the same fireplace, I'm more than sure."

When his face softens, I know he wants all of that too.

"As long as they all look like you, I don't care where we live." He laughs, leaning over the armrest for a quick, hard kiss.

"Well, there are five bedrooms to fill," I respond with a flirtatious smile.

"So, you're saying we should get home and practice? I like the way you think, Princess." He wraps a hand around the back of my head and pulls me in for a long, deep kiss.

I break away and motion to the gearshift. "What are we waiting for?"

He takes my not-so-subtle hint and throws the car into drive, my laughter bouncing between us as the force forward pushes me back in my seat. His voice grows excited as his thoughts spill out. "What did you have in mind? The living room floor? The laundry room is always fun. But the kitchen counter . . . or maybe we just spend the rest of the day in bed?"

"I want all of it. As long as it's with you, Heath, I want it all."

The End

WHOSE STORY IN THE SWEETNESS SERIES
WOULD YOU LIKE TO READ NEXT?

Email me at

authorheatherbentley@gmail.com

and let me know!

ALSO AVAILABLE FROM
HEATHER BENTLEY

beautiful lies

ACKNOWLEDGMENTS

I had just started this story when Carrie Fisher passed away. I never intended to name the heroine Leah (yes, the spelling change was intentional) or give her the nickname, but this was one of those celebrity deaths that stung. I very clearly remember six-year-old me watching her on the giant screen in total awe. It had nothing to do with her being a princess and everything to do with her being a sassy, fierce, intelligent woman. The big guns and killer hairdo didn't hurt either. So, with that said, thank you, Carrie.

I am so thankful for my amazingly awesome betas—Erika, Kristie, Kirsten, Marieke, Cassie, Jessica, Arielle, Karen, Genie, Kayla, and Tiara. You have all been so generous with your time and feedback, and I'm beyond appreciative for each and every one of you.

Kristie and Emily, I can't thank both of you enough for your friendship and support. I only hope I give you the same in return.

Heather, you are the ultimate beta, blogger, and friend. You didn't just help me with the title; you also found Heath his very own song[1]!

Robin, your insane eye for detail is only surpassed by your kindness. I appreciate every minute (and the thousands of messages) you put into helping me make this story what it is.

To all of the kick-ass bloggers who have been so gracious in supporting a new author—THANK YOU. Your endless efforts are what put books into readers' hands.

This book would be an ugly, jumbled mess if not for my cover designer, Sarah; my editor and formatter, Jovana (I'm still not over the mug debacle); and my proofreader, Marla. Thank you, ladies! You are all the best at what you do.

Sophie—aka Sophilicious, aka Cujo—thank you for warming my lap as I edited. You literally forced me to stay in my seat and get the work done. I think we need to make this a regular thing. Tell your mom I said so.

Speaking of, Christine, thanks, woman. You're the BE to my ST and the FRI to my END. I've got the keychain to prove it.

To my hubby—Thanks, babe, for supporting me as I continue on this journey. And to my boys—Thanks for not burning the house down or causing each other severe bodily harm while I worked.

---

[1] "Alone" by I Prevail

And I can't leave yet without thanking YOU. If you're like me, you have more books on your Kindle than you'll ever admit to, but you chose to spend your time with this one, and for that, I am truly humbled. Thank you.

ABOUT THE AUTHOR

Heather Bentley grew up in the suburbs of Chicago. Her first book was written at the age of nine on a flight to Florida that centered around her hopes that the DC-10 she was traveling on wouldn't nosedive to the ground in a ball of flames. And, yes, it was even illustrated. She continues to reside in Illinois with her family and still loves flying about as much as she did back then. Today, she writes new adult and contemporary romance and is the author of *Beautiful Lies* and *Sweetest Heartbreak*.

Amazon: bit.ly/AuthorHeatherBentley

Facebook: bit.ly/FBHeatherBentley

Goodreads: bit.ly/GRAuthorHBentley

Instagram: @hezwrites

Made in the USA
Middletown, DE
30 May 2018